She looked around the shop. Everything was set up for her first customer. Except for the garden spade in the middle of the floor . . .

The pointed end of the spade was tinged reddish brown. Carolina clay, probably. But this seemed darker. There were traces of it leading toward the warehouse door in the back of the shop. Wondering what happened and who she was going to chew out for it, she picked up the shovel. That's when she saw him. Her hands went numb, and the shovel clattered to the floor.

She wasn't sure how long she stood there looking at the man. Her first impulse was to turn around and run out of her shop, screaming for help. But she was made of sterner stuff. Or at the very least, she was morbidly curious. Years of being a cop's wife didn't prepare her for this. But her background as a researcher made her push her emotion aside and take another look.

The man was facedown in one of her attractive wicker baskets filled with anemone bulbs. It was part of the autumn scene she'd created, complete with scarecrow and pumpkins. He'd obviously fallen forward, dragging the scarecrow from its perch on the oak rocking chair. The straw figure looked forlorn, lying half under the man's weight like some bizarre teddy bear . . .

PRETTY POISON

Joyce & Jim Lavene

BERKLEY PRIME CRIME, NEW YORK

THE BERKLEY PUBLISHING GROUP
Published by the Penguin Group
Penguin Group (USA) Inc.
375 Hudson Street, New York, New York 10014, USA
Penguin Group (Canada), 10 Alcorn Avenue, Toronto, Ontario M4V 3B2, Canada
(a division of Pearson Penguin Canada Inc.)
Penguin Books Ltd., 80 Strand, London WC2R 0RL, England
Penguin Group Ireland, 25 St. Stephen's Green, Dublin 2, Ireland (a division of Penguin Books Ltd.)
Penguin Group (Australia), 250 Camberwell Road, Camberwell, Victoria 3124, Australia
(a division of Pearson Australia Group Pty. Ltd.)
Penguin Books India Pvt. Ltd., 11 Community Centre, Panchsheel Park, New Delhi—110 017, India
Penguin Group (NZ), Cnr. Airborne and Rosedale Roads, Albany, Auckland 1310, New Zealand
(a division of Pearson New Zealand Ltd.)
Penguin Books (South Africa) (Pty.) Ltd., 24 Sturdee Avenue, Rosebank, Johannesburg 2196,
South Africa

Penguin Books Ltd., Registered Offices: 80 Strand, London WC2R 0RL, England

This is a work of fiction. Names, characters, places, and incidents either are the product of the authors' imagination or are used fictitiously, and any resemblance to actual persons, living or dead, business establishments, events, or locales is entirely coincidental.

PRETTY POISON

A Berkley Prime Crime Book / published by arrangement with the authors

PRINTING HISTORY
Berkley Prime Crime mass-market edition / May 2005

ISBN: 978-0-425-20299-9

BERKLEY PRIME CRIME®
Berkley Prime Crime Books are published by The Berkley Publishing Group,
a division of Penguin Group (USA) Inc.,
375 Hudson Street, New York, New York 10014.
BERKLEY PRIME CRIME is a registered trademark of Penguin Group (USA) Inc.
The Berkley Prime Crime design is a trademark belonging to Penguin Group (USA) Inc.

PRINTED IN THE UNITED STATES OF AMERICA

10   9   8   7   6   5

1

Anemone

Botanical: *Anemone nemorosa*
Family: N.O. Ranunculaceae
Common names: Windflower, wood anemone

Anemone is originally derived from the Greek word ánemos, *meaning wind. It belongs to the buttercup family. The Chinese called it the flower of death. The Egyptians believed the anemone denoted sickness because of the flush of color on the backs of the white sepals. In Europe, it was custom to hold your breath while running through a field of anemones. They believed that even the air around the anemones was poisonous.*

IT WAS TOO LATE for Peggy Lee to stop when she saw the car. There wasn't even time to sound the air horn that scared away dogs and small children. It was like being in a slow motion movie.

The green Saturn Vue pulled out of the parking lot, and her bike glided right into the driver's side door. The over-sized front tire absorbed most of the shock. The impact jarred her but didn't knock her down. She put out her legs to brace herself and stared belligerently at the man behind the wheel.

The driver couldn't open his door with her bike nudged up against it. Instead, he opened his window. "I'm sorry. I didn't see you there. Are you all right?"

"I'm fine." She removed her helmet and feathered her fingers through her shoulder-length hair that was more white than red. "You could be a little more careful coming out like that. You know, share the road."

He squinted into the sunlight behind her. "I wasn't looking for traffic on the sidewalk. Aren't bicycles supposed to be in the street?"

"When the street doesn't have potholes big enough to swallow them." She moved her bike to the parking lot, checked the tires and the front fender. Nothing seemed to be wrong with her or the bike. She was lucky.

The driver parked his car beside the Starbucks coffee shop again. He waited while she looked over her bike. "Are you sure you're all right?"

"I'm sure." She frowned at her watch. "Except for being late. Of course, that isn't your fault. The city is tearing up Morehead Street again, so I had to come up East. Unfortunately, all the coffee drinkers seem to come this way, too."

He glanced down at the spreading coffee stain on his blue shirt. "Do you ride to work every day?"

She really looked at him for the first time. He wasn't too bad. A little ordinary maybe, brown hair and brown eyes. But he had a nice smile. Good teeth. Not that it mattered. She was too old to have those thoughts. She hadn't been a widow that long. "I'm doing my part for the ozone. Everything seems to be fine. Thank you for stopping."

"Wait!" He took a business card from his wallet. "Take this in case everything isn't fine. Call me if you need anything."

She glanced at the card, then tucked it into her pocket. "I will."

"Now the best thing you can do is not to use tap water on these at all," Peggy said as she held up the attractive, white African violet in the pretty, cobalt blue glass pot. "They're very sensitive to salt. Rainwater or bottled water is much better for them. If you think you have a salt buildup, as this little lady does, you'll see the white residue on the pot."

She pointed out the rime on the pot's edge. The women in the audience looked carefully at it. A few took notes.

"Take the plant out and repot it. If you're going to reuse the same pot, be sure to clean it thoroughly with about a teaspoon of chlorine bleach in some warm water. Fill the pot with fresh soil halfway, then gently replace the plant and cover the roots. Be sure to water often, before the plant dries out. Then drain the excess to avoid root or crown rot. Only fertilize once or twice a year in the summer and allow the excess to drain completely."

"What if it stops blooming?" a voice asked from the group of twelve women in the Kozy Kettle Tea and Coffee Emporium.

"Then give it more light. These plants are very affected by light. If they stop blooming, it's more likely you have them in a bad spot than that they need fertilizing. Be patient with them."

"Is it true you can only grow them if you've gone through menopause?"

Peggy laughed at the question. "Yes, and you can only dye your hair at midnight during the full moon or the color will run. That's an old wives' tale. Julie Warner has a very nice collection at her home, and I don't think she's gone through menopause yet."

There was some snickering in the audience. Everyone knew who Julie Warner was, of course. Her restored 1902 house was in every Charlotte magazine. Her name and face were in every society column. Her husband was Mark Warner, a senior executive with Bank of America. Of course, *she* had African violets that bloomed constantly.

"Any other questions?" When there was no response, Peggy nodded. "Thank you for coming this morning. Good luck with your African violets. Next week, we'll be talking about planting your bulbs for spring."

A light smattering of applause filtered through the group before they began to gather their pocketbooks and jackets to leave. The scent of coffee mingled with the aroma of freshly baked bread and spicy herbs.

Peggy picked up her tote bag. She smiled at the man behind the counter. "Would you mind if I leave this African violet and potting soil here a little longer? I don't think I can carry all of this with me."

He laughed. "Don't worry about it. Another cup of peach tea for the road?"

"No thanks, Emil. I have to get over to the shop. I got here late this morning. Selena called to tell me she was running late, too. I haven't even opened yet."

"It's barely after ten. You're not too far behind." Emil Balducci's thick gray mustache drooped a little on the right side when he wasn't smiling. That didn't happen often.

He was one of the happiest men Peggy had ever known. With his broad Sicilian features, craggy brows, and shadowed dark eyes, he was quite a ladies' man. Especially when his wife, Sofia, wasn't at the shop. "Thanks again for letting me have the garden club meeting here."

He held up his big, callused hand. "I enjoy the talks, and you bring in customers after the morning rush. Maybe you could have a garden club every day, hmm?"

"When they can clone a couple more of me, we'll talk. It's all I can do to keep up with this one. But we'll be back next Thursday."

Claire Drummond, a tall, gaunt woman with very large white teeth, approached her. "I really appreciate the advice, Peggy! I was wondering if you could come over and take a look at my terrarium sometime. It's developed some mildew or fungus that I can't get rid of."

"If I can't get there myself, I'll send someone else out." Peggy took her appointment book out of her bag and flipped through the pages. "When would be good for you?"

"Anytime really," Claire said. "Well, anytime in the next week. Kevin's out of town until then. He doesn't care much for dirt being all over. I try to do big projects while he's gone."

"How about day after tomorrow?"

"That would be great! Thanks!"

Peggy started toward the door that led into Brevard Court, anxious to open her shop. The autumn morning was gorgeous, with wreaths of mist hanging in the trees. After a hot, dry summer of milky skies and heat lightning, the bright blue Carolina sky was a blessing. The sun was warm despite the chill of November. It was a wonderful ride . . . until she ran into the Saturn.

Even then, she couldn't complain. Nothing really happened. Except she found out her heart could still race a little when she was talking to an attractive man. That was more of a surprise than running into the side of his car. Her husband, John, had only been dead two years. She never expected to consider a man as anything more than a friend for the rest of her life.

She shuffled her keys, looking for the right one that would open the door. Good smells were already emanating from Anthony's Caribbean Café and China King restaurant. Across the way, the Carolina Expert Tailor shop was busy, and a woman in a tight red business suit was smoking a cigarette outside of Cookie's Travel Experts.

Brevard Court was built at the doorway to Latta Arcade. Like a turn-of-the-century mini-mall, the shops continued along the inside arcade in the restored 1915 office building. The antique light fixtures and parallel rows of shop fronts created the feeling of walking into the past. The overhead skylight, which was part of the original architecture, kept shoppers dry. Its original purpose was to provide natural light for cotton buyers to inspect their goods.

The rent was a little steep, but Peggy loved the look and feel of the place. The Potting Shed had real heart-of-pine floors that squeaked when she walked across them. It wasn't huge, but it had a nice-sized warehouse space in the back to keep shovels, potting soil, and other essential items. She did a brisk business, even in the winter. Charlotteans were avid gardeners all year long.

One of the students who worked for her created a beautiful banner for the big storefront window. Red tulips linked to yellow marigolds. Purple hyacinths entwined with pink carnations. It made her think of spring when she saw it.

Her shop was the realization of a dream Peggy and John Lee had shared. An urban gardener's paradise. They saved money religiously toward it for ten years. It was going to be their retirement. They both loved plants and gardening.

Peggy was the daughter of a South Carolina gentleman farmer. She grew up walking barefoot through cornfields and soybeans in the rich coastal soil. She loved to help out with planting and harvesting. Her career as a botanist was a natural extension of her love of plants. She taught classes at Queens University for twenty years before retiring when she was fifty. She went back to teaching part-time to help offset expenses with the Potting Shed.

John called working in the yard his getaway. He came home, put his hands in the dirt, and forgot everything he'd seen and heard on the streets of Charlotte. He was amazing with trees and shrubs. He had azalea flowers the size of grapefruit. All of their neighbors were envious.

He was a police detective for twenty years. Walked a beat for ten years before that. Then he answered a late-night domestic dispute call that ended in violence. It would be two years in December since he was shot and killed on the sidewalk outside a south Charlotte house. The husband killed his wife as well as John Lee. He fled the scene and was never found.

When John died, Peggy took all the money they'd saved plus his pension fund and opened the shop. Her accountant almost had a heart attack. But there was prime space in the downtown area available. She'd wasted enough time.

Business was slow at first. There were times she was afraid she was going to lose everything. But the idea caught on as more people began to inhabit the expensive condominiums and apartments being built. Charlotte's inner city was coming alive, and Peggy's garden shop was part of it.

Humming to herself, Peggy took off her purple cape as she walked in the door and tossed her hat behind the counter.

Traffic was light on Thursdays anyway. Things would pick up around lunchtime when the personal assistants and office managers came out of the uptown buildings. They loved to eat lunch in the courtyard outside her windows where benches and wrought-iron tables and chairs were set. Then they wandered through the shops.

She switched on the lights and set up the cash register for the day. She was having some trouble with the computer she used for ordering unusual plants and supplies for her customers. But a good swat on the case set that right. The store was ready for the fall planting season but gearing up toward the winter months when most outside work was maintenance. Her seed catalogs were beginning to arrive to fill everyone's mind with visions of color for spring.

She looked around the shop. Everything was set up for her first customer. Except for the garden spade in the middle of the floor. Peggy glanced at her watch and wondered how late Selena was going to be as she walked around the counter to pick it up.

The pointed end of the spade was tinged reddish brown. Carolina clay, probably. But this seemed darker. There were traces of it leading toward the warehouse door in the back of the shop. Wondering what happened and who she was going to chew out for it, she picked up the shovel. That's when she saw him. Her hands went numb, and the shovel clattered to the floor.

She wasn't sure how long she stood there looking at the man. Her first impulse was to turn around and run out of her shop, screaming for help. But she was made of sterner stuff. Or at the very least, she was morbidly curious. Years of being a cop's wife didn't prepare her for this. But her background as a researcher made her push her emotions aside and take another look.

The man was facedown in one of her attractive wicker baskets filled with anemone bulbs. It was part of the autumn scene she'd created, complete with scarecrow and pumpkins. He'd obviously fallen forward, dragging the scarecrow from its perch on the oak rocking chair. The straw figure looked forlorn, lying half under the man's weight like some bizarre teddy bear.

She wanted to look away. She had her cell phone open but couldn't get her fingers to press the buttons. The terrible picture mesmerized her. She felt like one of those people she yelled at who gawked at car accidents. She knew what she should do, but the connection between logic and motor function failed her.

The man could be a homeless person. Despite the best efforts of the real estate management group who owned Brevard Court, there were usually one or two of them hanging around. Although his clothes seemed too clean and his trousers had a sharp crease down the legs. There was also the little question of how he came to be in her shop.

The courtyard door was locked when she came in. She locked it after the last customer left yesterday. He didn't come in that way without a key. The only other way in was through the back loading door. She wanted to check it. But she couldn't get her feet to move any more than she was able to dial 911.

He might just be unconscious. Peggy really wanted to think that was the case. There was only one way to tell.

She stepped carefully around the man on the floor until she could reach down and touch his neck. There was no pulse. He was as cold as last winter. There was some dried blood on his white shirt collar. It spread down his back to darken his suit coat and reached up into his hairline. There was a thin trickle of it on his right ear. Blood had pooled on the floor around him.

He definitely wasn't one of the college students who worked for her. She couldn't tell who he was with his face buried in the basket. And she knew better than to move him. How many times had John come home complaining about a disturbed crime scene?

But she couldn't help noticing some of the same details John used to tell her after coming home from a call at three A.M. Caucasian man. Probably about six feet tall. Fairly athletic build. Light brown hair. She couldn't tell the color of his eyes, and there were no visible scars. At least not from her perspective. There was a white mark on his outstretched wrist that looked like he was used to wearing a watch. His nails were manicured.

She stopped cataloging his vitals when her gaze reached his feet. He was wearing black nylon socks but no shoes. She glanced around the area. There was no sign of them. She heard a key rattle in the back door. It was locked, too. Not sure what to expect, her hand reached out for one of the rakes in the display.

"Morning, Peggy! How's busi—geez! What happened?"

Peggy looked up at her assistant. "I'm afraid he's dead. Don't touch anything."

Selena Rogers remained where she was, horror-stricken by the sight of the body. "How do you know he's dead? Maybe he's asleep."

"I touched him. He's stiff and cold. He's not ever getting up again."

Big blue eyes widened even further. "What happened?"

"I don't know. There's some blood. I don't think he died from natural causes."

"Did *you* kill him?"

"Of course not! Don't be silly! I don't even know who he is!" Peggy carefully stepped back around the body. Her hands were shaking, but she forced them to punch in 911. She turned away from the dead man. Selena's entrance broke the spell. She was glad to be able to function again.

"Was he killed right there, looking at the bulbs?"

"I don't know. He was dead when I got here." The emergency operator came on the line. Peggy told her what happened and her address. She closed the phone and sank down on the nearby garden bench. Her knees were a little weak, and she was light-headed. She despised those ridiculous women who fainted at the sight of blood and wasn't about to become one of them. "You might as well sit down, Selena. This could take a while."

It only took the Charlotte police department about a minute and a half to get a squad car to Brevard Court. An ambulance was there soon after. Peggy opened the door for them, then stepped aside.

The uniformed officer took a cursory look around the shop. He didn't seem particularly upset when he saw the man on the floor. He took out a small notebook and pen. "Are you the one who found the body?"

She looked at his name tag. "Yes I am, Officer Kopacka. This is my shop."

"Your name?"

"Peggy Lee."

He looked up. "Didn't you used to be a singer?"

"No." Like no one ever asked her *that* question. "That was someone else."

He asked her a series of rapid-fire questions. She answered as well as she could. When it came to the shovel, she admitted that she disturbed the evidence. "I didn't know at the time that it was evidence. It was just in the way."

"And what makes you think the shovel is evidence now?"

She shrugged. "The blood on the edge?"

He looked skeptical. "And you've never seen this man before?"

"Maybe. It's difficult to tell, since I can't see his face."

He scribbled down her answers, then addressed Selena. "What about you?"

"Me? I just got here. Peggy was standing over him when I walked in. I don't know what happened."

He looked back at Peggy.

"Hey, Kyle," his partner called, "you better come and take a look at this."

"Stay right here, both of you. I have more questions."

"I have plants to run over to Wachovia," Selena said. "Then I have class at noon."

"Not today. Even if you didn't see what happened, we still need your statement."

Peggy put her arm around Selena's shoulders. "Don't worry. It'll take a while to clear this up, but everything will be fine. I'll call Liz at Wachovia and postpone. You should be able to get out of here in time for class."

"Thanks." Selena shivered when she looked back at the dead man. "What do you think happened? If you just got here, too, how did he get into the shop?"

"I don't know."

The officer came back to them. "You ladies might as well get comfortable. We're going to have to wait for a detective. This man's been murdered."

"That's crazy!" Selena declared. "Peggy wouldn't hurt a fly!"

"Please don't help me, Selena. I don't think the officer was suggesting that I killed the man. Were you, Officer Kopacka?"

"Not necessarily."

"That's very reassuring. Thank you."

Selena moved closer to her. Her long black hair and cocoa skin emphasized her golden whiskey brown eyes. She was tall and thin, a long-distance runner at Queens University. After taking Peggy's botany class by accident last year, she went to work for her a week later. "I'm sorry. I didn't mean it the way it sounded. I'm just so nervous, you know? This is like being on one of those reality shows. Except for real."

"It's okay. I don't know how all of this happened. But I know we can clear it up. There wasn't a dead man here when we left last night."

"No." Selena stopped. "Was there a delivery? Not that they would've delivered him here but . . ."

Peggy pushed a strand of white hair out of her face. "I'm not sure. I'll have to take a look at the delivery log."

Emil crashed in through the courtyard door. "Peggy? What happened?"

"You can't come in here," Officer Kopacka told him. "This is a crime scene."

All five-feet-ten inches of Sicilian male bristled. His voice was still heavily accented, even after twenty years away from Sicily. "Hey! I'm a taxpayer! I'm entitled!"

"I'm sorry, sir. Nobody walks in on a crime scene unless the detective on duty says so."

"Okay. Where's the detective?"

"I'm all right." Peggy didn't want her friend to go to jail. He was a little prone to theatrics. This wasn't the time for it.

"I saw the squad car and the ambulance." Emil puffed out his chest. "Are you hurt?"

"I'm fine. I walked in and found a dead man in my shop."

He frowned. "A dead man? It's not that homeless bum you're always feeding, is it?"

"No." She wished he wouldn't be quite so much help either.

"Homeless man?" the officer asked. "What homeless man?"

"He comes and begs for handouts." Emil nodded at Peggy. "She always gives him something. I told her it was asking for trouble. Those kind are always trouble."

The officer looked at Peggy again. "Is that true?"

"The odd biscuit or two. Some spare change. It's not like I took him into my home."

"But he's always here?"

"He's not here today," Emil added. "He probably killed this man, then ran away."

"He's sixty-three and has arthritic knees," Peggy told him. "He could hardly run anywhere."

"Ha! You're too easy on him."

"You need to leave, sir," the officer interrupted their debate. "I'll be sure to note your remarks. Someone will talk to you later."

Emil threw his hands up as he was leaving the shop, "Okay! I'll be over there!"

The officer ignored him as he questioned Peggy. "Have you seen this homeless man lately?"

"I haven't seen him since Sunday," she answered. "But he didn't have anything to do with this. The dead man is in my shop. The doors were still locked when I got here."

"Maybe the homeless man surprised him."

"How would either of them get in?"

Officer Kopacka glanced around. "I guess we won't know until we investigate."

"I'd say she knows more about that than you do, son," a familiar voice joined the conversation.

Peggy turned back and smiled at an old friend. "Al! Thank goodness!"

Detective Al McDonald kissed her cheek. His heavyset black face sat squatly on a thick, muscular neck. Red-rimmed brown eyes were alert to the details of the shop around him. "How are you? I haven't seen you since Easter, right? The egg hunt in the park? I trampled on that patch of whaddyacallit."

"Violets. That's right. I'm fine. How's Mary?"

"Mary's okay. She's getting impatient for me to retire." He laughed, lines creasing his thick black face. "How's Paul?"

She rolled her green eyes when she thought of her son. "I don't know. I never see him anymore."

"You know, I never see him either. And we both work out of the same precinct. I think he's avoiding me."

"That makes two of us. I know he's in Charlotte some-where!"

"So, what have we got here?" he asked her.

Peggy told him what she knew. "I don't think I know the man, but it's hard to say. People are in and out all the time. And his face *is* down in the anemones."

Al nodded. "The crime scene boys are right behind me. You know the drill. This could take a while."

"Detective McDonald?" one of the younger officers called him.

"Excuse me a minute." He smiled at Peggy again and nodded to Selena.

"What are they looking at?" Selena whispered. "Do they think *we* did it?"

"Of course they don't think we did it! I'm sure they're looking for evidence." Now that Al was here, things would be in hand. He was John's partner for twenty years. There wasn't a man alive she trusted more.

Al came back to them after talking to the officer in a far corner of the shop. "I think you're right, Peggy. It looks like this man was murdered with the shovel, then robbed."

"So someone robbed him?" Selena deciphered. "It's sounding more and more like Homer."

"Homer?" Al asked.

"He's our local homeless man," Selena explained. "He lives out in the courtyard sometimes. You know, he asks for spare change and food."

Peggy shook her head. "Mr. Cheever wouldn't hurt anyone. He's a Vietnam vet who fell on hard times. He could be John."

Al looked skeptical. "John wouldn't have begged for money and food outside shops. I know you want to help this Mr. Cheever, but we need to talk to him, whether you think he's guilty or not. You know that better than these rookies."

Peggy didn't really know much about him. "He moves around the city quite a bit. He's had some trouble with the police."

"And you say his name is Homer Cheever?" Al took out his notebook.

"We call him Homer because he reminds us of Homer Simpson, the cartoon character?" Selena shrugged. "I guess we don't really know his name."

He looked up at her. "And you are?"

"Selena Rogers. I work here."

"And did you see anything unusual, Ms. Rogers?"

She glanced at Peggy. "I came in when she found the man—uh—body."

"What about this homeless man?" he continued. "How about a description?"

Peggy responded, "He's tall, very thin and pale. He has bad knees and wears a long black coat with holes in it. He has thinning brown hair and blue eyes. He's got a jagged scar on one side of his face. He told me that he's sixty-three."

"Okay. We'll put out an APB on him."

"He doesn't have a key to the shop," Peggy pointed out.

"Don't worry about it. We'll figure it out. You'll have to leave the shop closed until we're finished."

"I know. But I still think you're making a mistake looking for Mr. Cheever."

"Look," Al argued. "Maybe the victim got locked in here last night by mistake when you closed up. Maybe he was trying to get out and your homeless friend saw him and attacked him. Maybe Mr. Cheever was trying to break into the store. The jewelry, the wallet, even the shoes. Those are all things a homeless man might take."

"The dead man couldn't get in or out of the locked shop without a key," she reasoned. "There was no one here when I left last night. And unless he broke a window, Mr. Cheever couldn't get in without a key to rob him!"

"Stubborn as always, huh? Just let us investigate. I'll keep you posted. Okay?"

"I understand." *But I don't have to like it.*

"Excuse me." One of the crime scene investigators interrupted them. "Would you like to take a look and see if he's someone you know?"

Peggy hesitated. It *seemed* like a good idea when she said she'd help identify him. She got up from the bench and walked slowly toward the body. The man's face was mottled and pale, his lips white and slack. His eyes were half open, revealing his vacant stare. Blood smeared his right cheek. But she knew him despite his ghastly appearance. "Mark Warner!"

2

Water lily

Botanical: *Nymphaea odorata*
Family: Nymphaeaceae

Known as the queen of the water, it is found in shallow ponds, streams, and lakes. According to legend, a Brazilian Indian girl was killed when she tried to embrace the warrior in the moon. He transformed her into the giant water lily, the vitória-régia, *whose flower opens wide only at night. It is said that the* vitória-régia *opens itself to its utmost only during a full moon when the sky over the Amazon jungle is cloudless and particularly clear.*

"*THE* MARK WARNER?" Al peered at the man's face. "Are you sure?"

"I'm afraid so," Peggy muttered. "I've seen him around the shop lately."

"What's he doing here dead?"

"I wish I knew."

"Well, take your time. Do your best," Al cautioned the crime scene team. "Not like I'd expect anything else from you. But this one will be on the news every night for a week."

Peggy knew that meant her shop would be on the news, too. There was no way to know how that would affect her business. She felt a little guilty thinking about it that way.

"I have to go." Al took her hand. "I'll be in touch. You sure you're okay?"

"I'm fine," she assured him. "I'm going to stay here for a while."

Al kissed her cheek before he left. "That's fine. Someone can take you home if you need a ride. Don't be shy about asking."

"All right. Thanks."

"I can't believe it. My first case has to be someone famous!" A young Vietnamese woman in a blue crime scene uniform stood beside Peggy when Al was gone. Her huge, almond-shaped brown eyes and pretty face were half hidden by heavy black glasses.

"I suppose that makes it harder," Peggy sympathized. "Once the press hears about it, reporters will be everywhere."

"Yeah." She adjusted her glasses. "Sorry. That's my problem, not yours. I'm Mai Sato. I'm with the medical examiner's office."

"Nice to meet you. I'm Peggy Lee."

The younger woman did a double take. "Aren't you someone famous?"

"Only if you can get famous being a professor at Queens for too long."

Mai smiled. "Sorry to meet you under these circumstances."

Peggy watched the crime scene teamwork on the body, inspecting it for anything that might help them discover what happened. "Is there anything I can do to help?"

"We'll need your fingerprints, Professor Lee. Also those of anyone who works here."

"That's fine. I'll tell my people. But I'm afraid you'll find a lot more than their prints here."

"It will give us a base to use as a comparison, since your prints will come up most often. I could do your prints right now so you won't have to come to the precinct," Mai offered. "Do you own this shop?"

"Thanks. Yes, I'm here almost every day." Peggy

shrugged. "I teach botany, but that's only part time. I contract out the fieldwork for the shop to some students. It's mostly commercial plant care."

The assistant ME looked at the dead man again. "And you're sure this is Mark Warner?"

"Positive. As I said, I've seen him around the courtyard lately. He's been in the shop a few times. He never spoke or bought anything that I saw." Peggy put her hands into her pockets. "But I'm sure you'll want to have someone who knew him better actually make the final identification.

They sat down together. Mai carefully put Peggy's fingers on the ink pad, then rolled them on the paper. She put a tag on the prints before she slipped the paper into a plastic bag and sealed it.

Peggy thanked her for the damp towelette to clean her hands. "Now what?"

"If you could have all the people who work for you come in, we could do their prints and begin matching up who belonged here with who didn't." She gave Peggy a business card. "If they have any questions, they can call me."

"Thanks, Mai. I'll let them know. That's Selena over there. She works here, too. She might as well get it over with while you're here."

"All right. How many people have keys to the shop?"

"At least five that work here," Peggy answered. "Oh, and Mr. Balducci. I gave him a key in case he needed to come in for some reason."

"That's the sandwich shop owner?"

"Yes."

Mai sighed. "It looks like time of death will probably be around midnight. What was Mark Warner doing here in the middle of the night?"

WHAT WOULD ANYONE BE DOING at the shop in the middle of the night? Peggy asked herself that question several more times as the day progressed. There wasn't a ready answer. While some deliveries were made after store hours, she knew none were made that late. The gates and doors to Latta Arcade and Brevard Court were locked down after around seven or eight. Only shop owners could get in through the back loading doors.

The media picked up on the story and added to it, but they couldn't ferret out the answer either. Not that they didn't try. She refused to talk to any of the local reporters about the incident. She knew what Julie Warner was going through. It had been terrible for Peggy to hear the information about John's death repeated a dozen times on TV and banner headlines trumpeting it in the newspapers.

She was scheduled for an evening lecture at the university. It was tempting to postpone it after the day's events. But it wouldn't do any good to hide in the house. She knew that too well.

Peggy forced herself into a black business suit that she teamed with an emerald-green blouse. She never wore heels, using her mode of transportation as an excuse. Really, she refused to put her feet through that agony. There was no one left for her to impress. She wasn't a young woman looking for a man.

There were the usual joggers on the street as she pedaled toward Queens University. She recognized some of them as students. They huffed and waved as they passed her. She rode beneath a city crew beginning to put up Christmas decorations on the streetlights. Evening traffic swarmed around her as she merged with the cars streaming into the university parking lot.

Peggy quickly repaired the minor damage done to her hair by the brisk wind. She glanced at her watch, realizing she was about to be late for her lecture. Fortunately, she'd never been a stickler for time. A few minutes here or there weren't going to hurt anyone. That attitude always drove John crazy.

The auditorium was full when she finally walked out on the stage. The dean had been stalling for her, running on about future events scheduled in the auditorium. "Here she is at last! We were beginning to wonder if you were going to show up, Dr. Lee."

Peggy thanked him and squeezed his hand behind the podium. She kept her voice down as she said, "Thanks for covering for me, Phil. I'm lucky to be here at all tonight. It's not every day I find a dead man in my shop."

"Are you sure you're all right?" the dean whispered out of microphone range.

"I'm fine." She moved closer to the podium and adjusted the microphone. "Good evening. I apologize for being late. Let's not waste any more time. As many of you know, I'm Dr. Margaret Lee. I teach botany here at Queens. Let's talk about botanical poisons."

She pressed the button on the projector control as the lights came down in the auditorium. A picture of a sunlit vine came up on the screen. "This is a common plant you've probably seen many times. *Hedera helix* or English ivy. It's an indoor/outdoor ornamental vine. It contains saponins, which can cause poisoning in animals and humans. Humans who don't know any better ingest the pretty berries on this vine and go into comas. Not a good thing to do."

Pens scribbled, and fingers typed on laptops. For the next hour, she took the audience through a list of poisonous plants that could be found in the garden or home environment. She'd worked with botanical toxins and their antidotes as a hobby for years. It finally spilled over into her professional life last year when she was consulted on a poisoning death that occurred in the North Carolina mountains.

"In conclusion, just because a flower or plant is pretty or seems familiar doesn't make it safe. If you have children or pets who may not know the difference, be sure the plants you pick for your home or garden aren't toxic. I've shown you a few species to beware. Consult a good botanical guide or call your local poison control center if you aren't sure. Are there any questions?"

"Wouldn't it be better not to sell plants that are poisonous?" a young woman asked from the audience.

"Possibly," Peggy acknowledged. "But how many things in our homes *could* be harmful? You wouldn't let your two-year-old play with matches either. Or put antifreeze out in a pail for your dog to drink. Some common sense is warranted with everything, including plants."

Peggy fielded questions for half an hour before she called for the last question as the dean made wrapping up motions with his hands.

"Could any of these plants be used to kill someone?" a man asked from the back of the auditorium. His face was hidden in the shadow of the spotlight they used for plays.

"It's possible," she answered. "People are notorious for finding any means to an end, aren't they?" The audience laughed, and she thanked them for coming. She glanced back out into the crowd. The man who asked the final question was gone. She shivered, always wondering if she was giving away the seeds of someone's destruction.

As the group broke up, Peggy was surrounded by her students and other members of the audience who wanted to ask her more questions. She saw a familiar face from the corner of her eye; the man in the green Saturn she ran into that morning.

He smiled and began to weave through the crowd toward her. Peggy felt a little flutter in her chest. Since she knew it couldn't be excitement at seeing him again, she put it down to indigestion.

Before he could reach her, another man stepped between them. "Dr. Lee? My name is Hal Samson. I'm from Columbia, South Carolina. I wonder if I could bend your ear about a case I'm working on right now."

Peggy looked past the jostling students making jokes about poisoning obnoxious professors. The man from the Saturn was gone. A small sense of disappointment nipped at her and was quickly pushed aside. It was ridiculous anyway. She should know better. The man was at least ten years younger than her. Even if she was romantically interested in him, which she *wasn't,* what could he possibly see in her? It was just a coincidence that he was there.

"Dr. Lee?"

She glanced at the heavily bearded man who adjusted his glasses self-consciously and straightened his stained tie. "Excuse me, Mr. Samson?"

"Dr. Samson, actually." He chuckled in embarrassment. "I know this is a bad place. I wouldn't be here if it weren't urgent. I assure you, I would've gone through the proper channels."

Peggy reached for her cape from behind the podium. "Nonsense! You can buy me a cup of coffee at the cafeteria, and we can talk."

Over large mugs of strong brew, Dr. Samson explained his dilemma. "She presented with signs of liver and kidney failure, depressed circulation, vomiting, diarrhea. She was hypothermic. We admitted her right away and did a workup on her. I thought it was last-stage liver disease until her husband told me that she was perfectly healthy the day before."

She looked at the twenty-four-year-old woman's file. "I assume you've come all this way because you learned it was poison instead."

"Tox screen analysis found traces of protoanemonin in her system." He stirred more sugar into his coffee. "It's not something we see much of. Poison, I mean. I immediately questioned the husband about what she'd been doing prior to her illness. He told me she went to work and didn't feel well when she came home. Her symptoms became worse as time passed until he finally brought her to the hospital. I thought it might be an accidental poisoning. Maybe she worked at a nursery or greenhouse."

"Anemonin isn't an accidental poisoning," Peggy said. "She couldn't get it from working with plants."

"I don't mind bringing the police in on it, if that's the case. But my concern right now is for the patient. She won't last much longer. I have no idea where she got the anemonin or how she was exposed. Her eyes or skin don't show any sign of irritation. I've used activated charcoal to flush her stomach, but that's probably too little, too late. I'm keeping her going with heart and respiratory stimulants."

Peggy studied the photo of the attractive young woman. "How long has it been?"

"She's been in my care for about eighteen hours. Her husband says they thought she had the flu. I'm running out of time."

"You've done everything you can, Dr. Samson. Without knowing the size of the dose or how it was administered, no one could do any better. There's no real antidote, although I have heard of ginseng being helpful in some cases. It must've been a small dose or she'd be dead already. If she makes it through the next twenty-four hours, she has a chance of recovery."

He picked up the photo from the file. "She's a lovely girl. Her husband says they were trying to start a family. They've been married for two years. Are you sure this couldn't be an accident, Dr. Lee?"

"There's no accident to it, Dr. Samson. It's a difficult and lengthy process to come up with anemonin in its purest, crystal form. I hope she recovers so she can tell you how she was poisoned." She looked at the hospital chart again. It was disturbing to think that someone would do such a thing, but she knew it happened.

It was after nine when they walked out of the cafeteria. Peggy pulled her cape around her and shivered in the breeze that rattled down the street.

"Can I drop you somewhere, Dr. Lee?"

"No, thanks. I don't live far from here. And please call me Peggy."

Samson smiled. "All right. If you'll call me Hal. I'll be happy to keep you posted on my patient's progress. Maybe there's a logical explanation for the whole thing."

She held out her hand. "I'd appreciate that, Hal. If there's anything else I can do or you have any other questions, I'll be glad to help. I'll send you that information about ginseng, if you like."

"That would be great, thanks. It's been a pleasure meeting you." He shook her hand heartily. "I'm sorry it had to be under these circumstances."

Peggy agreed. She walked back with him to the auditorium parking lot. Hal Samson was exactly the kind of man she should be interested in, if she was ever interested in a man again. He was a few years older than her. Intellectual. His clothes were a little messy, but she wasn't exactly neat herself, especially when she was working.

But where was that little spark when they parted company at his gray Volvo? There was no flutter when he waved to her from behind the window. She watched him drive away and sighed. She just wasn't ready yet.

PEGGY TOOK OFF HER GLASSES and rubbed her eyes. It was two A.M. She'd spent the last three hours searching through her files for any new information she might've missed about treating anemonin poisoning.

Despite frequent updates from her colleagues in the study of poisonous plants, there was no new research on *Anemone pulsatilla*. The tiny flower was harmless enough and once used quite heavily for medicinal purposes. The oil caused skin irritation, and its primary component, anemonin, was still an active ingredient in other herbal preparations as a sedative.

Trying to get the thoughts of death out of her mind, Peggy did what every gardener does when they can't sleep: She took out her seed catalog. Scarlet runner beans and pink hibiscus were always soothing. She was thinking about planting some lilac bushes in her yard, even though they didn't do as well in the warm, damp Southern climate.

Despite the bright pictures, she couldn't focus on the catalog. The day's events weighed heavily on her mind, especially the dead man on the floor in her shop. There were so many unanswered questions.

If Mark Warner were a little less of a celebrity around

town, she wouldn't have known him. He wasn't there the few times she'd been at the Warners' home. But there were so many newspaper articles about him; he was almost as familiar as the mayor.

She suddenly remembered that a beautiful woman was at his side when he came to Brevard Court those warm fall days. She'd seen them together a few times in the shop. The pair didn't act businesslike toward each other: heads bent close together, stroking each other's arms. And the woman dressed a little expensively for a personal assistant.

Of course, everyone had heard the gossip about the Warner family. Rumor had it that Julie and Mark both fooled around on the side. Maybe those rumors colored her thinking about the man.

While Al's idea that Mark got locked in the shop by accident was ludicrous, what if he was purposely hiding? Was it possible that he planned to meet the tall brunette there after the shop closed? She'd have to check with Keeley and Sam to see if they were there the night before. They sometimes dropped off plants and supplies at night. Maybe they saw or heard something.

Peggy shook her head and flipped a page in the spring catalog without seeing it. That didn't make any sense either. The Potting Shed was too small for her not to notice if someone was still there when she closed up. And a man in Warner's position wouldn't skulk around in a garden shop waiting to be locked in. He'd simply arrange to meet the woman at a friend's house or a hotel.

Yet there he was lying dead in her shop. While none of the hypotheses made any sense, the result was incontrovertible.

A tiny chime sounded from a clock on the mantel across the bedroom. She jumped up and fumbled around for her slippers. With her glasses in one hand, she ran down the broad spiral staircase that led to the ground floor.

The house was chilly, as always, when the weather got cool. John had frequently complained about the quirks and problems of living in a big, rambling house from the turn of the century. Upkeep was ridiculous and sometimes improbable.

But Peggy loved the old house. She loved the feel of the cool marble stairs on her feet in the summer. She loved all the nooks and crannies. She kept a thirty-foot blue spruce growing in the entrance hall. Each room in the house had a fireplace. The ceilings were still the original plaster.

But the basement was her passion. Here she dabbled and played with Mother Nature. In her botanical lab, she cross-pollinated and modified, looking for new varieties of plant life for pleasure as well as medicinal purposes.

The basement sprawled the length and width of the entire house, but it still wasn't enough room for her pets. It opened into an acre garden that she cultivated by the season. Here she produced a black rose last summer. Under a two-hundred-year-old oak with branches thicker than her body, she grew purple mushrooms. Two years ago, she produced a small green melon that tasted exactly like a peach.

Tonight, she was going to view her night-blooming water lily for the first time. It was named Antares for the largest red star in the constellation Scorpius. A friend of hers who worked at Longwood Gardens in Pennsylvania sent it to her last month. She put it in her indoor pond and was quickly rewarded with gorgeous dark green and purple leaves.

An array of various heat lamps and ultraviolet lights guided her way through her experiments. She caught her breath when she saw the lily. It was as wide as a dinner plate. Its velvety scarlet petals were reflected in the filtered water where it floated. She immediately took out her camera and notebook. Then she pulled up her sleeves and started in on the real work. She was hoping to create the first rose to only bloom at night.

PEGGY DIDN'T LOOK UP AGAIN until she heard the doorbell ring at eight-thirty. She was wet from working in the pond and covered with dirt. "And that would be the police," she muttered to herself as she put the teakettle on to boil.

She never actually went to sleep last night. She took off her gloves, brushed the loose dirt from her pants, and looked at herself in the antique mirror that hung in the foyer.

Her green eyes seemed greener the last few years, more summer green than spring. She had more white in her hair. Like being blond from the summer sun, only older. The color ran out of her hair after John died. Until then, the red only had traces of white through it.

She touched the fine lines that ran from her eyes and mouth, not willing to spend the time or money to make them less noticeable. She still had a strong chin, like her mother. And too many damn freckles! Pushing her shoulders back under her purple sweater, she opened the door.

"Hey, Peggy."

"Hello, Al. Would you like some tea?" There was deep concern and embarrassment in her old friend's eyes. She didn't know the younger man at his side. But his gaze was impatient and irritated.

"We have a few more questions, Peggy. You know how it is. This is my boss, Lieutenant Rimer. Lieutenant, this is Dr. Lee."

"How do you do, ma'am?"

"I'm fine, thanks." She extended her hand to him after wiping it on her pants. "Nice to meet you, Lieutenant Rimer. You must be new. I don't think I recognize you."

"I transferred from Ohio recently."

"I hope you're feeling at home here?"

"Not really. Not yet anyway. My wife's from Charlotte. All her family's here. I'm still adjusting." He glanced around the room. "I don't want to take up too much of your time, Dr. Lee. Do you have someplace we could talk?"

"Will the kitchen do? I just put on the kettle."

"Sure, thanks."

She walked beside him through the foyer. "You know, these things take time. I moved up here from Charleston. I didn't think I'd ever get used to these cold winters. And all that red clay!"

Rimer laughed. "Yeah, I know. And what's with that white stuff they put on your plate at breakfast?"

"You mean grits? We had them in the Low Country, too. I come from a big family. We ate fried grits, boiled grits, and baked grits. It was a relief the last time I went home and my father had a box of Krispy Kreme donuts on the counter!"

Rimer sat down opposite Al at the big oak table. There was a yellow mum blooming from the sunlight that streamed in the window every afternoon. Smells of lemon balm and spearmint mingled with the strong aroma of chamomile as she steeped the tea.

"What else can I tell you?" she asked.

"Do you have any idea what Warner was doing in your shop?" the lieutenant began with an exasperated sigh.

"I can't imagine why he was there," Peggy answered. "Not for lack of trying. I thought about it all night."

"I feel like an idiot asking you these questions." Al ran his hand through his coarse, thinning black hair and brushed his bulbous nose nervously. "But you *did* find the body."

"Of course. John always told me the first person on the scene was the first suspect. I understand. It's logical."

He fidgeted some more. "Mrs. Warner told us she thought her husband was having an affair. She suggested that maybe it went bad. She said Mark was moody and distracted lately. Did you see him with anyone?"

"Yes. I remembered something early this morning. I know I may appear cool and collected about this, but there *was* a dead body in my shop yesterday. I almost fell over it!" She explained to them about the brunette she'd seen Mark with in the shop.

"What brunette?" Lieutenant Rimer demanded impatiently. "Do you know the woman's name?"

Peggy described the woman for him. "I never really got a close look at her. They were usually there around lunchtime. She could be someone he works with."

"But you didn't think so," Rimer insinuated.

"Not really."

"Did they act . . . friendly?" Al asked.

"*Very* friendly," she confirmed. "But there's a lot of that going on with the lunchtime crowd."

"So was she tall? As tall as him?" Al scribbled in his notebook.

"Not quite, but close." Peggy thought back. "Her hair was very dark brown, shoulder-length. Very good condition. She dressed well. Expensive shoes. She had very muscular legs like she bikes or runs regularly."

"What about her face?" Al questioned. "Eye color? Anything?"

"I saw them together, but they weren't close to the checkout counter. Lunchtime is always busy. I don't have time to do more than glance at people as they come and go. She always had her face turned away from me. I'm as preoccupied with celebrity gossip as the next person. I've heard the trash about the Warners. I wanted to know who was with him as much as any reporter."

"What trash?" Rimer asked.

"The gossips," Peggy explained. "They say Mark and his wife have been dating outside their marriage for years. Who knows if it's true or not. The Warners are a high-profile couple in Charlotte. I'm sure some of it is sour grapes."

"Do you think the brunette was hiding on purpose?" Al went back to their conversation.

Her cinnamon colored brows lifted. "If I were out with someone well-known like Mark and I didn't want anyone to know, I'd stay away from public places! She had to think they were safe. Or it didn't matter."

Al tapped his notebook with his pen. "Okay. We can check this out. Somebody else must've seen them together, too."

"What about the homeless man you mentioned yesterday?" Rimer wanted to know.

"Mr. Cheever?"

The lieutenant consulted his notes. "Officer Kopacka

has it in his report that you said a homeless man could be responsible for the murder."

"I never said that!"

"What *did* you say, Dr. Lee?"

Peggy collected her thoughts. It wouldn't do any good to go off half-baked while she was talking to this intent young man. "I didn't mention him at all. My assistant and Mr. Balducci said something about him."

"And who's Mr. Balducci?" Some of Rimer's notes fell on the floor.

She helped him pick them up. "He owns the sandwich café next to my shop. He was suspicious of Mr. Cheever."

Rimer shook his head. "So you *don't* think Mr. Cheever killed Mr. Warner. Who do you think killed him?"

"Well, I don't know *yet,* Lieutenant! But if I have any ideas, I'll let you know."

"Sounds like this mystery woman could be a good lead," Al added in a gruff voice.

"But even if Mark was having an affair with this woman, it doesn't explain how they got in and out of the shop without a key." Peggy got to her feet as Rimer stood up.

"We'll know more after the autopsy," Al told her.

"Don't worry, Dr. Lee," the lieutenant assured her, "we'll catch who did this."

"Call me Peggy," she invited. "But what I don't understand is how an autopsy will answer my question."

"Thanks. You can call me Jonas. It's difficult to explain how these things work, Peggy. We're getting information on Warner now. Where he was, what he did that night. If we need anything else, I'll have Al give you a call."

"I understand." She hoped John didn't brush people off that way or act like they were brain-dead.

"I'm late for a staff meeting." Jonas looked at Al. "I'll see you back at the office. It was nice meeting you, Peggy. I'm sorry I never met your husband. But I like your son."

"Okay, Lieutenant." Al sat down at the table as Peggy handed him a cup of tea. When the kitchen door closed behind his boss, he said, "That man has a chip on his shoulder a mile wide. But you had him eating out of your hand."

"I don't think I'd say *that*," she contradicted. "He's just not used to the way things are done here. He'll come around."

Al glanced around the kitchen. He recalled when his friend John Lee came back from Charleston with his blushing bride, Peggy. She still had that saucy look to her eyes and that pretty smile.

He grew up with John. They went to the University of North Carolina at Chapel Hill together before splitting up for a few years. Then they both joined the police department in Charlotte. "This is a great old house. John's grandfather built it in the twenties, didn't he?"

She nodded. "We found a box of letters in a chest upstairs that were from his grandparents. He always wanted to do something with them. Have them made into a book or something. But it never got done."

"That's too bad. Maybe Paul will be interested someday. I remember playing cards here on Friday nights and coming to barbecues. God, I miss those old times."

"So do I," she agreed. "You know, you *could* still visit from time to time."

"I know. I'm bad about that. Maybe when I retire, things will be easier." He looked everywhere but into her eyes. "There's gonna be press over this, Peggy."

"I'm not worried about it. I'm sure it won't hurt business, and everyone at the university already thinks I'm eccentric. I hope you can find out who did this."

"We will. The lieutenant's right about that." He struggled slowly to his feet. "I need to go. Anything else I can do for you?"

"No. I'm fine." She smiled at him. "Good luck with the case."

After she closed the door and locked it behind him, she slowly walked upstairs to shower and change. Al and Jonas didn't have the answers to the questions that plagued her all night. But working in research, she knew there were always answers if you knew where to look for them. And she couldn't resist the urge to dabble in the Warner investigation. It happened at her shop, after all.

3

Columbine

Botanical: *Aquilegia vulgaris*
Family: N.O. Ranunculaceae
Common Name: Columbine

Aquilegia, from the Latin word for eagle, refers to the clawlike petals. Columbines are classified with the buttercup family. They grace gardens from British Columbia through the Southern U.S. Columbine is a favorite food for hummingbirds. Thompson people, indigenous to British Columbia, believed that columbine brought good fortune in gambling. They rubbed the plant on the legs of horses and racers to increase their stamina.

TRAFFIC WAS HEAVY going from Queens Road to uptown Charlotte. Peggy navigated her bicycle down the tree-lined streets. A blast of late autumn air had shaken most of the remaining leaves down into the road. The combination of wet pavement and wet leaves made for several accidents. Angry drivers waited impatiently for squad cars to come. She passed them quickly, trying not to look smug. In the city, it paid to stay away from fossil-fueled engines.

Brevard Court and Latta Arcade were mostly deserted. Most of the shops didn't open until ten. She saw the Potting Shed's pickup and made a quick turn toward the loading area at the back of the shop.

Sam was helping Keeley unload flats of pansies. They were planting them in the plaza atrium that day. Pansies weathered Charlotte's outdoor temperatures most of the winter. Their deep purple, yellow, and burgundy were eye-catching.

"Some of those pansies look a little wilted, don't they?" Peggy asked, creeping up on them.

Surprised, Sam juggled a flat of pansies for a moment before he finally got his hands on them. "Damn!"

Keeley took a step back and put her hands to her chest. "You scared the crap out of me!"

Peggy grinned. "It's good for you once in a while."

"I'm glad you think so," Sam argued. "You just took ten years off of my future high-end consulting practice."

"I got twenty dollars off the bad flats because of their condition." Keeley noticed her boss looking at the wilted flowers. "The supplier said these were the best he could get right now anyway."

Peggy examined the plants. "They've had too much water."

Sam lifted another flat and glanced toward the shop. "How weird was it finding a dead guy in there?"

"It was pretty weird. I'm a suspect, you know."

Keeley dropped a flat of pansies. The plastic tray split open. Flowers and potting soil flew everywhere. "How could they think that?"

Peggy bent down to help her pick them up. "I found the body. That makes me a suspect."

"That's stupid."

"They might have another suspect. Julie Warner told the police that she thought Mark was having an affair."

Sam stopped unloading the pansies. "Not that he was having an affair with *you*?"

"No, Sam. Of course not. How *could* they?" Peggy patted his muscled arm.

Sam Ollson wanted to be a heart surgeon, but he looked more like a male model. Blond hair, always tan, perfect teeth, and shoulders a fullback would envy. He'd worked with her since she opened the Potting Shed the summer before he started college. "You know what I mean."

"I do. I'm having some fun. I stopped when I saw you to be sure you got my message about going to have your fingerprints made. The police won't let this go. Be sure you make the trip, or they'll come looking for you."

"I will," Keeley Prinz said solemnly. Her doe-brown eyes were wide in her creamy face. Her thick brown hair was streaked blond by the summer sun. She was an attractive, muscular young woman, the daughter of Peggy's best friend. She loved working outside and planned to be a forest ranger when she finished college. "Who do you think killed him?"

"I don't know," Peggy admitted. "Before Julie mentioned his affair, the police liked Mr. Cheever for it."

"Homer?" Sam grinned. "They gotta be kidding, right?"

"Mark's wallet and jewelry were gone. So were his shoes. They think Mr. Cheever hit him over the head and robbed him. I tried to tell the police it wasn't possible. They won't listen."

"Come on! Even if Homer wanted to, he couldn't get enough oomph to kill a man!"

Peggy answered quietly, "Mr. Cheever could be the suspect through default. Whoever did it left the shovel behind. Which probably means the person was wearing gloves and isn't worried about fingerprints."

"Or they got scared." Keeley shrugged. "Imagine what it must be like to kill someone. I mean, unless you *planned* to do it."

"Hitting somebody with a shovel doesn't seem too calculated to me," Sam observed. "It was probably a crime of passion. The police are right to look for Warner's lover."

"Were the two of you here night before last?" Peggy helped them unload the rest of the pansies and put them in the storage shed.

"We were here until what? Eight-thirty?" Sam looked at Keeley.

"Yeah. We picked up that order of tulip bulbs we planted

yesterday at Dr. Marshall's and dropped off the work order for the Langely estate where we planted the daffodils the day before."

"And you didn't see anything? Or anyone?"

"Nothing unusual." Keeley dusted potting soil from her hands. "I think we would've noticed a man in the shop!"

"Did you notice if Mr. Cheever was around that night?" Peggy wiped her hands on a rag.

"I didn't notice," Sam answered. "I kind of take him for granted."

"Me either," Keeley said. "But he's always around."

"He was here Sunday." Peggy didn't want to implicate her homeless friend in the investigation, but she wanted to know if he saw anything. If the killer thought Mr. Cheever was there when the crime was committed, he could be the next victim. "The police will ask questions when you go in to give your prints."

Sam smiled at her. "We can handle it. And we won't mention Homer unless they beat it out of us."

"Yeah," Keeley joked. "We know you're *hot* for him."

Peggy laughed. "Thanks! I don't want you to lie! But I'd like a chance to talk to him before they pick him up."

"You got it." Sam put on his sunglasses. "Anything else?"

"I'll call the nursery today and have them bring us some fresh flats. No one likes a wilted pansy!"

Keeley frowned. "Sorry. I was trying to save a few bucks."

"That's okay." Peggy assured her. "See you inside."

It was difficult to unlock the back door and make herself walk into the shop. Al had called a crime scene cleaning service for her, and it appeared they did a good job. There was no blood on the floor, but the old wood didn't give up the brown stain. She'd have to buy a rug to put over it and try not to think about it every time she walked in. The scarecrow was gone, probably taken for evidence. The pumpkins were strewn across the floor.

Something strange caught Peggy's eye as she was trying to put her autumn scene back together. She reached down and picked up a flower head from its precarious perch on top of a pumpkin. *Columbine.* "What are *you* doing here?"

"Did you lose something?" Keeley looked at the smooth wood floorboards with her.

"No. I wanted to make sure everything was cleaned up from yesterday." Peggy got up from the floor and pocketed the tiny red columbine flower. She could put it into a plastic bag later. It didn't belong there. Columbines grew wild in the Carolinas but not in November. The flower wasn't more than a few days old. She didn't have any columbine plants in her shop.

She wasn't sure what that meant, if anything. The crime scene team either didn't see it or overlooked it as being part of the decor. After all, it *was* a garden shop. A random flower head that didn't belong on her floor was hardly something that would spark police interest. And it wouldn't clear Mr. Cheever. Still, she didn't plan to throw it away. It might be a piece of the puzzle.

Sam moved the rocking chair back into position. "It doesn't look the same without Gus, does it?"

She smiled. "Getting a new scarecrow is the least of our worries. In some ways, all this publicity will be good for business. It should certainly bring in some new people. And that's good. Except for people who want to come and look at this stain on the floor."

He agreed. "There's that rug place in the Arcade. Would you like me to run down there and get something to cover it?"

"That would be great, Sam. Thanks. Take the checkbook."

The Potting Shed was always busy on Friday with gardeners stocking up for the weekend. The weather was supposed to be nice. Peggy urged everyone who came in during the week to take advantage of it. It wouldn't be long before winter set in, and they'd all be dreaming of spring.

True to her expectations, a steady stream of customers flowed into the shop as soon as they opened. Some were familiar faces there to pick up plant orders or buy potting soil. Some were strangers who walked slowly through, looking at the floor. All of them wanted to know about the murder they'd seen on Channel 9 news.

Everyone had an opinion. Most of the women felt Warner deserved to die for his much-rumored infidelity and was probably killed by some former lover. Most of the men were certain the homeless man was responsible and wanted to know when the city was going to clean up its act.

They all wanted to know Peggy's opinion. When she claimed not to have one, they looked embarrassed or disappointed and continued walking around the shop. Most handled a few garden implements or picked up a pack of bulbs. Few bought anything.

Around ten, the press came in and asked to talk to Peggy while they took pictures of the shop. She declined, even though the free publicity appealed to her. The Potting Shed was notorious enough.

Sam came back with a rainbow-colored rag rug. They moved the rocking chair and the wicker baskets out of the way and laid the rug over the bloodstain.

There was sudden silence in the shop, despite the twenty-five or so customers. It was followed by an audible sigh of disappointment. Several people put away their cameras and left. Peggy shrugged and rearranged the display on the rug. She didn't need gawkers there anyway.

She finally had to leave Keeley and Sam. She wanted to tell them about the columbine she found, but it seemed too vague. She certainly couldn't call it a clue. But on her way to her freshman botany class, she suddenly decided to make a quick stop at the downtown precinct. Maybe Mai would have more information. And maybe Peggy would tell her about the columbine.

There were several squad cars and the white crime scene van outside the redbrick building. It was strange being there after two years. How many times did she bring John's supper up there and wait for him in the parking lot? She only did it to spend an extra few minutes with him. Their lives were too hectic sometimes with his job, her teaching, and their varied outside interests. She wished now they'd taken the last vacation they had postponed.

She walked inside, and the memories continued to haunt her. In some ways, it was like nothing had changed. The badly painted walls and scuffed floors, the smell of strong disinfectant and day-old coffee. John's office had been in the back of the precinct. She hadn't been there since the day she cleaned out his desk. Who was sitting there now?

Several ragged men waited on an inside bench near the door. Peggy wondered if they were being questioned about Mark's death. All of them fit her general description of Mr. Cheever, but he wasn't in the group. She was glad they hadn't found him yet, even though he might be safer here. There was also the worry that he'd become a convenient fall guy.

She was distracted by a ficus as she waited to speak to the desk sergeant. Poor thing was shedding leaves faster than a poplar in autumn! She stuck her finger into the soil where the roots were showing. It was as dry as last week's casserole.

"What can I do for you?" the sergeant finally asked her.

He was new. She didn't recognize him. It was surprising how much the building stayed the same while the people came and went. Like they didn't have any effect on their surroundings. "I'd like to see—" she took out the business card and showed him, "Mai Sato. She's with forensics."

"I'll give her a call. Your name?"

"Peggy Lee."

He grinned at her. "Are you Paul's mother by any chance?"

"Yes, I am. Is he here?"

"Not right now. They've got everybody out on the street bringing in homeless men. He might be back soon." He picked up the phone and called Mai.

When he put down the receiver, she said, "You're killing that lovely ficus by keeping it too close to the door. Every blast of cold air is like a deathblow to it. It needs watering, too, and more dirt to cover the roots."

"I don't take care of the plants, Mrs. Lee."

She raised an eyebrow. "Who does?"

"I don't know. Whoever's handy, I guess."

"Thanks." She made a mental note to talk to Al about it after this was over. It might be another job for the Potting Shed.

While she was waiting for Mai, she looked at the little ficus again. When the sergeant was talking with another man, she moved it closer to his desk, away from the door. It would be protected from the worst of the weather anyway.

The battered hall door opened. "Dr. Lee! What brings you down here?"

"Hello, Mai! I wanted to check and see what was going on. Have my people come in to be fingerprinted?"

"Come on back. It's freezing out here. You know, it occurred to me after we talked yesterday that you could be Paul Lee's mother."

"Guilty as charged. You know Paul?"

Mai grimaced but didn't answer.

Peggy followed her down the hall that smelled like antiseptic cleaner, wondering what her son did to alienate the young woman. They turned into a dismal, windowless office. A desk was shoved into one corner, and a worktable took up the rest of the closetlike space. Stark fluorescent lighting made everything look surreal.

Mai shuffled the stacks of papers on her desk. Colored tabs and folders neatly organized each stack. "No one's come in yet. I hope you impressed on them how important this is. I'm sure none of them want to be mistaken for a suspect."

"I'm sure they don't. But all of them are students. You know what that's like. I'll call them again. Can you tell me anything more about Mark Warner's death?"

"Have a seat. I heard about your husband. I'm sorry for your loss. Since your son *and* your husband were on the job, I suppose I could give you a few details. It *did* happen in your shop."

"Exactly. Thank you." Peggy sat down carefully on a rickety ladder-back chair.

"Most of the tests aren't done yet. There are a lot of samples to go through. But we know there were no defensive wounds. The ME thinks he was standing with his back to the killer, not suspecting anything until he was attacked. The shovel damaged the brain stem enough that death occurred."

"That's terrible!"

"Yeah. The killer probably knocked him down, then stood over him to use the shovel with maximum effect." Mai demonstrated with a pen. "They found his car yesterday. It was parked in the deck behind the Bank of America building. It was in his space. There was nothing irregular about it. We think he left work and walked over to your shop."

"Which would support my theory that he was going to meet someone there secretly," Peggy added.

"Someone like who? Was he friends with someone who works there?"

Peggy told her about the brunette she'd seen with him.

Mai nodded. "That could explain a lot. But why pick *your* shop? There are a dozen hotels closer."

"I don't know. Maybe it was somewhere familiar. Somewhere they felt safe."

"I suppose that makes sense," Mai agreed, "in a weird way."

"But it doesn't explain how they got into my shop."

"True. Could he have had a key?"

"I don't see how."

"Maybe you should write down the names of all the people who have keys." Mai passed her a piece of paper. "A detective is bound to ask you at some point anyway."

Peggy considered carefully. "All my assistants have keys. Full time, that's Selena, Keeley, and Sam. There are two others who come in part time, Brenda and Dawn. They're all students. That's five. Emil has one. I have one. The pest control man has one. The cleaning service has one. That's all I can think of."

"You don't leave one anywhere, do you? Under a mat or taped somewhere on a window ledge?"

"No, nothing like that! My husband would turn over in his grave if I were that careless!"

Mai shrugged. "It's not unusual. Have you asked your assistants about that night?"

"The last two were there around eight-thirty. Selena works days. She left with me. The pest control man comes in once a month. It wasn't time for him. I don't know if Emil has ever used his key. Mint Condition, the cleaning service, comes in once a week. But that wasn't their night to clean."

"Well, that didn't help."

"I'm afraid not."

Mai glanced through the paperwork from the case. "Someone else is checking out Mr. Warner's clothes. We never found his shoes. So far the only unusual thing we found was a piece of some kind of flower petal in his pocket."

"Columbine?"

"Is that a flower?"

"I found this on the floor in the shop this morning." Peggy pulled out the flower head. "It might match what you found. We don't carry columbines this time of year."

Mai used tweezers to take the flower. She sealed it into a plastic bag. "How did we miss this?" She carefully labeled the sample.

"It's a flower in a garden shop. It doesn't really look like evidence."

"And it might not be," Mai told her. "But thanks for bringing it in. I'll let you know if it's anything."

The door to the office burst open. "Mom? I heard what happened. Are you okay?"

Peggy glanced up at her son. "Hello Paul! I know how to get to see you now. Have a murder at my shop."

Paul Lee was tall and slender like his father. But his red hair and freckles came from his mother. He had her green eyes and delicate nose. He smiled less often, especially since his father's death. "I'm sorry, Mom. I don't have a lot of time."

"Hogwash! Give me a hug." She caught him close to her. He squirmed away almost as soon as she hugged him. "I managed to see your father, even though he walked a beat."

"That was different."

There'd been a rift developing between them since John died. She opposed Paul joining the police department. He'd wanted to be an architect until his father was killed. They argued about his decision. Paul moved out on his own only a month after John's death and then became a police officer. Peggy felt like he was looking for revenge. "Never mind. I'm glad to see you anyway."

He lowered his voice. "So why are you here?"

She laughed. "I came to pump Mai for information."

Mai took off her heavy glasses, smiled, and shook her head.

He glanced at her. "I didn't notice you there."

"What else is new?"

"Don't give her a rough time, huh?" Paul demanded.

"Grow up!" Mai growled. "I only do my job!"

"Whatever! Can I see you out here for a minute when you're finished, Mom?"

Paul walked out. Peggy noticed Mai watching him. "You know him well?"

"No! Thank goodness! I see him around from time to time, that's all. I'm sorry, Dr. Lee, but he's a jerk."

Mai wasn't watching Paul like she thought he was a jerk. The young forensics officer seemed pretty interested in him. "Only my students call me Dr. Lee. My friends call me Peggy."

"Thanks." Mai glanced at the open doorway. "Maybe he's still grieving. Maybe that's why he's such a jerk."

"I'd like to think so. But I'm not really sure."

"I'm sorry! I shouldn't be talking about him that way."

"No, that's all right. He's my son, and I love him, but no one's perfect."

"Has he always been so . . . ?"

"Difficult?" Peggy queried. "Yes. I'm afraid so. Worse since his father died. He looks like me, but he has his father's moodiness. He was devastated when John was killed."

"Are you finished with her yet?" Paul looked in from the doorway. "She's answering questions voluntarily. I hope you've noted that."

"I have," Mai answered belligerently. "And after meeting her, I don't know what happened to *you*!"

Paul's face turned red, but he recovered quickly. "Save the sarcasm. I'm getting my mother out of here. Anything else, you'll have to contact her attorney."

Peggy glanced at him. "But I don't have an attorney, honey."

"Maybe you should get one," Mai warned. "We don't know how this is going to end up yet. And you *were* the one who found the body."

Peggy sighed and got to her feet. "We'll see. Thanks for your help anyway."

"Any time."

"Come over here," Paul invited his mother, closing Mai's office door with a loud bang.

She followed him into an unoccupied office.

"You shouldn't be here." He closed the door behind them.

"I wanted to know what they found out," she defended. "The dead man was in *my* shop."

"Look, Mom, this is embarrassing enough without you making it worse!"

"*Embarrassing?*"

"Yes." Paul's pacing was hampered by the tiny room stuffed full of furniture. "What do you think it's like with people knowing my mother found a dead man in her garden shop? Mark Warner, of all people, for God's sake!"

"You can hardly blame me for what other people think."

"I know that. And I don't blame you. But being here only makes it worse."

"In what way?"

"What do you think everyone will say when they know you were here asking Mai for details?"

Peggy shrugged. "That I was interested?"

"Look, Mom, stay out of it! Go home. Let everyone do their job! You were married to a detective, but that doesn't make you one."

She looked at her son's handsome face. "I'm going home. Well, actually, I'm going home *after* my class. For now anyway. But if I have a chance to solve even a small part of the puzzle, I will."

"Mom—"

"I'll talk to you later, Paul."

"*Mom!*"

She smiled and kissed his cheek. "Don't worry so much. Come by, and I'll make you supper one night."

"Dad always said you were too stubborn for your own good."

"I love you, too!"

Peggy showed herself out of the station after getting some water from the drinking fountain to use on the ficus. She half expected Paul to come out screaming after her. When he didn't, she took a deep breath and unlocked the chain on her bicycle. She glanced at her watch. It was eleven-thirty. The air was delicious with the smell of frying onions and peppers from the uptown sidewalk vendors. It made her stomach growl, reminding her that she only had tea for breakfast. She had just enough time to go home for lunch before her class.

THE WIND WAS BRISK and cold, but she welcomed it in her face as she pedaled into her driveway past the Chinese fountain and the frostbitten crape myrtles. She'd come to like having the four distinct seasons in Charlotte. Growing up at the coast, there was summer and a cool month. Then it was summer again. Or at least it seemed that way to her as a child.

"Good morning, Clarice," she called to her neighbor.

"Morning, Peggy!" the other woman greeted her. "I was wondering if you could tell me how close I should trim these roses? Last year, I think I trimmed too close, and they didn't do so well. John was always such a dear to help me with them, bless his soul."

"It's probably not how close you trimmed them." Peggy leaned her bike against the house, then walked around the neat wood fence that separated their yards. She ignored the little tug on her heart at the reminder that John was gone. "Give them plenty of lime and make sure they have enough water. They should do fine in a sunny place like this."

"Thanks, Peggy!" The neighbor's inquisitive eyes roamed over the shiny red bike. "You know, it's not safe for a woman your age to be riding up and down the streets on that thing. When are you going to start driving again?"

"After I finish the hydrogen conversion."

"Excuse me?" Clarice looked at her like she had two heads. "What are you talking about?"

She started to explain about her project converting her father-in-law's 1940 Rolls-Royce from a gas-burning pig to a more polite hydrogen-fueled vehicle. A sudden commotion in the backyard stopped her. Clarice's tiny toy poodle was barking like something was ripping him to shreds.

"Poopsie?" Clarice ran toward her dog, the effort straining her brightly flowered slacks.

Peggy ran after her. The apricot-colored poodle was dyed to match Clarice's hair. It was no bigger than a large squirrel, but it had cornered something in the garden. It was difficult to tell what it was. Even though it was massive compared to the poodle, the other animal was balled up in fright against the side of the fence.

"What is that *thing*? What the hell *is* that?" Clarice began to scream, staying a good distance away from the fray. She reached in her pocket for her cell phone.

Peggy shooed Poopsie away from the creature. She took off her purple cape and tossed it over the animal. She wasn't sure what her reasoning was except that it appeared to be wet and cold. Immediately, a huge square head popped up. Big brown eyes looked at her in question, and the animal let out a long, low howl.

"Yes! I need animal control! There's something in my yard trying to kill my dog!" Clarice stuttered over the words as she tried to get help from 911.

"It's a dog, Clarice. I think it's a Great Dane. But it's just a dog."

"I don't care what it is, Peggy. I want someone to come and shoot it and get it out of my yard."

While Clarice waited on hold, Peggy went closer to the whimpering dog. Poopsie continued to yap and growl until she told him to hush. She wasn't a dog lover. But she could see the creature was scared and in pain. "Easy, boy. Or girl. Whichever you are. I'm not going to hurt you."

Clarice shrieked. "Don't touch that thing! It could take off your whole arm. I don't know if my homeowner's insurance will cover you being bitten by a stray dog in my yard."

But Peggy didn't listen. She crept in close to the animal. He laid his head down and let her stroke his matted coat. His thin hair was tan, and his muzzle was black. His ears weren't cropped like most Great Danes. They hung down on the sides of his head. She could count his ribs. His hipbone protruded under his wet coat. As she touched him, a long tongue snaked out to lick her hand.

"They're on their way." Clarice closed the sequin-studded phone. "Will you *please* get away from that thing?"

"It's just a dog. He's scared and starving."

"And likely to eat Poopsie! Leave him alone until the animal control people get here."

Peggy moved away from the dog. He struggled to his feet and lurched after her.

Clarice screamed, grabbed up her dog, and ran into the house.

"You *are* pretty intimidating," Peggy told the Great Dane. He was rail thin, but his shoulder came past her waist. She wasn't sure how he had the strength to stand. "I have to go now. I'm sorry."

She started walking back toward her house. The dog followed. She stopped and looked at him. "You don't understand. I really don't have time for a dog. I'm sure the animal control people will find you a good home."

The dog whimpered and shook his head, his huge ears flapping up and down.

"I know. Those places are better at putting an animal out of its misery." She looked into the dog's eyes. "You must belong to someone. Maybe if I could keep you alive for a while, I could find your owner. But it's only for a few days. I'll ask around. If no one claims you, you're on your own."

Clarice rushed to meet the animal control truck as it pulled into her driveway. Between loud sobs and Poopsie's barking, she managed to tell the driver what happened.

While she was crying and thanking him for coming, Peggy got the Great Dane to follow her. She sneaked around through her garden and into her neighbor's yard on the opposite side. A few years back, a retired veterinarian lived two doors down. She wasn't sure if he was still there. But if she could get the dog to him, he might be able to help her.

The dog followed her silently. Peggy glanced back at him and wondered if she'd lost her mind. What was she going to do with a dog the size of a small pony?

While the animal control man scoured the neighborhood, Peggy knocked frantically on what she hoped was the veterinarian's door. When it opened, she shoved the dog into the house and followed quickly, slamming the door behind her.

"Can I help you?"

She looked at the man who'd answered the door. It was the man in the green Saturn. "I'm sorry. I must have the wrong house. I'm looking for Dr. Newsome, the old veterinarian. I think he used to live here. I came to one of his Christmas parties a few years back."

"I'm Dr. Newsome, and I'm a vet." He smiled at her. "You didn't look at my card, did you?"

Nice smile. "No, I'm sorry. I forgot about it. You're not as old as I remember. Or that wassail punch was stronger than I thought."

"I'm *Steve* Newsome. You're probably thinking about my uncle, Jack. He was a vet, too. He died last year."

She felt like a complete idiot. "I'm sorry I barged in here like this. I found this dog, and I'm trying to get him away from the animal control people."

He crouched down and patted the Great Dane's head. "Is *that* what this is? He's a mess. Maybe someone *should* put him out of his misery."

"No! I'm sure he must belong to someone. He probably wandered off. I don't want to be responsible for getting someone's dog killed."

"I was only joking, Peggy. I'll take a look at him. My uncle always kept a small exam room and supplies in case of an emergency. I think this bag of bones qualifies as an emergency."

She was surprised he knew her name until she recalled that he was at her lecture. "You were at the auditorium yesterday."

"I'm flattered you noticed! I was there because I get so many cases of animals poisoned by plants. I'd like to learn more about the subject."

"Well, Dr. Newsome—"

"Please call me Steve. We've bumped into each other so many times, I feel like I know you."

Her heart fluttered a little, but she maintained her look of skeptical indifference. "That wouldn't have anything to do with my face being on television and in the newspaper, would it?"

He laughed. "Not at all. Although the case has made for some interesting reading. I'm sure it was terrible for you to find that dead man in your shop."

"I've had better days." She glanced at her watch. "Can I leave him with you for a while? I have to teach a class, and I'm already late."

"Sure. No problem." He studied her face. "Are you always late?"

Her face turned red. *Stop that! You're blushing like a schoolgirl. Get a grip!* "Oh, you mean the lecture. Actually,

I'm usually very punctual. The last few days have been hectic. Now this!"

He ran his hand across the dog's back. "Would it be a bad time to ask you out to dinner?"

"I, uh, I don't know."

"You don't know about dinner with me or if it's a bad time?"

Peggy wasn't sure about either one. But he *was* going to take care of the dog for her. She supposed she could buy him dinner. Where would the harm be in that? "Dinner would be fine."

"Great. I'll pick you up at seven."

She couldn't stop herself from smiling. "Okay. I really have to go. Thanks for your help."

4

Pansy

Botanical: *Viola tricolor*
Family: N.O. Violaceae
Common Names: Johnny jumpup, wild pansy

The word pansy *is traced back to the French word* pensée, *meaning thought or remembrance. Cultivated some time after the fourth century B.C. in Europe. Legend says the pansy was originally white but turned bright purple when it was pierced by Cupid's arrow. It's said that you can see a loved one in the face of a pansy.*

QUEENS UNIVERSITY WAS over a hundred years old. Its campus was located in the Myers Park residential area of Charlotte. Graceful, spreading oak trees and lush lawns dominated the landscape in summer. But in November, even the gold and red leaves were gone from the skeletal boughs. Classes were in full swing with hundreds of students milling from building to building.

Peggy rushed into the science hall. She wasn't surprised to find her freshman class sitting on their desks, talking about movies. "Sorry I'm late. Let's get right down to business to make up the time."

One of the students raised her hand. "Could we talk about the murder you're involved with, Dr. Lee? What did the dead guy look like? Was it like being on *CSI* or one of those reality shows?"

Peggy couldn't fight the groundswell of questions about the murder. She perched on her big desk and answered as honestly as she could. The questions weren't so much personal as curious about the event.

Before she knew it, the hour was up. They managed to avoid discussing anything from her notes that day. "I'm assigning the next three chapters as reading material for the weekend. On Monday, there will be a test that includes a line drawing; all the parts of pistil and stamen from *Rhododendron vaseyi*. You should know this! If you have any questions, I'm available on E-mail. You have my address in your notes."

Her cell phone rang as the students started groaning and packing their book bags. She checked the number on her caller ID. "Hello, Sam. Is there a problem?"

"I found something. It was out in the dirt alongside the loading dock. I think it might have something to do with the murder. Can you come back to the shop?"

Peggy paused as a student wished her a good weekend. "I'll be there as soon as I can."

"I WAS OUT HERE cleaning up the mess you caused when you made Keeley drop that flat of pansies. Then I saw *it*." Sam walked quickly through the storage area to the loading dock, glancing suspiciously around the bags of peat moss, potting soil, and manure.

Peggy ran to keep up with him. "*It* what? Do you always have to be so dramatic? If you don't tell me what it is right now, I'm going to fire you!"

"As if!" He grinned. "Hey! It's my big moment. I have to *show* you."

They walked down the stairs alongside the dock. There was still potting soil and pansy flowers littering the ground.

"I don't see where you cleaned anything," she said.

"I didn't clean anything yet. But I found *this*." He pulled a key from the pocket of his blue T-shirt that said *Potting Shed*. "Don't worry. I put on my gloves before I picked it up. If there are any fingerprints on it, they should still be here."

Peggy sat down on the wood stair behind her. "Have you decided to become a detective instead of a doctor? Why is this fascinating? Do you realize how much traffic there was coming up Fourth Street?"

"Take out your shop key," he said, still grinning.

Peggy did as he suggested, wondering if he'd been out in the sun or smelling the manure for too long. The two keys were the same. She sat up straight. "Whose key is it?"

"Maybe it belongs to whoever let Mark Warner in the shop."

She scuffed her shoe in the dirt. "It could've been back here for a year, too."

"That's easy to find out. Let's see who has their key and who doesn't. I have mine. You have yours. Who else has a key?"

"Let's find out," she agreed. "But first, let's put that key in a plastic bag. I can take it over to Mai to check for prints."

"Who's Mai?" Sam wondered. "He sounds hot."

Peggy laughed. "*She* might be. You can meet her yourself when you go in to have your fingerprints made."

"A sister, huh? Oh well." He slapped himself in the head. "Sorry. I keep forgetting to go over there."

"If you're arrested for Mark's murder because the police don't know you work for me, you might remember."

"Why don't you let me take the key over there, and I can get my prints made at the same time?"

She started back into the Potting Shed. "How do I know you're not the killer, and the evidence on this key won't ever reach the police?"

The door closed behind her as Sam digested her words. "Hey! Wait up! Are you saying that I'm a suspect?"

Peggy was already in the front of the store by the time he caught her. They both waited for a customer to leave before asking Selena to produce her key.

"You guys look like a couple of vultures." Selena found her key and held it up. "I didn't kill anybody. Especially not with this key!"

"No one said you did," Sam replied with a suspicious tone. "Do you have something to hide?"

She stuck out her tongue at him. "No! Do *you*?"

"We know Mark Warner was murdered by one of his lovers," he said. "You could've been one of them."

"Eeuuww! That's gross! Do you know how old he was? He was like my *grandfather*!" She recovered from her disgust and glared at him. "Besides, *you* could've been one of his lovers, too."

Sam shuddered. "Eeuuww! You're right. That's gross. Except he had a lot of money. I could overlook a few things for someone who could help me pay off my medical school bills."

They both looked at Peggy to end the dispute. She took her time about it, checking the cash register receipts before she answered. "I don't know, Sam. You offered to take a piece of evidence to the police."

"Not because I'm guilty of killing someone!"

She laughed and squeezed his arm. "Of course not, sweetie! And neither is Selena. But once we figure out how Warner got into the shop, we might be that much closer to figuring out why. This key could be part of that."

Sam was satisfied with that. He started a list of key holders on his Palm Pilot. Peggy gave him the names of everyone who had keys. He put checks beside his name, Selena's, and Peggy's. "I'll talk to Keeley tonight. Maybe you could check with Mr. Balducci, the cleaning company, and the bug guy."

Peggy agreed and made a note for herself.

"What about me?" Selena asked. "I had to see the dead guy. Shouldn't I get to check something out?"

"You should," Peggy sympathized. "I have to leave again for a couple of hours. I'll be back to close up. In the meantime, keep an eye out for that woman we saw with

Mark for the past couple weeks. See if you can find some way to get her name."

"You mean the woman with the legs that could crack walnuts?" Selena chuckled and nudged Sam with her elbow. "Too bad you don't want to hook up with her. She'd show you *hot*."

He shuddered. "She sounds scary. If her legs can crack walnuts . . ."

"Maybe you're right," Selena agreed. "Maybe she killed Mark Warner."

"Let's find out who she is before we accuse her of murder," Peggy suggested.

"She looked strong enough to hit somebody with a shovel," Selena reminded her.

A group of customers came into the shop. The lunchtime crowd was gone, but late stragglers were still shopping for weekend projects.

"I have to go," Peggy said again. "Let me know what you find out."

THE REST OF THE AFTERNOON went quickly. Her second class was less impressed by the murder in her shop, so they went through the process of photosynthesis.

One student stopped after class to ask about her lecture on botanical poisons. He suspected one of the people who shared his house of killing his goldfish by pouring Drano into the tank.

"Drano doesn't qualify as being botanical," she explained. "A botanical poison is made from plants or plant substances. I think Drano is chemical. You'll have to do some research on the Internet."

"Have you ever seen a Drano poisoning, Dr. Lee?" he continued. "Do you know what the symptoms would be?"

"I really can't say. And I imagine it would be different for humans than for goldfish."

"What about other poisons? What would be something

you could use that would be fast acting and not leave any trace for the police to find?"

She frowned. The conversation was beginning to take a downward turn. "With today's crime scene investigation, there's no such thing. If you want to get revenge for your goldfish, I suggest you take up boxing or kung fu."

The young man took notes and thanked her for her time. He seemed unimpressed with her suggestion not to use poison and denied he was looking for revenge. She shook her head as he left. She couldn't be responsible for the facts. She hated to think any of her knowledge would be used the wrong way. But it was like the Internet. Just because you found out how to build a bomb on-line didn't mean you had to build one. People had been using poison for thousands of years. Still, she scribbled down his name and E-mailed the dean in case anything came of it.

She called Mint Condition cleaning service and asked about the normal cleaning day for the shop as well as who had the key. The owner assured her they had her key in safekeeping and that her regular cleaning day was Friday, as it was for the rest of the shops in Brevard Court and Latta Arcade. Peggy thanked him, then looked up the number for the bug guy.

It was the same story with him. He only came in once a month to spray for pests. His last visit was at the beginning of November, two weeks before Mark's death. He offered to show her the key to the shop, but Peggy assured him she believed he had it.

She crossed both names off of her list and considered the rest of the choices. It might seem like an extensive list of key holders to Mai. But to her, the rest of the people on the list were people she cared about. She didn't want to think any of them were involved with the murder. Yet what other possible explanation could there be?

After stuffing her books and papers into her backpack, Peggy got on her bicycle and rode back to the Potting Shed. Traffic was still heavy, but the weather was nice again. Between traffic lights, she thought about Steve Newsome and his invitation to dinner. It had been a long time since she dated. She wasn't sure she remembered how.

A car slammed on its brakes in front of her, forcing her to do the same. What was she thinking? This dinner wasn't a date. She was taking the man out for dinner because he helped her with the dog. He'd asked her because . . . well . . . because he was probably curious about the murder. He did mention it, after all.

By the time she reached the shop, she'd convinced herself there was nothing romantic about dinner with Steve. He was a man. A *younger* man. She was a widow who still loved her husband. The rest was pure fantasy on her part brought on by stress and sleeplessness.

As a compelling part of this hypothesis, she reminded herself that she was assuming responsibility for a dog. A *big* dog. She didn't need any other evidence to convince the jury in her mind. Obviously the stress and lack of sleep was leading to lapses in judgment.

"How did it go?" she asked Selena after a customer left the counter.

"Okay, I guess." Selena looked furtively around the shop and whispered, "I didn't see *her*."

"We'll just have to keep looking. She'll probably come in again."

Selena picked up her book bag from behind the counter. "I'm going. I have that English lit exam tonight, and I have to study for the French exam tomorrow, so I might be late in the morning. But I'll keep my eyes open while I'm waiting for the bus. Maybe *she'll* walk by."

"What will you say if you see her?"

"I don't know. Maybe I'll pretend I know who she is. You know like, 'Lucy! Is that *you*?' "

Peggy laughed. "Just be careful. She could be the one responsible for Mark's death. She might be nervous."

"I'll watch out for her legs. The rest of her didn't look all that dangerous. See you tomorrow."

Selena had only been gone a few minutes when the woman they were looking for walked into the shop. Peggy

knew Selena was going to be disappointed she wasn't there
to question her. But she couldn't put it off in case she didn't
come back again.

She didn't want to take Selena's hypothetical approach
and pretend to know the woman. Besides, she had the advantage of being in the shop. Thinking quickly, she took some
scraps of paper and approached all of the customers who
were there. "We're having a giveaway. A beautiful Christmas wreath. Just the thing to brighten up the holidays. All I
need is your name and phone number."

A few people reminded her that they were already on her
mailing list. Peggy apologized for not knowing them and
took their names. She saw the brunette coming toward her.
With a firm hand on her pen and a smile on her face, she
greeted her.

The woman smiled. "I can't think about that right now.
I've had a personal loss. Maybe some other time."

"I'm so sorry." Peggy put away her pen and paper. "Are
you here for flowers for the funeral?"

"Not exactly. We liked the courtyard and the stores here.
We used to come over at lunchtime." She spoke like she felt
awkward talking about it and shifted her glance around the
shop.

"That's so romantic." Peggy sighed. "My husband passed
away two years ago. We were going to open this shop together but didn't have the chance. He loved to garden. Did
your husband enjoy plants?"

The expression on the woman's face was almost comical. Her tone lowered a notch. "He wasn't *my* husband.
And that's where the problem comes in with sending flowers to the funeral. If you know what I mean."

"Oh! I *understand*. It happens. I could arrange to send
something anonymously. That way, *he'll* know you cared,
but his wife won't be suspicious."

"I didn't say he was married." Her shoulders sagged, and
she sighed. "But he was."

Peggy touched her arm. "Of course he was. Or he

would've been *your* husband, wouldn't he, dear? I'm sure he was proud to be with you."

"Thank you." She took a deep breath as if to firm her resolve. "All right. I'd like to send something. You take Visa, don't you?"

After their conversation, Peggy was certain that Ronda and Mark were having an affair. She helped the distraught woman pick out a lovely pot of cyclamen, explaining that it meant good-bye. After all, Ronda wasn't interested in sympathizing with the widow so much as saying good-bye to her lover. Even though the transaction served her purpose, Peggy was still intent on helping her customer.

Twenty minutes later, Ronda McGee left the Potting Shed. After learning her name from her Visa, it only took Peggy two minutes to look her up on the Internet. She was married to Mark's boss at Bank of America, Bob McGee.

She called Al right away and left him a message. She didn't know if the information would help him. He probably already knew about Ronda. But she wasn't going to take any chances with Mr. Cheever's life.

Sam called in a few minutes later. "I talked to Brenda and Dawn today. Both of them have their keys. How about the cleaning and bug people?"

"They're fine. I knew they would be. But something interesting happened." Peggy picked up the Visa receipt. "The brunette who was in here with Mark before he died came by and ordered some flowers for his funeral."

"Did you ask if she has a key?"

She laughed at him. "No, I didn't. Did you take that key to Mai?"

"Yeah. She was okay. I got my fingerprints made. I saw Paul. He grunted at me and left right away."

"That's my son. What did Mai say about the key you found?"

"She didn't say much of anything. The prints on it were blurred. She didn't think they could get anything from it and didn't seem to think it meant much. But she kept it anyway."

"Check with Keeley tonight. You have that delivery to make to South Park Mall, don't you?"

"More pansies, right? Yeah. I'll be glad when autumn's over. I'll talk to you tomorrow. We can compare notes."

Peggy hung up and glanced at the big clock by the door. It was almost six P.M. Time to close up. The shop looked empty, but their new policy was to walk through and check it out. Maybe they could avoid any other unpleasant surprises.

The courtyard outside was deserted. The lights had been on for an hour already with the early fall twilight. She saw Emil and Sofia locking up for the night and hurried out to catch them.

Sofia put her heavily ringed hand to her throat as Peggy approached them. Her dark eyes widened dramatically. "You startled me! After that murder, who knows what to expect?"

"Sorry," Peggy said. "I needed to talk to you a minute."

"I took a precaution anyway." Emil brought out a huge handgun and pointed the barrel in Peggy's face.

"Stupid!" Sofia slapped his hand.

Peggy's knees shook. It wasn't bad enough he had the gun in her face, Sofia had to surprise him!

"What?" He put the gun away. "I was only showing her."

"You were showing everyone else, too! You want the robbers and murderers to know you're armed?" Sofia slapped him again. "You're such an idiot sometimes."

"A gun is dangerous if you don't know what you're doing," Peggy managed to say in a strangled voice. "John worked a few cases where the person breaking in took the gun away from the homeowner and shot him with it."

"It's not loaded," Emil assured her. "It's just to scare the bad guys. They don't know I won't kill them dead."

"If you meet one, you'll be forced into showing him what you'll do," Peggy answered.

"Did you want something important?" Sofia asked her, tapping her foot impatiently.

"I was wondering if you still have the key to my shop."

"Sure." Emil took the key out and showed her. It was

attached to a ring that held at least fifty keys, but he went to it without hesitation. "Did you lose yours?"

Peggy explained about the key they found behind the shop. Emil grumbled about people being careless and asked to see the key he gave her for his shop. Sofia complained about standing in the cold courtyard.

"Thanks anyway," Peggy said. "I guess I'll go and close up now."

"You want us to wait for you?" Emil offered.

"No, thanks. I'll be fine. See you tomorrow."

Music from the French restaurant kitty-corner from the Potting Shed spilled out into the empty courtyard. The wind swept away a few sandwich wrappers left behind by careless diners. Peggy shivered in the chill and hurried back into her shop.

If the last two days weren't enough to put her on edge, Emil's gun in her face did the trick. She felt like going into a closet, locking the door, and cowering in the corner. She didn't want to think about what could've happened if the gun was loaded.

She pulled the old-fashioned shade down on the door, then turned the key in the lock and switched off the light. Her bike was in back, but she was thinking about keeping it behind the front counter in the future. The darkness waiting for her by the loading dock wasn't very appealing, especially since one of the back lights burned out that evening.

Peggy wrote a note to remember to ask the maintenance people to replace the light and put it on the front counter. She wasn't a high-strung person by nature, but surely anyone would feel a little frazzled in her place.

Footsteps on the hardwood floor caught her attention. Panicking, she realized she'd left the door unlocked while she was with the Balduccis. She glanced behind her, looking for something to defend herself with. Her gaze fell on a rake a customer forgot to take with him. With nothing else in easy reach, she held the implement in front of her and waited for the footsteps to reach the front of the shop.

"Peggy?"

It was Julie Warner. Peggy's heart rate decreased, she put the rake down, and the words tumbled out of her mouth, "What are you doing here?" Realizing how rude the question sounded, she rephrased it as she turned the light back on. "Julie. I'm surprised to see you here."

Always well-dressed, the widow looked chic and tiny in her elegant black suit. She wore a Jackie Kennedy pillbox-style hat with a black veil that covered her face. "I'm sorry if I startled you. I thought you saw me come in while you were outside."

"No, I didn't. But that's okay. I thought the shop was empty. What can I do for you?"

Julie's face was very pale behind the black webbing, but her tone was resolute. "I want to see where it happened."

Peggy debated with herself. Was it an odd request? What should she say? "Mark was right here when I came in." She hoped her voice didn't sound as awkward as she felt.

"Where *exactly*?"

This probably wasn't healthy. But didn't she walk by the spot where John was killed? "I'll show you."

Julie followed her soundlessly to the colorful rag rug that hid the bloodstain on the floor. Peggy didn't plan to show her that part. "He was right here. Facedown in a basket of bulbs. The police took everything around him for evidence. This is all that was left."

The widow didn't move or speak. She stared at the spot like she could see through the rug to where her husband's lifeblood had pooled. Then she took a deep breath and reached a black-gloved hand into her pocketbook.

Peggy jumped back and put her hands up in a defensive stance.

Julie looked at her strangely as she withdrew her checkbook. "Is something wrong, Peggy? I'd like to reimburse you for the damages. It wasn't your fault this happened. You shouldn't be hurt by it."

"Sorry. It's been a long day." She lowered her hands and felt like an idiot. But after Emil's gun . . .

"I understand. And I apologize for getting here so late. There were so many arrangements to be made, people to call. I came as soon as I could."

"That's all right. Don't worry about the expenses, Julie, please. My insurance will take care of it. I'm glad you came. I felt the same way when my husband was killed. I couldn't be there with him when it happened. I just wanted to see the place."

Julie put her checkbook away and smiled. "I appreciate your kindness. You know what I've gone through with this since it happened to you, too. The press is terrible. My children don't understand. It's like the world has turned upside down, and it's all I can do to keep from falling off."

Peggy couldn't help herself. She hugged Julie, expensive suit, veil, and all. She might be wealthy, but that didn't protect her from tragedy. It was like holding a child; she was so small, so fragile.

Both women were wiping tears away as they separated. Julie straightened her hat and cleared her throat. Peggy blew her nose on a tissue, then put her hands in her pockets.

"I should go." Julie moved toward the door.

"If there's anything I can do . . ."

"Thank you. I hope you'll come to the funeral."

Peggy unlocked the front door. "I'll try. I'm so sorry for your loss."

When Julie was gone, Peggy locked the front door again. She walked through the shop, holding the rake like a weapon. But this time, she was alone. Quickly, she turned off the light and locked the back door behind her.

She was tempted to call a taxi. Her hands were shaking, and her knees felt weak. She probably needed to go across the courtyard and have a big glass of wine to steady herself. But she refused to give in to her trauma. Like everything else, fear was meant to be handled head-on. She wasn't good at cowering.

She forced herself to get on her bike despite the eerie shadows and creaking sounds from the loading dock. Then she realized it was after seven. Steve was going to have further proof that she was always late. The thought gave her impetus to pedal faster down the busy streets.

"I'm so sorry," she said as she rode into her driveway.

Steve got out of his car when he saw her. "That's okay. I wasn't about to eat the car interior or anything. You don't drive?"

"I do. I mean, I have a license and a car. But I prefer using the bike to get around the city. I'm close to the school and my shop. I don't need to contribute to the problem of global warming."

"That's right. You teach botany, specialize in botanical poisons, *and* run a garden shop. No wonder you're always late."

She stowed her bike in the garage. "I'm not *always* late. But despite you impugning my integrity, I'm willing to apologize for being late tonight by making dinner for you."

He smiled at her. "I won't turn down a home-cooked meal. Although I think I should point out in my own defense that I *did* offer to buy you dinner."

"You did?" She tried not to notice how her pulse fluctuated at his words. "I thought I was buying *you* dinner for taking care of the dog."

His face was shadowed, but there was laughter in his voice. "And here I was fooling myself all day that you thought I was attractive and you couldn't wait to go out with me."

Peggy was glad for the shadows as she felt a blush come over her face. She searched in her pocketbook for her keys and told herself to calm down. "Speaking of the dog, how is he?"

"Were we talking about the dog? Okay. I can take a hint. The dog seems to be fine. He's undernourished and needs to gain some weight, but he mostly looks bad. His body is basically sound. I think he needs a good home."

"I'm willing to provide that until I can find his owner. I'm going to print up some flyers tonight and put them out tomorrow. He's an expensive dog. Somebody must be missing him."

"Maybe," Steve said. "But did you notice that his ears aren't cropped? If he was pedigreed, the chances are his owner would've taken care of that. He's definitely not a show dog. He doesn't recognize any commands. If you're going to keep him, you'll have to have him trained."

She finally got the front door open. "I don't plan on keeping him that long. As you noticed, I'm pretty busy. I don't have time for a dog."

"Then you plan to nurse him back to health so you can give him to the pound and they can put him to sleep?"

"Are you always so absolute?" Peggy let him walk by her, then shut the door.

"Are you always so optimistic?"

She turned on the lights in the foyer.

"Wow!" He looked up at the blue spruce. "Are you getting ready for Christmas?"

For a moment, Peggy panicked. How could she do this? Everything that meant something to her and John was around her. How could she let another man into her life? How could she explain all those things she and John thought were special? Steve, or any other man, would probably think she was crazy. She could argue with herself that she wasn't attracted to Steve that way. But she knew it wasn't true.

"I planted it here when I moved in thirty years ago," she explained.

Her heart was racing as he walked around the tree. She didn't know what to expect from him. She promised herself she wouldn't give up on moving forward in her life, even if he acted like a jerk. Not everyone could like or appreciate her for what she was. John did, but he was exceptional. Maybe she was greedy to think she could have more than one exceptional man in her life.

"It's great!" Steve looked back at her. "I wonder if I could get one to grow in *my* foyer."

5

Hibiscus

Botanical: *Hibiscus rosa-sinensis*
Family: Malvaceae
Common Name: Queen of tropical flowers

Hibiscus is native to Asia and the Pacific islands. It signifies peace and happiness. The red hibiscus is worn behind the ear by women of the Pacific islands. If she wears it behind the left ear, she is desirous of a lover. Behind the right ear, she is already spoken for. But if she wears a flower behind each ear, she has a lover but would like another.

PEGGY MADE SCRAMBLED EGGS and toast for dinner. She apologized to Steve for not realizing her cupboard was bare. "I only shop when there's no food in the house."

"Yeah, me, too. Don't worry about it. This is great. What kind of herbs are in the eggs?"

"These are green scallions that I grow myself. They're a little sweeter than the ordinary ones. I'm glad you like them." She poured them both another cup of orange spice tea.

He sat back in his chair. "I like your house, too."

"It was built in the 1920s. It belonged to my husband's family. He was a direct descendent of Robert E. Lee." She took a sip of her tea and smiled. "Of course, since you aren't from the South, that doesn't mean anything to you."

"That's not true. I'm very impressed. I grew up in Cleveland, but I came down here over the summer every year. My uncle and my mother were the only ones left of their family. They were pretty tight. Now both of them are gone. I always loved his house and this neighborhood. So when he died, I moved my practice down here."

"How is it you and your uncle both had the same last name?" She turned her back and took out two strawberry tarts she bought last week at Harris Teeter. They smelled all right. No mold spots. Praying they weren't stale, she gave one to Steve on a napkin.

"Thanks." He put the tart on his plate. "My mother never married. I never knew my father. I don't know why she moved to Cleveland instead of staying here where her family was. But that's my life story."

She smiled as she tasted the tart. It wasn't too bad. "I'm sure there's more to it."

"I suppose. Let me see. I'm forty-five years old. I have all my own teeth and hair. I graduated somewhere in the middle of my class at the University of Ohio. I've never been married. I can't tell you exactly how much money I make because only my accountant knows that. I'm afraid to ask."

"You're very honest."

"And obnoxiously absolute." He saluted her with the tart, then ate it. "Pretty good. What about you?"

Peggy didn't want to go there. "You know, I want to pay you for your work with the dog. More than just some scrambled eggs."

"Okay. I'll have my accountant send you a bill. Are we going to talk about the dog every time it starts getting personal?"

She had a good mind to ask him to leave. He was smart-mouthed and intrusive. Instead, she stirred a little more sugar into her already sweet tea. "I was married for thirty years. He was killed two years ago. I guess I'm used to people knowing everything about me. I don't like to dredge up the past."

"Fair enough. We won't dredge. How about showing me around your beautiful home?"

She took him on a quick tour. Now that they'd eaten, she was nervous. He made her uncomfortably aware of herself. What did he want from her anyway? She was seven years older than him. He had to realize it. Part of her wished he'd leave and she'd never see him again. The other part of her wanted so much more.

Most of the twenty-five rooms in the house weren't being used. She pointed out her bedroom, glad the door was closed, then hustled him down the main staircase. "I have my laboratory in the basement."

"Like Frankenstein?"

She laughed. "I suppose so."

"Would we have to start talking about the dog again if I ask to see it?"

"No. I take people down there all the time."

He wiggled his eyebrows. "Yes. But do they ever come back?"

She couldn't resist spending a few more minutes with him. He was as enthusiastic about her plants as she could've wanted him to be. He asked questions and paid attention, even when she described her work as "natural selection or genetic modification that remains within the natural bounds of cross-pollination."

She realized she was rambling beyond what a layman could grasp and started talking about her night-blooming rose. She showed him the water lily, pleased when he bent his head and smelled it. Even more so when his tie dangled in the water, and he didn't make a fuss. The lights gleamed on his dark hair.

"You know, I was surprised to see you here." She tried to make normal conversation, worried he'd think she was all compost and hybridization. "How did you know where I live?"

"It wasn't too hard." He looked at a big red hibiscus. "I knew your name. You're listed in the phone book, address and all. Why? Did you think I was secretly an FBI agent?"

"No. Of course not! Just wondering. I'm incurably suspicious."

"You probably should be." He smiled at her in a way that made her skin tingle. "You live alone. Someone could take advantage of you."

Peggy led the way back upstairs to the foyer. Steve marveled again at the size of the tree. "You do decorate it for Christmas, don't you?"

"I have in the past," she answered. "Not the last two years, since . . ."

"Your husband died?" he guessed.

"Yes." She lifted her head. He might as well know the worst of it. "I didn't want to do it without him."

"I think that's understandable." He nodded as he walked around the tree again. "But if you decide to do it this year, I'll be glad to give you a hand."

"Thanks." She hesitated, wanting to ask him to stay for more tea. Feeling she should let him leave right away. More confused than she'd been since she was a teenager. "Can I ask when I can pick up the dog without you making a big deal out of it?"

"Of course." He slipped his arms into his jacket. "I wanted to keep him overnight to be sure he was okay. You can pick him up tomorrow. Or I can bring him by."

"I wouldn't expect you to do that. I'll pick him up. Thanks."

"That's fine. I'll try to have your bill ready. Or you could make me dinner again."

Peggy picked a spot on the wall and stared across his shoulder. It helped not to look into his gorgeous eyes. Why did she think he was so ordinary? "I think I should pay you. You are a professional. And you're in business to make money."

He took a step closer to her. "I'm also a man who'd like to spend more time with you, Peggy. If we can get past talking about the dog. Or not. Either way, I'd like to see you again."

She could hardly breathe. Her voice squeaked when she replied, "I'd like that, too."

"Great. We'll work with that." He put his hand on her arm and lightly kissed her cheek. "Good night, Peggy."

"Good night, Steve."

She rested her head against the door after it closed behind him. She was as light-headed and weak-kneed as she'd been when she found Mark Warner's body. "I guess that says it all!"

Her answer was to bury herself in her work. The phone rang while she was grafting some of her water lily to her rose, humming "Till There Was You" from *The Music Man*. Not wanting to put it down, she let the machine get it. It was Paul. She hastily set the sample down and grabbed the phone.

"Mom? Are you all right? You sound kind of breathless. Have you been running?"

"Just to answer the phone. I was in the middle of an experiment."

"I'm calling because Clarice Weldon tracked me down. She said there was a strange man going into the house with you, and she was worried. She thought I should know."

Peggy took a deep breath and said a little prayer for patience. "I appreciate the phone call. But you know Clarice! She wasn't really worried, just nosy."

"Who was he?"

"Are you nosy, too?"

"Mrs. Weldon was looking out for you. I asked her to keep an eye on things since I can't be over there as much as I'd like. You're not exactly a teenager anymore, Mom. I don't want you to get hurt."

"Don't worry about it, Paul. I'm fine. The man Clarice saw is a veterinarian. He's taking care of my dog."

"When did you get a dog? You don't even *like* dogs!"

Peggy didn't want to answer that question. She didn't even know the answer. A timer went off behind her. It seemed like a good excuse. "Gotta go, sweetie! Call me, and we'll have lunch *without* Clarice!"

Paul complained but finally said good-bye.

Peggy hung up and went back to work. She thought about her son for a long time, wondering how she could mend their relationship. He didn't think she understood about his need to find John's killer. But she empathized all too well. She just didn't want to lose Paul, too.

BY MIDNIGHT, HER BACK WAS killing her from leaning over the pond. Exhausted but satisfied with the progress of her project, she dragged herself upstairs to shower and change. A thin trail of water and dirt followed her up the wide marble stairs. She pretended not to notice. It would still be there tomorrow for her to clean.

Afterward, she sat down in front of her computer monitor for a game of chess. She'd been playing on-line with various people from around the world for about a year. She never knew their real names, only the names they logged on with. It was exciting to play masters of the game, pitting her skill against people she wouldn't have met except for the Internet.

Tonight, she was playing against a new opponent. His screen name was Nightflyer. She was white and took the first move. Pawn to f4.

"Good evening, Nightrose."

She read the words in the chat box and responded to her screen name. *"Hi there."*

Black pawn slid to e5. *"You're taking some time out to relax tonight."*

Peggy studied her next move. *"I try to be here at least a few times a week."* She moved forward. White pawn takes black pawn on e5.

Black pawn moves to d6.

The game progressed. Peggy gave as good as she got. The two players were well matched.

"About that poisoning in Columbia . . ."

Nightrose's white knight moved to f3. Peggy realized what was in the chat box after she made her move. *"I don't know what you mean."*

Black queen takes white pawn on g3 and checks white king. *"The young woman succumbed about an hour ago."*

Peggy watched the black queen put her king in check. But she was too astounded by the chat to think about her next move. *"How do you know about that? Are you Dr. Samson?"* White pawn takes black queen on g3.

A smiley face appeared in the chat box. *"Are you sure about that move?"*

"Are you Dr. Samson?"

Black bishop takes white pawn on g3. *"Checkmate. You're not playing well tonight, dear."*

"Who are you? You're not Dr. Samson."

"You're right. Care to try again?"

Before she could reply, the phone rang, startling her away from the computer.

It was Hal Samson. "I'm sorry to call so late, Peggy. But I thought you'd want to know. My patient died about an hour ago. The police are involved now. They believe the husband might be responsible for the poisoning."

"Were you on-line playing chess a few minutes ago?" It sounded ridiculous, but she had to know.

"No. I've been with the girl's parents since it happened. I would've called you right away except for that. Why do you ask?"

Peggy looked at the computer screen. Nightflyer had left the game room. It couldn't be a coincidence. "I'm sorry, Hal. Her chances of recovery were slim. I assume there'll be an autopsy."

"There will. I'll be happy to send you the results, if you're interested."

"Thanks. Maybe we can learn something from her death." She paused, reluctant to open the subject again, but she couldn't help it. She had to know. "Was there anyone else involved with the case who knew you approached me about it?"

"No. I didn't see any reason to tell anyone else. Why? Is something wrong?"

She told him what happened during her chess game. It seemed significant to her.

He didn't think so. "It was probably someone who knows your screen name, Peggy. If they know you at all, they know you work with poisons. That's not much of a coincidence to me."

"You're probably right," she acknowledged. "I shouldn't be up playing chess with strangers in the middle of the night anyway."

"If you're not sleeping, I could get you a prescription for that," he offered. "Not getting enough sleep is bad for the nervous system."

"Thanks anyway, Hal. I'll be fine. I don't envy you having to deal with people's loved ones after such a tragic death. Please keep in touch."

Peggy hung up the phone and logged back in for another chess game. There were several immediate answers to her challenge. But none of them were Nightflyer. She realized she'd never seen that name before.

Hal was probably right about turning off the computer and going to bed. But a cold chill slid down her spine, and she stayed up for a few more hours. The event haunted her. She wouldn't be satisfied until she knew who Nightflyer really was.

PEGGY WAS AT THE Potting Shed the next morning when Mai called from the precinct. She wasn't officially open on the weekend, but a few good customers needed to come in for supplies now and then. It gave her a chance to do some straightening up and check the inventory for Christmas. Unlike most retail establishments, her garden shop had to get through fall before plunging into the holidays. Seasons were important to gardeners.

"Peggy, I just found out!" Mai told her. "They picked up Mr. Cheever last night. They're letting him sleep it off in a cell before they question him. But he had Mark

Warner's personal possessions. It doesn't look good for him."

"Thanks for letting me know. I wonder if I could see him."

"I doubt it. We contacted his daughter in Rock Hill. She's supposed to come in. They might let her see him, but you're not a relative. Until they get everything settled, the police will be the only ones talking to him."

"You mean until he's charged with murder." Peggy pursed her lips in frustration. "Does he have a lawyer?"

"Not until he asks for one. He hasn't been formally charged. Maybe he has an alibi or something that can clear him."

"Maybe. I hope so. Thanks for calling anyway. By the way, was the flower I gave you a match for the petal you found in Mark's pocket?" Peggy could hear Mai shuffling through her papers.

"It was. We sent it off to Atlanta to be identified. We don't have a botanist on staff."

"It was a columbine. But I'm not on the payroll. You'll have to do it the hard way. I'll talk to you later."

Peggy could hardly wait for the last customer to leave. She usually hung around the shop most of Saturday, encouraging customers to stay for tea and conversation. Sometimes she had lunch with a few good friends. Today, she had too much on her mind to appreciate her gardening paradise. She locked up at ten-thirty and rode her bike to the uptown precinct. She had to figure out a way to see Mr. Cheever.

The sergeant at the desk recognized her this time. He worked there when John was alive. Mai had been called away to a crime scene in south Charlotte, but Al was in his office. He sent Peggy back without bothering to call for permission.

Al was surprised to see her. "Peggy! What brings you down here?"

She sat in a chair by his desk. "I'd like to see Mr. Cheever. I heard you arrested him last night."

"Word sure gets around." He shook his head. "But you *know* better! You can't see him. They brought him out of detox a little while ago. He's a bit disoriented, but otherwise he's okay. Unless you're his lawyer, nobody sees him today but us."

"You could arrange it for me. I really need to talk to him, Al. I feel responsible for him being a suspect in this case."

"It's not possible. Please don't ask me."

"Hogwash! You could make it possible."

"The lieutenant would ream my butt. I can't get you in there. You don't realize all the heat we're taking on this murder. This family has friends in important places. But there's nothing for you to feel guilty about, Peggy. We would've heard about him one way or another. There's nothing you can do for him now. Go home."

She got to her feet. "You know I'll find a way to see him."

Al rubbed his eyes with his hands. "Go home before I lose my pension. Mary would do lots worse things to me than the lieutenant. *You* don't scare me."

Peggy was seething as she stormed out of the office. She passed the sergeant without speaking, pushing the sorry little ficus away from the door again. He stared at her but didn't ask why she did it.

She didn't have a lawyer who represented her interests. But she did have a friend who was a lawyer. She went to his house, only to find he was playing golf.

She stalked him at the Myers Park Country Club. Park Lamonte flatly refused her request to represent Mr. Cheever. He had a plate full of pro bono work already taking up his time, and the case was too high profile. Besides, he was friends with the Warners. It would represent a conflict for him.

"You wouldn't really have to represent him," she urged. "Just pretend you will so we can talk to him."

Park looked at her like she was crazy. "That's only breaking about half the rules I could be disbarred for. I can't do it, Peggy. I'm sorry. You know I would if I could."

"Could you recommend someone else? I'll pay his fee. It doesn't have to be pro bono."

He put his arm around her shoulders and grinned. "If you've got the cash, Peg, any knee-jerk attorney can take the case. Hell, a second-year legal student could do the work. It won't matter anyway. The man's already tried, convicted, and hanged in this town."

She scowled at him when he kissed her cheek and invited her over for dinner one night. "I hope *you're* never in a tight spot and someone says that about you!"

"I hope not, too. Go home, Peg," Park advised. "This is too big to beat. If this man is your friend, plan to visit him in prison. That's the best you can do for him. Don't waste your money. Let the state pay for an attorney."

But she wasn't going to let that happen. She didn't know where to find an attorney on a Saturday. All the law offices she called were closed. She knew the court would appoint a lawyer for Mr. Cheever, but that wouldn't solve her problem of getting in to see him.

Sam was waiting at her house. "Where have you been? I've been trying to reach you for the last hour."

"I've been trying to get a lawyer for Mr. Cheever. They picked him up last night. He had all of Mark's stolen personal effects." She rested her bike against the side of the house. "No one wants to take the case."

Sam slapped his hand against his leg. "I guess that's it then. It doesn't matter *who* has their keys."

"Why? Did you find someone with a key missing?"

"I'm not sure. Last night Keeley asked to borrow my key to get into the shop. She told me she left hers at home. Which may be true. I didn't pursue it."

"Why not?"

He scratched his head. "I have to work with her, Peggy. I got this far. Maybe you could go the rest of the way."

"I'll talk to her. First, I have to find a lawyer desperate enough to take this case." She started toward the front door.

"If you're looking for desperate, I think I can help with

that. My sister, Hunter, is a criminal lawyer. She had a falling-out with one of the partners in the law firm that hired her when she got out of school. Now she's trying to make it on her own."

"What kind of falling-out?"

"The senior partner hit on her, and she broke his arm. She's a black belt."

Peggy laughed. "Sounds like my kind of woman. Could you give her a call?"

AN HOUR LATER, Sam and Peggy met Hunter Ollson at the Mecklenburg County Jail. Peggy rode over with Sam in the Potting Shed pickup. They had to circle for ten minutes before they could find a parking place.

"Peggy, this is my sister, Hunter."

"Nice to meet you." Hunter put out her hand and shook Peggy's with enthusiasm. "I appreciate the opportunity to represent your friend. I've been following the case, and I made a few calls on the way over here."

"I'm impressed. Is everyone in your family a go-getter?" Peggy looked at the two siblings. They were both specimens of good Nordic genetics. Hunter was as blond, tall, and muscular as her brother. There was a no-nonsense look in her fierce blue eyes that made Peggy glad she was on her side.

"As I understand it," Hunter continued, "you want to be my legal assistant. You want to talk to your friend, right?"

"Yes. I need to understand what happened. He may even know who committed the murder. I'm sure he's innocent."

"That's fine. We're not breaking any laws, just bending a few. Take this." Hunter handed her a heavy briefcase. "I like my coffee black, no sugar."

Peggy wasn't sure what she was getting into. It seemed unlikely she'd have the time to fetch coffee for Hunter. Maybe she didn't explain the situation well enough. Whatever, she didn't want to argue about it while they were standing on the steps.

Sam leaned his head close to hers. "She's kidding, Peggy."

"Thanks. Good sense of humor, too."

Hunter said good-bye to her brother, then dashed up the stairs, leaving Peggy to trail behind her. She barked out requests as she walked. Peggy scrambled to find some paper and write them down.

When they reached the front desk, Hunter produced her credentials, told the officer on duty she'd been hired to represent Mr. Cheever, and demanded to see her client at once.

Peggy was impressed and uncertain about her attitude. She half expected the officer to turn them down. But he nodded and buzzed them through the side door. They passed through another weapons search, then walked down the dismal gray hall to the visiting area.

"You're doing fine," Hunter confided to Peggy. "I hope I wasn't too hard on you. They expect lawyers to talk to paralegals like that."

"I think I can handle it." Peggy replied. "I should've asked about your fee for representing Mr. Cheever."

Hunter smiled, showing dazzling, perfect white teeth. "Don't worry about it. I'm still living at home with my parents. I'd do almost anything for a thousand dollars. Besides, this case could bring me the notoriety I need to pull in the rich basketball players who need legal assistance."

They were escorted to a small room. A brown plastic table and several chairs were pushed together in the middle of it. Mr. Cheever was brought in as they sat down.

"Let me know when you're ready," a burly deputy told them as he left, locking the door behind him.

"Do your thing. Keep it down though. Uncle Sam is watching." Hunter nodded at the camera in the corner.

Peggy took Mr. Cheever's hands in hers. "Do you know who I am?"

The dull brown eyes squinted at her. "I'm not real sure. Are you Jane?"

"I'm Peggy Lee from the Potting Shed. Who's Jane?"

"My daughter. They said she was coming to see me."

"She'll probably be here later. I brought you a lawyer who's going to defend you. You have to tell her everything you saw the night Mark Warner was killed."

"Who? I didn't see anyone killed."

"I'm Hunter Ollson, Mr. Cheever. Do you understand why the police brought you in?"

"They said I took something."

"That's right. You took some things from a man in Peggy's shop. Do you remember that?"

He nodded, gazing into the distance like he was trying to remember. "He was lying on the floor."

Peggy squeezed his hand. "Yes! He was on the floor. How did you get into the shop?"

"The door was open. I walked in. He was asleep. He didn't need his shoes or that other stuff. It was cold. I couldn't find my shoes."

"But he was already dead when you got there," Hunter clarified. "That makes you guilty of robbery, but not murder. That plus diminished capacity should get you off, no problem."

"He's not at his best right now," Peggy told her. "He's usually quoting Shakespeare and singing arias from *Madame Butterfly*. I don't know why he's like this, but maybe you should ask to have a doctor see him."

"Okay. The important thing is that he's innocent."

Peggy got Mr. Cheever's attention again. "Do you remember seeing anyone else at the shop the night Mark Warner was killed?"

"That woman."

"What woman? What did she look like?"

"She ran out. I heard them yelling. I saw the door open and went inside. He was on the floor."

"Did you see her face?" Peggy asked him.

Mr. Cheever stared at the wall behind her. "I'm hungry. Can I get something to eat? Where's Jane?"

Hunter took Peggy aside. "I think we should have a doctor see him before he says anything else. If he's been injured or he's sick, it would be better to have it documented.

We don't seem to be getting through to him right now. Let me see what's going on, when they plan to arraign him or whatever. I don't know if he's even been charged yet."

Peggy agreed. She hated to leave him there, but she got what she came for. He couldn't possibly lie in his condition. He was barely able to put two sentences together. He went into the shop because the door was open. Mark was already dead.

She sat back down with him while Hunter made the arrangements and found out what was happening. Peggy tried to talk to him again, but he was rambling about food and his daughter. Most of what he said didn't make any sense.

When Hunter returned, the deputy took Mr. Cheever back to his cell.

"He's very hungry," Peggy told the deputy. "Could he have something to eat?"

"Sure. We'll get him something."

Hunter waited until they were alone, then took Peggy's arm and bent her head close as they stood in the hall. "The DA has already formally charged him with first-degree murder and robbery. He'll be arraigned this afternoon. They're going to take him to have some tests done. We'll see what happens."

"Can you be there with him at the arraignment?"

"Of course. And I'll be entering a not-guilty plea, although we may have to consider diminished capacity if something's happened to him."

They walked out of the visiting area directly into Al and Jonas. Peggy ducked her head, but it was too late.

"What in blazes are *you* doing here?" Jonas's nasal Northern accent filled the entryway.

Peggy started to speak, but Hunter inserted herself between her new friend and the irate police officer. "She's my temporary legal assistant. I'm representing Joseph Cheever. If you have any legal questions, please address them to me."

Al shook his head and purposely didn't look at Peggy. Jonas glared at all of them, then marched into the visiting area.

"I guess that settles it then." Peggy waved to Al. "See you later."

"Peggy . . ." Al started, but it was too late. Peggy and Hunter were walking out the front door.

"What's going on with her?" Jonas demanded.

"I honestly don't know. I'll talk to her." Al knew from past experience that nothing he said would make any difference, but he would definitely talk to her.

Peggy and Hunter congratulated each other when they reached the steps. They both hugged Sam, leaving him with a confused look on his face.

"I'm staying here for a while." Hunter took her briefcase from Peggy. "The assistant DA is on his way. I need to know what they have on Mr. Cheever."

"Thanks for your help," Peggy replied. "Please keep me in the loop."

"Does this mean we're still trying to find out who killed Mark Warner?" Sam asked her.

"Yes, it does." Peggy told him about the interview as they drove back to her house. "I was right. They may want to blame this on Mr. Cheever, but he didn't do it. From what he told me, the killer may be a woman." She went on to tell him about Ronda McGee and her floral purchase. "She looks pretty strong. I think she could've done the job."

"But what would her motive be?" Sam considered the matter seriously as he negotiated the afternoon traffic. "Unless maybe Warner was refusing to leave his wife for her."

"I don't know yet. Why does any human take the life of another?"

"You're not going all philosophical on me, are you? I get a lot of that at school, you know."

"It's a valid question," Peggy argued. "People kill people for many different reasons. Ronda may have a motive we can't begin to understand."

Sam turned into her driveway. "Looks like you have company."

A Charlotte-Mecklenburg squad car was parked behind a green Saturn. Peggy groaned. "Oh no."

6

Crocus (wood crocus)

Botanical: *Crocus sativus*
Family: Iridaceae

The crocus was highly valued in ancient times. Used in rituals, it was also a food and a source of dye. Its petals were scattered on the ground at social gatherings and on the bed of newly married couples. Crocus essence was used as a perfume. The stamens of autumn-flowering Crocus sativus *are also known as saffron.*

STEVE WAS WALKING the Great Dane in the front yard. Even though the dog was thin, it was all he could do to hold the leash. He tried to pull the animal toward Peggy, but it resisted, almost pulling him into a flower bed.

Paul made a beeline for his mother. "Who *is* that man? Is he the one who was here last night?"

Sam laughed. "I've got some studying to do. Give me a call later, Peggy. Hey, Paul."

"Hey, Sam." Paul turned back to his mother. "Is that *your* dog?"

Peggy frowned. She wasn't crazy about his tone. "For now. I plan to look for his owner. I don't want him to be taken to the pound."

A huge, whooping shriek came from behind them. Clarice was about to come out and join in the conversation when she saw the Great Dane. Poopsie barked from her arms. "There it is! I knew I wasn't imagining it. I'm going to call 911."

"You don't need to call anyone." Peggy called the dog to her, and he immediately came running, dragging Steve behind him. "This is *my* dog, Clarice."

"That's the man who was here last night," Clarice told Paul.

"The dog may look puny, but he's all muscle." Steve gave Peggy the leash, trying to catch his breath.

"Who are you?" Paul demanded. "Let's see some ID."

Peggy put her hand on Steve's as he started to take out his wallet. "This is my son, Paul. Paul, this is Steve Newsome. He's a vet. He brought my dog to me. That's all. You don't have to harass him."

Paul stared at her hand on Steve's. "A vet, huh? How much is he charging you for that flea-bitten mongrel?"

Peggy kept her Irish temper down with an effort. "I think we should go inside and talk about this. My daddy always told me it was ill-bred to stand outside and air your dirty laundry."

Paul didn't argue. He marched straight to the front door and waited for her with a mutinous look on his narrow face.

Clarice pouted. "Peggy, that dog is too big to live here. We only have that little fence between it and my Poopsie. Unless you plan to put up a bigger fence, it will have to go."

"I plan for the dog to stay inside except when I walk him. I'll talk to you later, Clarice."

"Maybe I should go." Steve handed her a bill for his services. "This is for you. If it's not high enough, I can tack on more. I'm flexible. There's a note on there about what you should feed him, further care. Basic stuff. If you have any questions or need help walking him, let me know."

"Thanks. I'm sorry about all this."

"That's okay." He smiled at her. "Paul looks like you, you know. I'll talk to you later."

Using a combination of pushing and pulling, she managed to get the dog into the house. Then she made Paul move the squad car so Steve could back out of the drive. She hoped her son would leave, too, but he pulled back in, slammed the car door, and confronted her.

"Let's go inside and have some tea," she suggested before she lost her temper.

Paul followed her into the kitchen. He sat down at the same table where he'd eaten as child. "What's going on, Mom? You've never wanted a dog. Is that dude threatening you?"

"Don't be ridiculous." She put the kettle on the stove. "I met Steve by chance. And I felt sorry for the poor dog. Just look at it."

A loud crash made her run into the dining room. The dog was on top of the eight-foot table. A Waterford crystal bowl that had been in her family for five generations was shattered on the floor. She groaned, and the dog whined, moving close enough to lick her face. Then he jumped down and ran into the kitchen. Before she could get there, she heard another crash and Paul swearing.

"Get this damn dog off of me!"

The dog had made a running leap, knocking man and chair over. He was standing on top of Paul, wagging his tail and licking his face.

Peggy grabbed the leash and pulled the dog into the large pantry. She turned on the light and closed the door as the kettle started to whistle. "There now. Let's have some tea."

They sat beside each other, ignoring the dog's plaintive whines from the pantry. Peggy sipped her orange peppermint tea and mentally tried to force her son to talk to her.

Paul sniffed the brew. "What *is* this?"

"Tea. I mixed it myself."

He pushed the cup away. "I'm not really thirsty, thanks anyway. Mom, you don't realize what it's like in the real world. You've got your little shop and your students. It seems safe. But that dead man in your shop should be a warning to you. There are people out there who could take advantage of you. You're a helpless widow with some money and a big house. Lots of men would like to get their hands on you."

Peggy stifled her laughter. He was serious. He was always serious. "I appreciate what you're trying to tell me. I always try to be careful."

"Really? Is that why Al called me from the county lockup to tell me you sneaked in to see a man accused of murder? I don't call *that* trying to be careful."

She tried to be tolerant. She knew how hard his father's death was on him. But she was only going to take so much. "Paul, I've been in this world a long time. I think I can handle myself."

"Mom—"

"Drink your tea, Paul. It's good for you."

He took a sip and made a face. "You can't help your homeless friend, you know. They found all of Warner's stuff in his backpack. He was wearing Warner's shoes, for Christ's sake! He stripped them off of a dead man. Case closed."

"All I've done is found him a lawyer," she explained. "But just because he was cold doesn't mean he killed the man. What was his motive? He can get free shoes at the shelter."

"I never knew you had such a soft heart." Paul smiled and shook his head. "First a homeless man, then a dog. What's next?"

Peggy got up and put her arms around him. "Don't you remember the one-legged frog we found in the backyard that summer? We took him away from a black snake who wanted him for lunch. We kept him alive by catching flies and tying strings on them so he could eat them. I've always had a soft heart, honey. It's not going to change now."

"I guess you're right. And I'm sorry. I'm overreacting because I feel guilty leaving you here all alone. I want things to be different between us from now on."

"Because I can't take care of myself?"

He kissed her cheek. "No. Because I love you."

"I love you, too. You know this will always be your home, too."

"I can't move back in, Mom. Thanks for offering. I might be seeing someone. I'd like you to meet her, if things work out."

Peggy took a deep breath. *That was close!* "I'd love to. Just let me know when."

She watched Paul leave, waving to him from the doorway. This was a good thing. She didn't want him to live with her again, but she wanted their relationship to be closer. She heard a loud thump from the pantry and ran back into the kitchen.

The dog managed to knock down a ten-pound bag of white flour. He was covered in it. She looked up at the shelf. It was a good five feet off the floor. It seemed impossible that he could reach it. But the proof was standing in front of her, a ghost dog with a large, dopey grin and a wagging tail.

"I really didn't want to live with *you* either," she scolded him. "But we're stuck with each other until I find your owner."

The dog barked and wagged his tail even harder, showering everything in the pantry with flour. Peggy sighed and dragged him to the big sink in the laundry room. Getting him into it was a whole other thing. By the time she was finished with him, she was covered in flour and only half of the dog was really clean.

Deciding they both needed some exercise, Peggy put on her gardening clothes and gloves. She found a rope, attached it to the dog's collar, then tied it to the porch. He bounced around on the grass until he came to the end of his tether. Then he whined and stared at her as she started in on separating her wood crocus bulbs.

While her backyard was an experimental garden, her front yard was as normal as any of her neighbors'. There was a huge circular bulb bed set to bloom according to the various seasons. The little wood crocuses were always the first in spring. Their purple heads peeked shyly from under the brown dirt while there was still ice on the ground. It only took a few days of sun and warm temperatures to bring them back.

After that, the tulips and hyacinths argued for space in March and April. May brought the irises, followed by the cannas in June and July. The dinner plate asters filled the garden in August. Mums began flowering in September and stayed around until November. The bulb bed was always busy.

"What are you still doing here?" Peggy found a small pink rose blooming beside a large piece of white quartz. The poor little thing was leggy and almost brown with frost, but it held its head high. A small azalea bush sheltered it from most of the cold temperatures. She gave it a dose of water and fertilizer, then continued separating her bulbs.

She separated and replanted about half the bulbs in the bed. Then she covered the whole thing with peat to protect it over the winter.

She turned her gaze on a small area near a stone bench. It had been one of John's favorite places to sit. A leafless Japanese cherry tree draped its branches across one side. A brass sundial kept pace with the day. It was a gift from Paul for John's birthday the year he died.

Peggy knew the tree needed pruning. She didn't know if she had the heart to do it. She could still remember John bringing it home one afternoon. He'd been so proud of it.

She took out her pruning shears and straightened her spine. Memories or not, the tree needed a good trim. Her cell phone rang as she approached the tree. She let out a sigh of relief, even as she chastised herself for being a coward.

"Hi Peggy." Keeley's voice sounded distant on the phone. "I got your message. What's up?"

"I was calling to see if you lost your key for the shop." Peggy came right to the point. "Sam found one in the back by the loading dock, and it doesn't seem to belong to anyone else."

For a long moment, there was no reply. Peggy thought her signal might be bad.

Keeley finally said, "Maybe. I'll check. I never seem to need it, since Sam's always there."

"Is something wrong?" Peggy wished she could talk to her in person. "You sound strange."

"You know me. I'm always strange. Anything else?"

"The police arrested Mr. Cheever for killing Mark Warner. I went to see him. He told me he saw a woman run out of the shop that night."

"That's terrible. I hope he has a good lawyer."

Peggy told her about Sam's sister. "She's quite a character. I think you'd like her. How would you like to come over for a brainstorming session later? Maybe we could come up with something to help Mr. Cheever."

"I'd love to, but I have to study. Maybe later?"

"Sure, Keeley. I'll talk to you later."

Something was definitely wrong. She sounded preoccupied and nervous. Peggy put away her cell phone and was about to start on the tree again when a cardinal flew by, swooping down close to the dog. The Great Dane jumped up and missed the bird, but he kept jumping at it anyway. The nylon rope that said it could be used to tow a car snapped. The dog ran off, following the bird.

"Oh, no!" Peggy heard a scream from Clarice's backyard followed by Poopsie's frantic barking, and ran next door.

Both Poopsie and his larger counterpart were standing on top of Peggy's neighbor. Covered with mud and screaming, Clarice was trying to push the dogs off of her. With the cardinal resting in a large crape myrtle above her head, the Great Dane wasn't moving. His booming bark sounded around the enclosed garden like a fog horn.

Peggy grabbed her dog's collar and finally managed to pull him away. The cardinal flew off, unaware of the commotion it caused.

Clarice staggered to her feet, refusing Peggy's offer of

help. "That animal is a menace! If I see it out of your yard again, I'm going to call animal control."

There wasn't much point in assuring her that the dog wouldn't get away again. Peggy dragged the dog as he licked her and wagged his tail. "You're going to have to come in here while I print up some flyers to take around. My life is complicated enough without a big lug like you causing a disaster every five minutes."

After making sure there was nothing he could knock down, she put him in the laundry room with a pail of water to drink. Then she went upstairs to shower and change clothes.

There were a dozen E-mails waiting for her when she turned on her computer. One of them was an invitation from Nightflyer to play chess again at eight that night. It was sent through the gaming site, so it didn't include an E-mail address. She saved the E-mail anyway.

She had to find out how he knew about the poisoning death in Columbia. It was too eerie to let go. There was probably a simple explanation; he worked at the hospital or something. But she planned to meet him on-line that night and ask him.

The flyers were simple to make. She used Microsoft Word to create the document, then printed twenty copies. Surely there weren't that many Great Danes lost on Queens Road in the last few days. Arming herself with a stapler, she checked on the dog. He was sleeping in the far corner of the laundry room on top of the furnace vent. He looked up and started to get excited when he saw her. Peggy quickly shut the door.

She didn't bother putting on her cape. The sun was still warm. She put the first flyer on the electric pole right outside her house. Then she stapled one on every pole as she walked down the street.

"Looking for the owner?" Steve's voice took her out of her world of worrying about the police stopping her for putting up signs on the street.

"Yes." Peggy was glad she'd changed clothes on the off chance that she might see him. People had told her that her cranberry wool slacks and matching sweater were flattering. She brushed a lock of hair out of her eyes and dropped the stapler. So much for trying to seem elegant or sophisticated.

He picked it up and smiled at her. "Looks like you could use some help."

"Thanks." She couldn't seem to come up with more than one word at a time. He looked even better today than she remembered. She loved the sound of his voice and the way his eyes crinkled when he smiled.

"Which way are you going?" he finally asked after a few minutes.

"I thought I'd go this way." *For goodness sake, he's just a man!*

They walked together, stopping to staple a flyer on each pole. Peggy held up the paper, and Steve stapled it. Traffic moved quickly past them. Saturday afternoon shoppers and soccer moms whizzed by in SUVs and minivans.

"Do you know how the investigation's going on that man who was found dead in your shop?"

Peggy explained about the police picking up Mr. Cheever and visiting the jail. "I know he didn't do it. But the police won't look for anyone else with him in custody."

Steve stapled another flyer. "That was pretty cool that you got into the jail to talk to him. It's too bad he didn't see what happened."

She didn't elaborate on the woman Mr. Cheever saw running out of the shop. She needed a chance to sit down with Keeley before she told anyone else about that. "I wish there was something more I could do to help him."

"Unless you get a confession from the real killer," Steve considered, "it doesn't look good for him."

Peggy realized they'd come to an intersection. She could see the Warners' front door from where she was standing. "I think I'll take a flyer to a friend's house over there. Maybe she knows something about the dog."

He studied the house. "Unless the pictures on the nightly news are distorted, that's Mark Warner's house. Doing a little investigating?"

"Maybe. A little. I know Julie Warner. She came to the shop the other night. I thought I might stop in for a cup of tea."

"Maybe I should go with you. You might need someone to distract her while you look through her garbage for the murder weapon."

She laughed. "You watch too much TV. Besides, the police already have the murder weapon."

"Does that mean you'd rather I didn't go with you?"

"Of course not!" She took a deep breath and slowed down. "If you'd like to come along, that's fine."

Julie and Mark Warner had a huge estate on a full five acres of parkland. The house had over fifty rooms. They had two children, a son and a daughter. Everything they did was the envy of every society-minded woman in town. Probably even down to Mark's untimely demise.

They walked right up to the front door of the mellow redbrick Georgian-style house. It was decorated with an elaborate wreath made from magnolia and holly leaves, trimmed with acorns and pinecones. Peggy admired it, then used the heavy brass door knocker.

A tall, thin Hispanic woman answered. "Miss Julie is out for the day. Making funeral arrangements."

"What a terrible thing this has been for her," Peggy sympathized. "I hated to bother her. I thought I could ask her help, and it might take her mind off of everything for a few minutes."

"Maybe I could help. What is it?"

Peggy showed the flyer to the housekeeper. "Have you heard anything about this, Emma? Your name is Emma, isn't it? I think I remember you from the last time I was here."

The woman smiled. "Yes. And you're Mrs. Lee from the garden shop, right?"

"That's right! You were here the day I came to look at Julie's delphinium. It was breathtaking, wasn't it?"

"It was. She has such a gift for growing things." Emma shivered. "But come inside out of the cold. Is this Mr. Lee?"

Peggy assured her that it wasn't and introduced Steve to the housekeeper.

"Come in, come in. I know Mrs. Warner would want me to fix you some tea since you're here. Dr. Newsome, maybe you can take a look at my cat. She's been sick for a few days."

Everyone knew Julie Warner did her own decorating. She had exquisite taste and style. Her house was a mandatory stop for house and garden tours. It was her crowning achievement. Crystal chandeliers shimmered in the sunshine coming in from sparkling windows. Everything in the house was from the early 1900s or a faithful reproduction, from the rugs underfoot to the tapestries on the wall. Above the fireplace was a life-sized portrait of Julie with her children.

"How's she holding up?" Peggy asked while Emma poured each of them tea in pristine white cups. The strong aroma told her it was a blend of pekoe and hibiscus.

"She's good, I guess. It's a brave face. She deserved better."

"Everyone does. Thanks, Emma."

"You're welcome." Emma sat down beside her at the scrubbed oak table. "Mark Warner was a *snake*."

Peggy heard the white-haired cook catch her breath, but she never stopped kneading the bread dough on the floured board. "That's pretty harsh!"

"I know. But it's true. Everybody knew it. He treated Miss Julie like she was worse than a dog! Running after anything in a skirt. Not caring everybody knew. The man deserved to die and *that's* the truth!"

Steve choked on his tea, apologizing as he picked up his napkin.

Emma glanced at him, then continued. "He could be doin' it with anyone! Miss Julie never knows when he's comin' home. Once he even gave her a *disease*."

Peggy was more surprised the housekeeper shared that information than she was by the fact. "That's awful!"

"She was pregnant with the boy when the doctor told

her. It wasn't serious. He treated it. But she knew how she got it. Threatened to leave him."

"Why did she stay?"

"She got all this." Emma waved her hand around the huge kitchen. "And he always promised it wouldn't happen again."

"There was a woman who was at my shop with him." Peggy pressed her for more information. "Tall, athletic. Dark hair. Anyone you know?"

"Sounds a lot like Mr. Warner's secretary, Angela Martin."

"Really?" Peggy was surprised by the housekeeper's response. Was there another woman in Mark's life besides Ronda McGee?

"Yes. But he promised Miss Julie it was over between them."

"But she didn't make him fire her?"

"Mr. Mark says he can work with her without cheatin'. He says what happens at work is his business, and he can't let someone go without good reason."

"So she was still working for him?"

The housekeeper nodded. "Last I heard. They should check on what she was doin' that night. Maybe they'd find the killer."

"Did you tell the police that?"

"No. They didn't ask me. Besides, Miss Julie won't hear nothin' bad about that man. But he deserved what he got, no matter. I hope his *puta* gave it to him good!"

"Did the police ask what Julie was doing that night?" Steve questioned.

Emma waved her hand. "Miss Julie wouldn't kill that man! She got too much to lose! Besides, that night she was up with the boy. He was sick all night, coughing and running a fever. I saw her with him."

When they were getting ready to leave, Emma took Steve to see her cat. The animal was curled up in a basket lined with an old blanket.

Steve crouched down to pet the white Persian's head. "How long has she been this way?"

"I'm not sure. Sometimes she gets outside. A few days. I know it hasn't been a week."

He examined the cat, looking in her eyes and touching her stiff legs. "It looks like she got into something outside. I can't tell what without doing some tests. If you'd like to bring her by, I'll be glad to see if I can help her."

"Thank you, Doctor." Emma took a business card from him. "Could I bring her by later today? I get off at five."

Steve agreed. Peggy thanked her for the tea, and they left the house.

"Who would ever guess they were so unhappy?" Steve walked beside Peggy down the front sidewalk. "I didn't know them personally, but they were always smiling for the camera in the newspaper."

"If ever a woman had a motive to kill a man, it seems to me that Julie did. But I don't think she's physically capable of the task. And Emma gave her a good alibi."

"You were really thinking that Mrs. Warner killed her husband?"

"Somebody did. To save Mr. Cheever, I have to find out who."

SHE WAS TEN MINUTES LATE for her chess game with Nightflyer. Hal Samson began sending the preliminary autopsy results for his poison case. He told her the police had questioned and released the woman's husband. A South Carolina biohazard team was looking for the possible point of poisoning. They ruled out the bank where she worked and concentrated their efforts on her home.

"I thought you weren't coming." Nightflyer's words appeared in the chat box.

Peggy made her first move on the chessboard. Black pawn to f4. *"I was busy."*

"Looking into that anemonin poisoning?"

She barely noticed his move. *"How do you know about that? Are you on Dr. Samson's staff? If you are, you should know that discussing this could be a breach of your hospital contract. You could be fired."*

"I'm not on staff at the hospital."

"Then who are you?" She moved. Black bishop takes white rook on e4.

"With your suspicious mind, I'm surprised you haven't accused me of poisoning the woman."

"Did you?"

The game proceeded forward with no response from Nightflyer. Peggy admired his skill at chess. It was all she could do to keep him at bay. They chased each other across the virtual chessboard. Her gaze stayed glued to the screen while she waited impatiently for his reply. Would he admit to poisoning the woman?

White queen checks black king at g8. *"Check."*

"Are you going to answer my question?" She typed, ignoring the game. He had her in check in less than ten minutes. But she was preoccupied. Maybe he introduced the subject to win the game.

"No, Peggy. But I might know who's responsible."

She knew the game was lost and didn't pay attention to her next move. *"You can tell me, and I can tell the authorities."*

"What fun would that be? Watching them try to figure it out is better than chess. Checkmate."

She didn't know which part of their on-line relationship was more frustrating. She wasn't a great chess player, but she was pretty good. Better than most players she faced. To have him kick her butt so quickly was demeaning. On the other hand, the game meant nothing in comparison to the poisoning case. How could he have that privileged information?

"Why are you telling me this? Do you want attention? Why not go to the police and get your face on television and in the papers?"

"I don't want their attention, Peggy. I want your attention."

"You have it. What do you want me to do?"

"Meet me here again tomorrow night. Midnight."

She wanted to say no. She didn't want to talk to him again. She could feel the hairs on the back of her neck rise when she read that he wanted her attention. No single woman living alone wanted to think some strange man was out there stalking her. And she just *knew* Nightflyer was a man.

But she agreed to meet him again. If he had information about the poisoning case, she felt duty bound to pursue what he knew. Even though he told her he wasn't responsible for the poisoning, how could she believe him? He could be a killer.

"Good night, sweetheart. Until tomorrow night."

Peggy started to reply, but Nightflyer was already gone. She sat and stared at the screen for a long time, trying to decide what to do. Should she tell the South Carolina police? She wasn't sure Nightflyer said anything he could be arrested for. But if they found out who he was, they might be able to get a lead on where the anemonin came from.

She poked around on the game site again. There wasn't a list of E-mail addresses for members. In fact, there was no membership required to play. It was something that drew her to the site. She didn't like to leave her name and E-mail address all over the Internet. She wished she'd been a little less picky. If the site required membership, it would be easy to find out his real-world identity.

A long, deep howl drew her away from the computer. The dog had been quiet in the laundry room all evening. She took him out for a walk at ten. He shouldn't have to go again. But that disturbing howl was followed by another, this one longer and louder than the first. Imagining Clarice calling the police, Peggy ran down the cold marble staircase and opened the laundry room door to see what was wrong.

The dog was whimpering and howling from his place on the vent. As soon as he saw the door open, he ran head-first into her. Peggy almost lost her footing and grabbed the counter for support. The dog nudged her with his huge head, then licked her arm and hand until she was soaked.

"What's wrong, boy?" She patted his head and rubbed his belly. He responded by wagging his tail so hard that his whole body shook.

There didn't seem to be anything wrong with him. He had plenty of water. He'd eaten a huge amount of dog food earlier in the day. She patted his head one last time, then closed the laundry room door and started back upstairs.

The howling began again. This time when Peggy went back to the laundry room, the dog bounded out and headed for the main staircase.

"Oh no, you don't!" She chased him, and he ran up the stairs. He smelled the carpet when he reached the second floor. Immediately, he followed his nose to her bedroom. By the time she caught up with him, he was happily ensconced on her bed. His head was resting on her pillow.

"You're not sleeping in my bed," she told him in her strongest teaching tone. "Come on. Back downstairs."

But no matter how hard she tried to get him out of her bed, he wouldn't budge. She brought out some crackers to try and lure him back to the laundry room. He didn't move. Finally, she admitted defeat but promised that this was only a battle and not the war.

"I suppose I'm going to have to come up with a name for you. I can't go on calling you dog. Maybe if you have a name, you'll listen better. It doesn't mean I'm going to keep you. Don't get your hopes up. If someone doesn't come to claim you, I'll get in touch with the Humane Society. There must be someone who wants a big horse like you."

7

Snowdrop

Botanical: *Galanthus nivalis*
Family: Amaryllidaceae
Common Name: Candlemas bells

The name galanthus is Greek, meaning milk-white flower. Nivalis is Latin, meaning resembling snow. The legend of the snowdrop: After being expelled from the Garden of Eden, Eve sat weeping. An angel comforted her. As the angel talked with Eve, he breathed on a snowflake in his hand. It fell to earth as the first snowdrop. The flower bloomed, and hope was born.

SUNDAY PASSED TOO QUICKLY with Peggy grading test papers and walking the streets looking for the dog's owner. She gave out flyers at church that morning. Myers Park Presbyterian was within walking distance of her house. It was possible someone would recognize the dog's description. Too many people suggested she call the pound. She wasn't going to do that, even if she had to keep the dog for a while herself.

She pushed aside the urge to call Steve and ask him for advice about getting the dog to sleep in the laundry room without howling. It seemed to her things were moving very quickly between them, and she felt out of place calling him. Instead, she spent half a day on the Internet looking for dog training tips and possible names for the beast.

He followed her from room to room all day as she worked with her plants and polished furniture. She finally went to sleep with the dog beside her in bed.

Early Monday morning, she left for the Potting Shed. She didn't have any choice but to bring the dog with her. He ran alongside her bike as she pedaled hard to keep up with him down Queens Road. Runners who ignored her before stayed out of her way. People waiting at bus stops quickly moved into the plastic shelters.

They reached Brevard Court in record time. It took Peggy a few minutes to catch her breath. The dog looked at her and wagged his tail as she tied his leash to an old radiator still in place behind the checkout counter. He lay down on the smooth wood floor and didn't move as she got ready to open the shop.

"Are you Peggy Lee?"

A woman's voice surprised her as she was taking out the new chrysanthemums. She was very attractive, tall and thin, with shoulder-length burnished red hair and bright green eyes. Her coat and shoes were new but not expensive. She clutched a worn brown leather pocketbook like she was afraid it would get away.

"Can I help you?" Peggy wondered if this was yet another of Mark's conquests. At this rate, she was going to make enough money from flowers for the dead man that the police might question *her* motives.

"I'm Jane Cheever." She held out her gloved hand. "You helped my father."

"Of course! Sit down. Would you like some tea? I have some excellent orange spice. It will only take a minute to put the kettle on the hot plate."

"No thanks." Jane sat down on the bench anyway. "I wanted to meet you. And I wanted you to know I appreciate your efforts to help my father. I can't believe a stranger would go to so much trouble for him. How did you meet him?"

"He spends some nights in the courtyard outside the shop," Peggy answered, thinking nothing of it. "We've had some intense philosophical debates. He's very intelligent."

"Yes, well, he's also very misguided." Jane looked up at the window across from her, still gripping her pocketbook. "It was very embarrassing to have someone call about my homeless father. The police looked at me like it's *my* fault he's homeless."

"I'm sure they didn't think so." Peggy tried to comfort her. "He's a good man. Down on his luck, I know. But I don't believe he'd hurt anyone."

"Maybe. But he's not *really* down on his luck. I'm afraid he's lied to you about that. He was living with me and my husband. He didn't like the rules. We thought he shouldn't be wandering around all night. That he should take his medication. We got into an argument, and he left. That was two years ago. I haven't heard from him since. Not that I didn't look for him. I couldn't find him. I even called in a missing persons report on him. I hate people calling him homeless. He *has* a home. He chose not to live there."

Peggy understood, even empathized, but that didn't change the fact that Jane's father could go to jail for the rest of his life. "Have you seen him?"

"No. They said I could after the arraignment. I think that's today."

"I saw him Saturday. Something's wrong with him. You know how he quotes things and knows everything about literature? He wasn't like that. He barely knew who I was."

Jane's lips pressed tightly together. "Maybe now he'll listen to me. He's a stubborn old man. Maybe it would be better for him to go to jail. At least I'd know he was being cared for. He wouldn't be out on the streets."

"Don't say that!" Peggy's temper rose. "No one is better off in jail. Especially for a crime they didn't commit."

"Why are you so sure he didn't kill that man? The police said they found him with his wallet and shoes. He could've knocked him down to take them. Maybe he didn't *mean* to kill him. It might have been an accident. But he's still responsible."

"Hogwash! I know your father well enough to know he

wouldn't hurt anyone, no matter how desperate he was. I'd think you'd know him that well, too. I realize this is an emotional time for you, but he needs you to stand up for him. You can't let him down."

Jane lowered her head. "You're right. I'm sorry. I just get so *desperate*. My neighbors remember him from when my mother was still alive. He was an English teacher for forty years. When my mom died, he snapped. He wasn't the same anymore. Everyone knows he's been arrested for murder now. Even in Rock Hill, we keep up with what's going on in Charlotte."

Peggy didn't know what else to say. She glanced around until she saw what she needed, then handed Jane a little plant. "Here you go. Snowdrops are for hope. That's what we need right now. Plus a little faith. People don't change. Your father is a good man underneath everything that's happened to him. We have to find out who did this terrible thing before the system runs over him."

"What can we do?" Jane looked at the plant in confusion. "They told me they have an airtight case against him."

"We'll see about that! You go and find out when the arraignment is. I found a lawyer for your father, but it would be nice for him to see a friendly face in the courtroom. I wish I could be there, too. Just remember he was there for you when you were a child. Do you have children, Jane?"

"Yes. Two. A boy and a girl. They don't even remember their grandfather."

"He's confused and frightened. He needs you now. Wouldn't you like to think, despite any disagreement, your children would be there for you when you really need them?"

Jane nodded and took Peggy's hand. "Yes, I would. Thank you, Mrs. Lee. I almost let my embarrassment overshadow the fact that I love him."

"Call me Peggy. Let me know what you find out. Give me your phone number, and I'll keep you posted if I learn anything else."

Selena came in as Jane was leaving. She started to walk

behind the counter and stopped dead. "Whoa! Where'd the horse come from?"

Peggy explained the situation with the dog as she continued to set things up in the shop. Emil brought some of his new brew for them to taste. "I call it Holiday Cheer. What do you think?"

"It's good!" Selena said, staying carefully away from the dog. "How'd you get it to taste like gingerbread?"

"That's my secret!" He smiled at her. "I worked all summer on it."

"It's very good," Peggy added. "I like the name, too. Maybe you could serve it at my holiday open house in the beginning of December."

He considered the idea and agreed. "I could give samples with little name tags on the cups. What a great idea! What day are you having this?"

"The first Tuesday of the month. You know how slow Tuesdays are around here. I'm sending out invitations to all my customers."

"Are we serving food?" Selena was excited by the prospect. "If we serve food, all the college kids will come. We're always looking for free food."

Emil shook his head. "What good are they? Always trying to get something for free. Peggy needs paying customers. So do I."

"But you *could* invite your friends," Peggy consoled her. "And I plan to have some food, too."

"Sounds great!" Selena smiled at her and refused to look at Emil. As he was leaving, she stuck her tongue out at him. "He's no fun."

"We *are* running a business," Peggy reminded her.

"Yeah, I know. Bottom line. Gains and losses. I hear it every day."

Sam came in with a worried look on his face. "Where's Keeley? She was supposed to help me with the plants at Bank of America. I tried to call her, but her roommate says she's been gone since Saturday. Did you talk to her about the key, Peggy?"

"Yes. I talked with her Saturday afternoon. She seemed a little . . . disoriented."

"What's up with the key?" Selena glanced between them.

Peggy explained briefly. "Keeley seems to be the only one who's missing hers."

"What does that mean?" Selena asked. "Are you saying Keeley let Mark Warner and his girlfriend into the shop?"

"I don't know." Peggy told her what Mr. Cheever said about seeing a woman run out of the shop that night. "It could have been Keeley."

Selena groaned. "Are you kidding me? You think Keeley and Warner . . . yuck!"

Sam laughed at her. "He had money. Chicks like money. They don't care what the dude looks like who's got it. Or how old he is."

"We don't know why the woman was running out of the shop," Peggy reminded them. "*If* the woman was Keeley, maybe she found Mark and panicked."

"We have to find her." Sam got out his Palm Pilot. "This is no good. I only have her number at the apartment. I already called there. They don't know where she is."

Peggy took out her cell phone. "Keeley's mother is one of my best friends. Maybe she knows what's going on."

There was no answer at Lenore Prinz's home or from her cell phone. Peggy left her a message and put away her phone. "I guess I'll give you a hand with that delivery, Sam. Can you keep an eye on the shop, Selena? It's Monday. It shouldn't be very busy."

Selena agreed. "But you're taking the dog with you, right?"

"You brought the dog?" Sam went around the counter and crouched down beside the Great Dane. "I love this guy! What are you gonna name him?"

"It doesn't matter," Peggy said. "I'm not keeping him. Just looking for his owner. He's friendly, Selena. He looks like a horse, but he won't hurt you. Unless he knocks you down."

Sam was rolling on the floor with the big dog licking him

on the face. "You should keep him. He's awesome. And you could use the company. Your house is big enough for him."

"Maybe you should call him Horse, since he's big like one," Selena suggested, still keeping her distance from the dog.

"You can tell you're a city girl," Sam teased her. "A horse is much bigger than this. This is more like a pony. Maybe you should call him Magic Pony."

"No, no! My Little Pony," Selena added. "You could get him a pink sweater and booties. Man, I used to love those little ponies."

"Thanks for the suggestions." Peggy laughed. "If I name him, it's only so I can communicate with him. I'm not going to keep him. I don't have time for a dog. This one howls at night unless I let him sleep in my bed. He follows me all over the house. And he eats a bag of dog food a day."

"He loves you," Sam explained. "He slept in your bed?"

Selena couldn't believe it. "Sounds to me like you must get along pretty well. Maybe you should keep him. Just don't bring him here anymore."

Peggy pulled on the gloves and work jacket she kept in the shop. "I think we should go now, Sam. We need to take care of those plants at Bank of America."

He followed her out of the shop, suggesting different names for the dog. Peggy sighed. It was going to be a long day.

THE POTTING SHED HAD A contract to maintain the plants on the executive floors of the Bank of America Corporate Center. This meant replacing dead plants, pruning back leggy ones, misting, repotting, and fertilizing. It wasn't a difficult job because the office workers were happy with whatever bit of greenery they could get in the sterile work environment.

Peggy specially chose plants that were hardy and easily maintained: philodendron, a few ficus, and diffenbachia. Even so, she never thought about people pouring their coffee into the pots or shredding the leaves walking by them. The shop made money on the contract, but she hated to see the plants abused that way.

Armed with a small cart that contained everything she needed, Peggy took the elevator to the next floor after dropping Sam off to take care of his part. Fortunately, she kept her pass from her first meeting there. She couldn't get in with Keeley's pass. Security was tight in the bank building.

She tsked when she saw the philodendron that Keeley put in less than a month before. The leaves were torn and yellow. Some of the plants had been moved away from the sunlight. They'd become smaller and had less growth to adjust to the change in light.

Carefully, she put the pots back where they belonged. She pruned and fertilized some of the yellowed plants. One was nearly dead. It smelled like an old coffeepot. She transplanted it into a new pot with fresh soil.

Glancing up from her task, she caught a glimpse of Ronda McGee disappearing behind a set of file cabinets. There was only one way to find out what the wife of the senior executive vice president was doing when her lover was murdered. Peggy put down her mister and went to ask her. "Excuse me, Ronda?"

The woman turned around sharply. "No. Is there something I can do for you?"

Peggy couldn't believe how much the two women looked alike. She recalled the housekeeper's words about Mark's secretary. "Oh, I'm sorry. My mistake. You were Mark Warner's personal assistant, right?"

The woman shrugged. She wore an elegant pink silk blouse and expensive burgundy wool skirt. Her narrow feet were encased in worn but fashionable Gucci shoes. Her shoulder-length brown hair gleamed like sable in the overhead light. "That's right." Honey-colored eyes narrowed as she looked at Peggy suspiciously. "Do I know you?"

"Actually, I only saw you from behind," Peggy confessed. "You look a great deal like Ronda McGee, Bob McGee's wife."

She smiled slowly, showing even, pearly teeth. "I suppose we *do* look a little alike. Especially from behind."

"I'm Peggy Lee. I own the Potting Shed over in Brevard Court. We do the plant maintenance on this floor."

"Angela Martin." The tawny eyes were still uncertain about the connection. "I don't quite see how you guessed I was Mark's PA. Did that have something to do with my looking like Ronda?"

Peggy laughed, denying the truth. "Of course not! I think I saw you with him once. You made a very striking couple."

Angela's pretty face grew more anxious. She put a manicured hand with long, lacquered red nails on Peggy's arm. "Let's step in here."

Mark Warner's name was still on the embossed brass plate outside the door. But inside the office, the desk and credenza were bare except for the computer. Boxes stacked along the wall were filled with personal possessions, making way for the new senior executive vice president who would take his place.

Angela's hand was strong and insistent on Peggy's arm. The PA closed the oak door and faced her. "I don't know who sent you, but it was over between Mark and me last year. He kept me on because I have seniority and I'm bitch enough to take him to court if he tried to get rid of me."

The ending of the affair between Mark and Angela would coincide with what Emma told Peggy. But as long as she had the other woman's attention, Peggy thought she might as well dig for more information. "Ronda McGee took your place with him, didn't she?"

"If you want to call the revolving door of women in Mark's life taking my place, then yes. She started seeing him a few days after we broke up. But I don't flatter myself that I was the only woman he was seeing. Mark got bored easily. He and I were over before his wife threatened him. Not that he cared about her threats."

"He was seeing someone else as well as Ronda?"

Angela smoothed her hand down the sleek side of her hair. "You'll have to ask him that. I only know he's been with a lot of women. Julie reacts when something comes up that might embarrass her. Otherwise, she lets him do what he wants. She knows one woman isn't enough for him."

Peggy decided to go for broke. "Where were you the night Mark was killed?"

"Are you with the police? I thought they already arrested the man who killed Mark."

"A suspect is in custody," Peggy repeated the phrase she often heard on the police scanner when John was alive. "That doesn't mean the investigation is over."

"In that case, I was washing my hair. I decided to stay in that night. I watched *Sleepless in Seattle* on HBO. Then I went to bed. I ate a pint of chocolate chip cookie dough— Ben and Jerry's, in case you have some way of testing for that. I've seen *CSI*."

"Was anyone there with you?" Peggy continued, letting Angela think she was with the police. "Can anyone back up your story?"

"No. I was alone all night. I didn't know I needed an alibi. What possible reason would I have to kill Mark? He owed me. We had an understanding. Now I have to start all over with a new executive VP. Mark being dead isn't good for me at all."

"Thank you. I appreciate you talking with me."

"Do I need a lawyer?"

"No. We just needed a few answers." Peggy opened the office door. "But don't leave town until the investigation is over."

The sultry brunette frowned. "Not like I can go anywhere. At least not until I know if I can keep my job. This new VP is coming in from Ohio. I hope to God I don't have to sleep with him to have some influence again."

Peggy finished up her plant care with a nervous eye on the elevators. If Angela decided to call the police, she'd be in trouble. Not that she actually told the woman she was with the police. But she'd allowed her to think it. Al and Jonas wouldn't like her talking to Angela.

But no officers came up to the floors where she was working. She met Sam at the truck outside in the parking lot when she was finished. He smiled at her and asked, "How'd it go?"

"The plants were in pretty good shape," she told him. "How about you?"

He pulled two pieces of pink memo paper from his jeans pockets. "Two phone numbers. Stockbrokers like college men."

She understood. "I always wondered what kept you working for me."

"Not the guaranteed dates, sweet as that may be. Do you know what it costs to become a doctor these days? Do you know how much Home Depot pays? I was lucky you didn't have any idea what you were doing when you got started. You pay me way too much for what I do."

"Aren't you worried about telling me that?"

"Nah. You need me now. You couldn't do it without me."

Peggy's cell phone rang while she was laughing at him. It was Lenore Prinz. She wanted to know if Peggy could meet her at the hospital. "I'll be there as soon as I can. What's wrong?"

"Who was that?" Sam asked as she closed her cell phone.

"It was Lenore. Keeley's in the hospital."

SAM DROPPED PEGGY OFF at Presbyterian Hospital. "I'll be back in about an hour. I'm going to drop these plants off at CPCC. Will you be all right?"

"I'll be fine. I'll see you then." She got out of the truck and walked up the long, narrow sidewalk into the large brick building. The sound of ambulance sirens filled the morning air. She hadn't been to this place since John died. They'd brought him here after the shooting.

Peggy sighed and tried to put it behind her. She'd held a grudge against the hospital for too long. John was dead before they brought him in. Al told her there was nothing they could do. She believed him. To go on feeling there was some kind of dark cloud hanging over the place was ridiculous. Still, she had to swallow hard as the revolving door closed behind her, pushing back the sunshine.

She asked the receptionist at the front desk for Keeley's room number. With her own doubts and memories tucked firmly away, she took the elevator to the second floor.

Lenore met her in the lounge. Her usually placid face was agitated. Thick, dark hair sprang up around her head like a lion's mane. She'd never found a way to tame her coarse, curly hair. She reached for Peggy's hands and squeezed them. "Thanks for coming."

"Of course." Peggy sat down beside her friend on the green plastic chair. She and Lenore grew up next door to each other. Lenore's parents owned the tobacco farm that bordered her parents' farm outside Charleston. They went to school together and dreamed of where their lives would take them. Somehow, they both ended up in Charlotte. "What happened?"

Lenore looked away. Her dark eyes, so like Keeley's, closed. "She was pregnant, Peggy. She never even told me. Something happened. She lost the baby."

"How is she?"

"She's okay. She was only about ten weeks. The doctor said the baby wasn't viable."

"I'm so sorry," Peggy said. "I didn't know Keeley had a serious boyfriend."

"I didn't either. Apparently, he wasn't someone she was very proud of. Probably one of those tattooed, pierced types. I don't know what young people are coming to these days."

"Keeley's a good person and a hard worker. Even if she wasn't sure about introducing him to her family and friends, it doesn't mean she was ashamed of him. Sometimes you just want to make sure. Can we see her?"

Lenore sighed. "I could've seen her an hour ago. I don't know what to say to her. I was hoping you could talk to her.

She thinks so much of you. Sometimes I think you should've been her mother. She and I have always had problems communicating."

Peggy patted her hand. "Only if you'll take Paul. He and I have the same problem. But you know what it's like trying to live your own life, not just doing what your parents expect of you."

"Maybe. I don't know if I can remember back that far. Mama and Daddy have been gone for so long. You're lucky to still have your parents."

"Sometimes I'm not so sure about that." Peggy stopped when she saw the horrified expression on Lenore's face. She sometimes forgot that her old friend didn't share her sense of the ironic. "Never mind about that. I'll go and talk to Keeley. But you have to talk to her, too."

"After you see her, I will," Lenore promised. "Thank you, Peggy. I'll think of something to say to her."

"Something that doesn't sound like Bible scripture thundering down from Reverend Jacob's pulpit, I hope."

Lenore smiled. "He was loud, wasn't he? I still remember how many times I was about to drift off, and he started shouting. Mama used to say it was enough to scare the devil right out of the county."

"But not what a young woman wants to hear from her mother after a thing like this."

"I know. Don't scold. You live in their world, Peggy. You have to expect the rest of us to be a little shocked by it. The idea that my daughter was with a man before she was married is still hard for me."

"She's twenty-one years old," Peggy reminded her. "Just remember that you love each other."

KEELEY WAS SITTING UP in bed when Peggy entered the room. She'd known the girl all of her life. She held Lenore's hand when Keeley fell off of her bike and got a concussion at twelve. She took care of her many times when her parents went away on business. Now she looked at her and felt a little like her mother. She wasn't sure what to say.

"I suppose Mom sent you in here because she couldn't face me," Keeley guessed.

Peggy hugged her. "How are you? The doctor said you're fine, but he can't see the important part of you."

Keeley looked up at her. "Which part is that?"

"Your heart. I know it must be aching."

"It was a stupid mistake, Peggy. I probably would've gotten rid of it anyway. It wasn't anything yet. Just some tissue."

"But you didn't. And you can't convince me that you didn't know about it from the beginning. You're too smart for that. Did you think *he* wanted the baby?"

"Yes." Keeley's bottom lip quivered. "I thought he loved me. How could I be so stupid?"

Peggy put her arms around her again. "Because you loved him. You wanted what everyone wants. There's nothing wrong with that. You're not stupid for falling in love and believing someone loved you in return."

Tears ran silently down Keeley's pretty face. "Even if he was married?"

"Please don't tell me—"

"It was Mark. I'm the one he was meeting at the Potting Shed. I was probably the last person to see him alive."

Peggy didn't want to believe it. "Have you told anyone else?"

"No. I told the doctor I didn't know who the father was. I didn't go to the police yet to give them my fingerprints because I was scared they'd find out."

"Tell me everything about that night." Peggy put her pocketbook on the side table and sat down close to Keeley. "Don't leave anything out."

The story poured out of her in low, uncertain tones. She met Mark at Bank of America while she was working with the plants. He asked her out for lunch, then for dinner. After a week of expensive restaurants and gifts, Keeley met him at the Omni Hotel. They went there a couple of nights every week for the past three months.

"He was funny, you know?" Keeley wiped the tears from her face. "He knew how to have a good time. I liked being with him. Then he called me one day and said it was over. I knew I was pregnant. He started coming to the shop at lunchtime with that other woman. I think he was trying to show me that he didn't care about me anymore."

"But he agreed to meet you one last time," Peggy surmised. "You told him you were pregnant."

"Yes. I thought it would make a difference to him." She laughed. "He offered me money to get an abortion. He said he wouldn't leave his wife."

"So you met him at the shop that night, let him in, and argued with him about the baby. Then what?"

"I guess I got a little hysterical. He was drunk anyway. Slurring his words and unsteady on his feet. I didn't want to talk to him anymore, so I ran out. He was still alive when I left. When I got home, my key was gone. I thought I left it in the back door, but I must've dropped it in back." She gripped Peggy's hand. "I'm *so* sorry I didn't tell you. I was so afraid everyone would think I killed him."

"*Did* you kill him, Keeley? You were upset. You weren't thinking about what you were doing. The shovel was handy."

"*No!* I didn't kill him. I can't believe you even have to ask me that question!"

"I'm sorry, honey." Peggy hugged her. "But the police will ask you more than that."

"Why do I have to tell them? I didn't kill him. Maybe Homer did."

Peggy stood up straight. "Let's stop thinking of him as a cartoon character. His name is Joseph, not Homer. He's in jail, and he'll probably go to prison for a crime he didn't commit either. You have to tell the police what happened."

"How will that help Mr. Cheever? It'll only make *me* a

suspect. Then he won't be in jail, I will. Is that what you want?"

"Of course not. But someone killed Mark. If nothing else, your recollections of that night could cause the DA to question what happened."

"But if it wasn't me and it wasn't Mr. Cheever, who did it?" Keeley asked. "Who else was at the shop that night?"

8

Holly

Botanical: *Ilex aquifolium, Ilex opaca*
Family: Aquifoliaceae
Common Name: Christmas holly

The word holly *comes from the word* holy. *Holly has always been associated with Christmas. There are over 150 species of holly. English holly* (Ilex aquifolium) *and American holly* (Ilex opaca) *are the species most commonly grown as Christmas decorations. The American holly has duller leaves and more spines than the English holly. Holly berries are potentially dangerous if eaten. Twenty berries can kill an adult human.*

HUNTER CALLED FROM THE COURTHOUSE as Peggy was leaving the hospital. "Mr. Cheever was held over for trial. No bond. The DA made it sound like he was a risk to himself and others. I couldn't exactly claim a homeless man had strong ties to the community."

"What happens next?"

"Without a lot of fancy footwork to prove the case, the trial should come up pretty quickly. Maybe right after the beginning of the year. The forensic evidence is all in their favor. They found him with Warner's possessions. He admits he took them and said Warner was on the floor 'asleep.' His fingerprints are all over everything. Mr. Cheever doesn't remember what happened. I won't even be able to use him on the witness stand. He's his own worst enemy."

Peggy stood next to a badly pruned holly bush. It was cut back so far, there were no red berries on it. For some reason, the one beside it wasn't pruned to within an inch of its life. It had mounds of berries. It reminded her of all the possible suspects popping up in Mark's death. "Suppose you could show it was *possible* someone else was responsible for the murder?"

"That would be fine." Hunter's voice faded in and out on the cell phone. "Creating reasonable doubt in the minds of the jury is the only thing that's going to save your friend. I have to tell you, I pleaded not guilty for him today. But I think we should be going for diminished capacity. He's not all there. I don't know if it's drinking or something else. They kept him at the hospital for more tests. The doctor thinks it's possible he had a stroke."

"Is there anything I can do?"

"Not really. Unless you have some evidence that can create reasonable doubt."

Peggy considered her words carefully. "I might have some evidence. I don't know exactly what to do with it. Can you meet me somewhere?"

THEY MET AT the Potting Shed at six when it closed. Peggy was straightening up when Hunter walked in. She'd already sent Selena home. She didn't want anyone else to hear what she had to say.

"This is where it happened, huh?" Hunter put down her briefcase and looked around the shop. "I recognize this area from the police photos. Warner was on the floor in the middle of your autumn collage."

"That's right. Some other facts have come up since then." Peggy took out two cream cheese and sprout bagels, handing one to Hunter.

"Thanks. Have you told the police?"

"I wanted to tell you first. The police don't seem too interested in anything but Mr. Cheever anyway."

Hunter unwrapped her bagel. "Tell me what you know, and we'll see."

Peggy told her what she knew about Ronda McGee, Angela Martin, and Keeley as she poured them each a cup of lemon balm tea. "I can't believe Keeley was involved with him. I promised her mother no one else would know unless it was absolutely necessary."

"I guess that depends on how you gauge something being necessary." Hunter sipped her tea. "The DA could ask for the death penalty. I think it's unlikely, given Mr. Cheever's current state. But the best scenario possible puts him in a hospital for the rest of his life. That seems pretty necessary to me."

"I know. But what good will it do to shift the burden of guilt from one innocent person to another?"

"Are you sure she's innocent?"

Peggy wiped her lips with her napkin. "I've known her since she was born. She did something stupid, but I don't believe she killed Mark. She loved him and thought he was going to marry her. I wouldn't want to see her on trial for the murder any more than I want to see Mr. Cheever there. There must be another way."

"What about the other women?" Hunter wiped cream cheese from her hand. "Angela and Ronda. Do they have alibis for that night? Isn't it possible one of them could be guilty?"

"I don't know about Ronda," Peggy admitted. "Angela said she was in all night by herself. Not much of an alibi, but she didn't have a motive to kill him either."

Hunter considered the prospects as she polished off the rest of her bagel and some cookies that Peggy brought from the Tea and Coffee Emporium. "We could hire a private investigator to find out everything about Warner's relationships with these women. Even if we don't find anything that proves one of them was responsible, I could use the possibility of their guilt to show the jury Cheever wasn't the only one who had access and motive for the crime. I could use Keeley as a last resort if the other two don't work."

"I'm afraid a private investigator is out of my price range," Peggy admitted. "Maybe I could keep looking around and asking questions. You said we have a while before the trial. If it gets too close and I don't find anything, I could turn everything over to an investigator."

"I guess that's okay. I spoke with Cheever's daughter after the arraignment. She doesn't have much money either. I wish the court would've appointed me, then the state would pay for Cheever's defense."

Peggy laughed. "Like that would've paid for a private detective! Don't worry. I'm sure we can work this out. I'm glad you're on our team."

"Let me know what you find out," Hunter said. "And don't go too far. You don't want the police coming after *you*."

Peggy agreed, and Hunter left a few minutes later. After the other woman was gone, she turned out the lights and locked the front door. The dog let out a long, low howl that sent goose bumps down her spine. "What's wrong, boy? Are you ready to go home?"

He came over and snuffled her hand. She wiped the dog slobber on a rag, then picked up his leash and led him out the back door. After she locked up, he growled low in the back of his throat and came to full attention, staring into the shadows that surrounded the loading dock.

"Do you see a rat or something?" Peggy asked loudly to deal with her sudden sense of fear. It was silly. She'd never been afraid walking out behind the shop before. Of course, she'd never had a dead man in her shop before either. She patted the dog's head and quickly pulled out her bicycle. "Let's go home. We've both had a rough day."

The dog wouldn't move. He stood like a statue, growling and glaring at the dark end of the loading dock. Peggy wasn't scared of shadows or things that went bump in the night. But the dog's fierce expression and challenging stance made her nervous. She finally got him to walk away and got on her bike. It was a relief to be away from the area. She was going to have to hound the maintenance people until they got that back light replaced.

As she turned out of the drive into the street, she thought she saw a small light, like a flashlight, at the top of the loading dock. When she looked again, it was completely dark behind the shop. The dog whined when she stopped as she tried to decide what to do.

She started to go back, then reasoned with herself; if she thought someone was back there, she'd be better off calling the police and letting them handle it. What would be the point of her checking it out? It wasn't like she was up to tackling a would-be thief.

Taking out her cell phone, she started to dial 911. Uncertainty stayed her hand. Unless she had something more to say than she thought she saw a flashlight, she didn't want to call. If she started calling the police every time there was an unusual sound or the dog growled, she'd be in a mess. She stayed where she was and watched the shadows as cars passed her in the street. There was no sign of the light again.

Sighing at her flights of fancy, taking a deep breath to clear her mind, she urged the dog toward home. It had been a strange week. No wonder she was quick to panic. Once she got home and had a nice cup of tea, she'd feel better.

A car she didn't recognize was waiting in her drive when she got home. She parked her bike beside the house. A man opened the car door and got out. "Peggy Lee?"

Her heart was beating fast and her knees were wobbly. "Yes?"

Paper rustled. "I saw your flyer. I think you might have my dog."

Peggy gave a sigh of relief. "You startled me. I wasn't expecting someone to come to the house."

The young man moved into the streetlight and frowned at her. "I'm sorry. I looked up the phone number on the flyer. I live about a block from here. I couldn't wait to come and take Jo-Jo home."

The dog whined and barked at the man. She patted his head and soothed him. "He seems to know you."

"Sure he does." He clapped his hands together. "Come on, Jo! Let's go home!"

But the dog backed away from him. He looked up at Peggy and whined, butting his huge head against her leg.

"He seems to know you," she amended. "But he doesn't seem to like you very much."

"That's ridiculous! I paid a fortune for that dog. He's damn well coming home with me."

Peggy stood between the man and the cowering dog. "I don't think that's a good idea. I'll have to ask you to leave now."

"Not without my dog." He reached his hand for the leash.

The dog lunged at him, barking and growling like he'd take his hand off. Jo-Jo chased his owner back to the car and put his massive paws on the window even after the man was inside. His teeth grated against the glass as he tried to get at him.

"That's enough." Peggy called him back.

"I'll be here tomorrow with my lawyer," the man promised when the dog went back to her.

She ignored the car leaving the drive and turned to the dog. "Let's go inside. It looks like we have some thinking to do."

The phone was ringing. She closed the door and locked it, took the leash off of the dog. He immediately fell on the floor at her feet as she answered the phone. She wanted to collapse there, too. Her life had taken on a weird, frantic aspect that didn't want to go away.

"Hi Peggy. Hal Samson. I wanted to let you know what's happened. The police decided not to press charges against the husband. There was no proof he was involved in his wife's death. They aren't sure where to go from here."

She took off her gloves and sat down on the bench by the door. "I'm glad for the husband if he was innocent, but that still doesn't answer the question of how the poisoning happened, does it? She was murdered, Hal. They can't want to overlook that fact."

"They don't. But apparently, there's no reason to suspect the husband beyond the obvious. I talked with the detective tonight. They're going to continue to investigate. But they're stymied right now, and that puts the case on the back burner. It seems murder by poison doesn't happen often in Columbia."

"I suppose that's true of almost everywhere. A gun is so much easier," Peggy commiserated. "I'm sorry I couldn't be more help, Hal. I wish we could've saved her. Would it be too much to ask her name and address? I'd really like to send a plant for her funeral. I feel as if I should know her name."

"I don't think it would be a breach of ethics for me to tell you. After all, you worked on the case. Do you have a piece of paper and a pencil?"

Peggy took down the woman's information, then promised Hal they could meet for lunch one day and said good night. *Molly Stone*. She stood looking at the woman's name for a long time. She was very young. Who would want to kill her?

The police were putting the case on the back burner. How often was John unhappy with that decision? But like the decision to charge Mr. Cheever with Warner's death, many police decisions were made for expediency rather than taking the time and money to find the truth. It was a sad fact for the officers as well as the public they protected but part of the reality of life.

She rubbed the dog's head. "Let's go and eat something. It looks like I'm going to be buying more dog food after all."

After a light supper and a quick check on her plants, Peggy went upstairs with the dog at her heels. Her mind was buzzing with questions that had no answers. She put on the green satin pajamas Paul gave her for her birthday last September. The dog was already asleep in her bed. She turned on her computer and logged on to her favorite gaming site.

Nightflyer was already there. She typed in her screen name, and he answered immediately.

"Busy day?"

She laughed. *"LOL! You could say that."*

"Too bad about your friend."

"Which one?"

"The one who got indicted for murder. What now?"

Peggy shifted uneasily in her chair. *"Now we play chess."*

"I know you've been snooping around. Two murders at the same time. That's a lot to handle. No wonder you're so busy. I don't see what you can do about the one in Columbia."

Getting angry with his apparent omniscient knowledge, she fired back, *"You don't know as much as you think, my friend. The Columbia police aren't through investigating that death."*

"But we both know it will be pushed aside for now."

"If you know that, maybe you know who did it."

"Maybe I do, Nightrose. Shall we play?"

Peggy beat him in the first game. It was a surprise to her. She suspected that he let her win. Especially when he challenged her to a second game and thoroughly squashed her.

"One more to decide the victor?" She typed into the chat box.

"Not tonight, dear. What are you going to name that dog?"

The same feeling she had leaving the store that night came over her. She almost looked around for a surveillance camera. *"Stalking is illegal."*

"Perhaps. But PROVING it is difficult."

"Who ARE you?"

There was no reply. His name vanished from the gaming site roster. She wasn't sure what to do. She supposed she could mention Nightflyer's insinuations to Paul, but he hadn't threatened her in any way. She didn't want the police ripping her computer apart if they took her seriously. She turned off the light on the desk, deciding to wait and see what happened.

SHE WOKE UP AT EIGHT the next morning with the dog barking and jumping in her bed. Someone was pounding on the front door. Guessing it was the obnoxious man who tried to claim the dog, she put on her robe and ran down the stairs, ready to do battle.

Instead, it was Al. "Peggy, I know this man is a friend of yours, but you can't go around pretending to be with the police, questioning people about the murder. It was bad enough that you snuck in to see him in jail. It's illegal to impersonate an officer."

"Good morning to you, too." She closed the door behind him, watching as he paced the foyer.

"Well? What do you have to say?"

"John always said not to admit anything. I wasn't there, and I didn't do anything."

"Peggy, this is serious. Rimer likes you, but he's not gonna let you screw this up. We have our suspect. We made our arrest. The man had everything but Warner's blood on him."

"Let's talk about that, Al. How do you suppose he managed to get the watch, the wallet, and the shoes without getting any blood on him?"

"Maybe he did get messed up. He's homeless. He could've dropped his jacket or whatever in a trash can, and we'd never find it."

"He's worn the same coat for two years. He doesn't get rid of things."

"Maybe he does when he gets blood on them." Al stopped and glared at her.

"What about *his* story?"

"You mean the phantom woman who ran out of the shop?" He laughed. "Did you expect him to confess? You were a cop's wife too long for that."

"No, I didn't expect a confession. But aren't you even interested in finding out if a woman was in the shop before he got there?"

"We've questioned everyone, Peggy. Even Angela Martin, his PA. You weren't the only one who knew he was having an affair. No one else had motive and opportunity like Cheever did. He probably didn't mean to kill him. He meant to knock him down and take his stuff. He hit him too hard. I'm sorry, but he still has to pay for his crime."

Before Peggy could argue the point, there was another knock on the door. It was the man from last night who tried to claim the dog.

"I'm back for my dog. Here are my documents. I bought him, got his shots, and cared for him. This is my lawyer. He's prepared to go to court, if necessary." The lawyer stepped forward, looking uneasy.

Al joined them, flashed his badge, and the two men backed down. "What seems to be the problem?"

"I'm glad you're here, Detective." The lanky young man nodded his head and grinned at Peggy. "I want to have this woman arrested for not giving my dog back."

Al raised a black brow at Peggy. She told him the story of how she found the dog and put out flyers to locate his owner. He looked at the man's papers. "Looks like everything's in order. Why didn't you give him the dog back?"

"The dog didn't want to go with him. He chased him and almost bit him."

"Peggy, a lot of runaway kids don't want to go home with their parents either. But the law says they have to. The man owns this dog." He handed the papers back. "You have to give it to him."

The man in the doorway rubbed his hands and laughed. "See? I told you I'd get him back."

Peggy picked the leash up from the side table. "Here you go. If I ever see that dog running around like some half-starved scarecrow again, I'll call the Humane Society and *my* lawyer will sue you for animal cruelty."

The man jerked the leash out of her hand and approached the dog confidently—until the animal picked up his scent and began snarling at him. "Nice boy. Good Jo-Jo."

"Well, if everything is in order," the lawyer in the plain gray suit started to move away from the door, "I'll be going."

Jo-Jo's owner managed to get a headlock on the dog. He tied the leash around his neck like a choke collar. The dog tried to pull away but ended up coughing and gasping for breath.

Peggy wanted to kick the man. The look on her face must've given her away. Al put a large hand on her shoulder to hold her back.

"Thanks, Detective." The man put out his hand to shake Al's.

"I think you'd better go, son. In case you haven't noticed, there's more than the dog who'd like to bite you."

"I suppose that was necessary." Peggy watched the man shove the dog into the backseat of his BMW.

"The animal was his property. Sorry."

She bristled. "I don't want the dog. But I don't want to see it mistreated."

Al sighed. "Just remember what I said about interfering in this investigation."

"What investigation? It seems to me that you aren't investigating anymore."

"Whatever you want to call it, don't get involved. Okay?"

"I have to go to work. I'll see you later."

HER BOTANY CLASS WENT SMOOTHLY. The students forgot her notoriety in their unhappiness about her test. She sat at her desk for a few minutes after everyone was gone. The tests looked pretty good. She knew most of the students would never be involved in any future botanical pursuit. For most, this was an easy science credit. She'd been teaching there long enough to know the kids regarded her as an easy class. She didn't mind. The few students who were serious about the subject were enough to keep her going.

"Ready for lunch, Professor?"

Peggy looked up at Steve. "Were we supposed to have lunch together?"

"I was in the neighborhood and thought I'd stop by. Do you have other plans?"

"No. I'm glad to see you. You've saved me from sitting here and going through all these tests."

"Consider yourself saved. Where would you like to go for lunch?"

They decided to take Steve's car and go to the Mimosa Grill. Peggy had never been there, even though it was across the street from Latta Arcade. Steve loved their food.

"I saw the Rolls in your garage. That's a classic," he observed after they were seated at a table by the window.

"It belonged to my father-in-law. My husband never drove it. I'm restoring it and changing the engine to run on hydrogen. There's too much fossil fuel emission without my adding to it."

"That's a challenge," he admitted. "I'm impressed. Do you have mechanical experience?"

"No." She picked up the lunch menu. "But how hard can it be? The combustion engine is pretty basic. Have you ever worked on a car?"

He laughed. "A little. When I was in college, I had this old Ford that had to be worked on every day. I swore once I was making some money I wouldn't ever work on a car again. But I'll be happy to give you a hand if you need one."

There was no mistaking his warm tone or the meaning in his eyes. Peggy mumbled something she was pretty sure he wouldn't understand and stared at the menu. When the waitress finally came, she ordered a vegetable plate and sat back.

There were a few awkward moments where they made small talk about the weather and the Panthers' winning streak. Peggy drank too much iced tea and had to excuse herself. She looked at her face in the small, dimly lit bathroom. Her cheeks were rosy, and her green eyes were sparkling. She was excited to be there with Steve, and she felt guilty at the same time. Was she supposed to be interested in another man already?

When John died, her sister told her she'd find someone else. At the time, she was horrified. Yet here she was, only two years later, thinking about another man. It defied her sense of logic. But she couldn't argue with the emotions pumping through her body.

Lunch was there when she got back. She determined between the bathroom and the table that she wasn't going to sit there like a block of wood. She sat down, smiled at Steve, and asked him about his veterinary practice.

He looked surprised but played along. "It's slow. I knew it would be. Starting over in a new town isn't easy. But I like being here. I think it'll work out."

"Did Emma bring her cat to you? That kind of thing could get you in with a large group of people. They all use the same housekeepers, landscapers, and vets."

"She brought the cat." He sipped his coffee. "Unfortunately, it died. I don't know if that's going to get me in anywhere."

"That's too bad. But if you hang in there, I'm sure things will work out."

"Speaking of animals, which seems to be a safe subject," he teased, "how's that big horse of a dog doing?"

Peggy told him about the owner coming to get the dog. "There wasn't anything I could do to save the poor creature. He looked at me so pitifully, slobbering and pathetic."

"The man or the dog?"

She was laughing at his words when she saw Paul. He was walking by the restaurant, going toward Founder's Hall. When he saw her, he stopped and stared, then went to the door. She wished they'd chosen a spot at the back of the restaurant. This whole thing with Steve was too new for her to defend. *She* wasn't even sure what she was doing.

"Isn't that your son?" Steve asked when he saw Paul walk in.

"Yes. Do you suppose it's too late to hide?"

"Why? Are you embarrassed to be with me?"

"Of course not," she denied, then recapitulated. "I was brought up in a very Southern, conservative family. We don't get embarrassed. We're *uncertain*."

They were both laughing when Paul stalked up to their table. "Mom."

"Paul." Peggy's tone was defiant. She was too old to be shamed by her son.

Paul stared at Steve but didn't speak to him.

Steve wasn't happy with the situation and got to his feet. "Would you like to join us?"

"I don't think so."

"We weren't really introduced the other day. I'm Dr. Steve Newsome. I'm a veterinarian. I live a few doors down from your mother."

Paul ignored Steve's outstretched hand. "I'm her son. I could live at home with her again anytime I want to."

Peggy didn't know whether to laugh at him or spank him. She wished the latter were possible. "Paul, was there something you wanted?"

"No, I guess not. I saw Al this morning. He told me you were running around town asking people questions about Mark Warner. I hope he impressed on you that this is *police* business."

"He did. But thanks for asking."

"Mom—" Paul began to speak but didn't finish. "I'll talk to you later. When you're *alone*."

"Nice to see you again," Steve said as Paul left.

"Sorry. He's a little overprotective sometimes. When he isn't totally ignoring me."

"Kids, huh? I'm glad I was never one of them." Steve glanced at her untouched lunch. "Would you like to go?"

"No. I'm fine. Paul will have to get over himself. As for that part about him living at home again . . ."

"We could always sneak over to my place." He smiled at her, then took a bite of his honey-baked ham on rye.

Peggy's toes curled in her shoes. She ate some of her

green beans, forcing them down her throat with a large
swallow of tea.

"So what's this about you getting in trouble for investigating Warner's murder?"

Peggy was glad to tell him about it. Talking about the
case kept her mind away from disturbing images of meeting Steve in her garden at midnight. She told him most of
what she knew without mentioning Keeley.

"Wow! You *are* involved. Who do you think did it if it
wasn't your homeless friend?"

"I suppose that's the bad part," she confessed. "I don't
have any idea. But there are plenty of other suspects. That's
good for Mr. Cheever but bad for the police and Julie
Warner. It's terrible not knowing who killed someone you
loved."

"You talk like you have personal experience with it."

She explained briefly about John's death. "This late in the
game, we'll probably never find the man who killed him."

"I'm sorry. No wonder your son doesn't like me."

They finished eating and walked out into the sunshine.
Tryon Street was congested with traffic. There was an accident waiting to be cleaned up right outside Latta Arcade.

"I guess I'll just walk across to the shop," Peggy said,
feeling awkward again.

"Is that where the infamous Potting Shed is? I've never
been inside Latta Arcade."

"Really?" She took a deep breath, then slipped her arm
through his. "I guess I'll have to introduce you then."

She told him about the history of the Arcade as they
walked through it to reach Brevard Court. Without pausing
for breath, she pushed open the door to her shop and
walked inside. It was busy with lunchtime traffic, shoppers
loading up on fall planting specials.

"I'm glad you're here," Selena said from behind the
counter with ten customers in line. "I can use the help."

"Would you mind?" Peggy asked Steve. "I need to help
her get caught up."

"No, that's fine. Is there anything I can do to help?"

"Yes," Selena answered. "This gentleman wants a hundred-pound bag of potting soil. His car is parked in back."

Peggy frowned. "You don't need to do that, Steve."

"No problem," he answered. "Where's the potting soil?"

Selena grinned at Peggy after showing Steve the back storage area. "Who's *he*?"

"Never mind," Peggy answered, ringing up the next customer in line. "Just don't ever do *that* again!"

"Hey, if he likes you, he better like your shop, right?"

Peggy didn't answer. When Selena was caught up, she walked back to the loading dock to find Steve helping another customer with a fifty-pound bag of bird food. The woman waved as she pulled away from the loading area.

"Thanks for your help," Peggy said, embarrassed. "I didn't expect you to do this."

"Not a problem. Are you free for dinner tonight?"

"Not really. I have so much to do. Tests to grade. My experiments are at a critical point."

"Just don't tell me you have to wash your hair."

She stared at him. "I'm sorry. I might need a little time. I wasn't expecting this to happen."

"Take all you like. I'm not going anywhere." He kissed her lightly on the lips.

A sharply indrawn breath followed by a wild whooping noise caught their attention. Steve slipped his arm around Peggy as they faced the back door.

Sam ran out laughing. "Wow! Peggy's got a boyfriend."

"Sam, this is Steve Newsome. He's a veterinarian who lives a few doors down from me," Peggy introduced them. "Steve, this is Sam Ollson. He's going to be a doctor someday. Right now, he works for me."

"Nice to meet you." Sam shook Steve's hand. "Make sure you get her in by ten, or I'll be out with my shotgun."

"That's not funny," she told him. "We just saw Paul."

"Right. He's *really* got a shotgun."

Peggy didn't laugh. "What are you doing here? I thought you had classes today."

"I did. But I couldn't get you on your cell phone." Sam waggled his eyebrows. "Have you heard the news yet?"

"We were having lunch," she said. "What news?"

"Keeley turned herself in to the police. She all but told them she killed Mark Warner."

9

Blackberry

Botanical: *Rubus fruticosus*
Family: Rosaceae
Common Names: Blackberry, dewberry

In France, it was believed the color of the fruit turned black when the devil spat on it. In England, it was bad luck to pick the fruit after Old Michaelmas Day, October 11. Brambles of blackberry were planted around graves to prevent the dead from rising as ghosts.

PEGGY AND HUNTER'S FRIEND, JANICE, another attorney, met Lenore at the downtown precinct. After Keeley's announcement to the press about her involvement with Mark Warner, she turned herself in to the police. Al and Jonas had been questioning her since then.

"Thank God you could come." Keeley's mother ran to Peggy and hugged her. "I haven't even had a chance to deal with this pregnancy issue. Now this! I feel like I don't know my own daughter anymore."

Peggy introduced Janice to Lenore. "What is Keeley telling them?"

Lenore shrugged. "I don't know. Why did she think she had to do this? Wasn't the rest of it bad enough?"

"I think I know why she did it," Peggy said. "It's my

fault. I talked to her about Mr. Cheever going to jail for the rest of his life. I didn't know she'd do anything like this."

"You knew what a fragile state of mind she was in." Lenore moved away from her. "How could you do this? What if they arrest her for murder? Did you want to save your friend and doom my daughter to a lifetime in prison?"

"Lenore," Peggy tried to reason with her, "you know I think of Keeley as a daughter. I wouldn't do anything to hurt her."

"Then why did you tell her to turn herself in to the police?"

Janice took over, hushing them as a few officers passed coming into the station. "We have to stick together here, ladies. Let's not assume the worst at this point. I'll go in there and see what's going on."

Lenore nodded, crying.

"Thanks, Janice." Peggy went to Lenore and put her arms around her. "We'll wait here until you come out."

The police parking lot was starting to fill up with vans from the major local news stations. Peggy could see them setting up from the window. The reporters weren't allowed in the precinct, but they'd be waiting when they came out. Lenore excused herself and went to the rest room. Peggy put her pocketbook on the chair beside her to save her place.

She felt completely responsible for Keeley's ill-advised confession. She should've waited to talk to her until she was out of the hospital. Losing a baby wasn't an easy thing. She should've taken that into consideration. She was so eager to find a way to save Mr. Cheever that she might have done something that would cost Keeley dearly.

"Hi, Peggy." Mai walked into the station. "How are you? Are you here about the new development in the Warner case?"

Peggy explained what happened. "Are you here because of Keeley?"

"Hardly. Nothing moves that fast around here. I'm working on another case." Mai held up her digital camera.

"It's a simple break-in over on the north side. I hope you aren't expecting to see your friend."

"No. I brought a lawyer for her. And I'm here with her mother." Peggy introduced Lenore as she joined them. "But if you have any information you can give us, we'd appreciate it."

Mai nodded, the light shining on her silky black hair. "I'll see what I can do. Just don't expect too much. No one is going to like this case blowing up in their face."

Al and Jonas came out of the side door, passing Mai on her way to her office. The station was crowded with officers and other personnel. Reporters watched anxiously, peeking in every time the outside door opened.

"You!" Jonas focused on Peggy, the frown on his face becoming darker. "Did you have something to do with this?"

"Only minimally," she answered. "I'm sorry it isn't going well for you. I think the case is much more complicated than you're giving it credit for. There's more involved than just a homeless man looking for new shoes."

"You know, I really like you, Peggy. On a personal level. But professionally, I wish you'd go home and make some tea or something. Quit messing around with my investigation. I thought Al made it clear. But I guess when it comes to you, Al is fluff."

"Lieutenant!" Al protested. "I did what you asked. She didn't tell me she knew about this girl."

"Well it's too late now. The whole damned city knows. We have to do some damage control to save our butts."

"What about Keeley?" Peggy demanded. "What's going to happen to her?"

Jonas smiled nastily. "Maybe she could take your friend's place in jail. How would that be?"

Peggy didn't back down from him. "I think you need a colonic. You sound a little backed up to me. I have just the thing. I could run home and get it for you."

He looked puzzled for a moment, then shook his head. "Go home. Leave the police work to us. No tonic or witch's brew is going to help this situation."

Janice emerged from the inner door. "My client is ready to speak with you again, Lieutenant."

Lenore grabbed her arm before she could follow the two detectives back to where they were holding her daughter. "Money is no object, Janice. Please save my daughter."

"I'll do my best," Janice promised, not quite disguising the gleam in her eyes at the mention of money. "We should be out soon."

Peggy and Lenore sat back down to wait. Peggy didn't know what to say that could make it better. She apologized to her friend, then glanced at the little ficus she'd moved away from the door. It was doing quite well.

"You know I didn't mean those things I said," Lenore answered. "I know whose fault this is. What did I do wrong, Peggy? Keeley has always been so high-spirited. She and I are like aliens together. I don't understand her at all."

"You'll be fine." Peggy patted her hand. "A few years from now, Keeley will have her own family, and things will be different. All of this will be a bad memory."

They waited for another two hours. Peggy called the school and canceled her afternoon lecture. Lenore fell asleep with her head back against the wall, a testimony to her sleepless night at the hospital. Peggy woke her as the door opened, and she heard Janice's voice. Keeley came out before her lawyer, teary-eyed and eager to leave.

"What happened?" Lenore was on her feet at once, clinging to her daughter. "Are they letting you go? Are they going to arrest you?"

Janice silenced them and hurried out of the station. A barrage of reporters shouted questions and videotaped them leaving. They made it to Janice's car and drove to a parking lot to talk.

"I'm okay, Mom," Keeley assured Lenore. "They didn't charge me. But they might want to talk to me again. I didn't kill Mark. I guess they believed what I told them."

"It's more that they have a stronger case against Mr. Cheever," Janice explained. "They'll probably check back through their forensic evidence now that they have your fingerprints. If they find anything that could link you to the crime, it will be a whole different scenario. If you think they might find anything, you should tell me now."

Keeley shook her head. "There's nothing for them to find. I didn't even touch him that night. Why would I? He made it clear where he stood about me and the baby. He might've fooled around a lot, but he wasn't leaving his wife for anyone else."

Peggy hugged her. "Everyone makes mistakes."

"Especially with men," Janice finished. "The stories I could tell you!"

Lenore and Peggy stared at her. Keeley sniffed and waited to hear more.

"Well, that doesn't matter. It's good you didn't touch him. We'll wait and see what happens," Janice cautioned.

Peggy left the other three women in Janice's car. She'd brought her bicycle in the trunk and decided to ride to the Potting Shed. She knew Selena and Sam would be anxious for information about Keeley. Steve had told her he was going back to work. She'd left him with everything up in the air between them. But right now, her whole life seemed to be that way.

Before she could get to the shop, she found herself face-to-face with Ronda McGee. The tall brunette ran to catch up with her as soon as she saw her go past the wrought-iron gate into Brevard Courtyard. "Peggy? Could I have a word with you?"

"Of course." Peggy glanced at the Potting Shed. It didn't look exceptionally busy. She felt guilty that Selena had to miss her break, but she'd been looking for a reason to speak with Ronda again.

They sat in the courtyard and ordered coffee from Sofia. The smell of frying food from the French and Caribbean restaurants spilled enticingly out to the afternoon shoppers who were enjoying the beautiful weather.

"I saw that girl on television this morning," Ronda began. "I realized what it might look like to you. After all, I was seeing that bastard, too. I didn't want you to get the wrong idea."

Peggy sipped her coffee. "As I understand it, he was seeing a number of women."

"That's right." Ronda fidgeted with her spoon. "I guess I knew at the time. But I didn't have any expectations of marrying him. Certainly not having a child with him! I'm happily married. I have two children already. I was just looking for some fun, you know?"

Peggy realized there wouldn't be a better opportunity to question her. Ronda was worried about being put in Keeley's position, except with far greater consequences for her personal life. "What exactly did happen between you?"

"I knew Mark for years. He worked with my husband. I don't know what made me think about going out with him. It was one of those things." She played with a strand of her hair and bit her lip. "We had dinner a few times. We stayed at this cute little bed-and-breakfast that was part of a winery. He didn't drink alcohol, you know. He was allergic to it. But we still had a good time. We both knew we weren't serious."

"What happened the night Mark was killed?"

Ronda hesitated. "This might sound bad, but it's the truth. My husband was out of town. I was supposed to go to Blumenthal to see *Oklahoma!* with some of my friends. Mark called and asked me to meet him at the Omni. I agreed, thinking I could cover my tracks by going to the performance, disappearing for an hour, then coming back before the show was over."

"That was quite a plan," Peggy said. "Wouldn't your friends have missed you?"

"Of course! They wouldn't say anything though. Half of them are having affairs, too. We cover for each other." Ronda said it like it was the most obvious thing in the world. "Anyway, I got this phone call. I couldn't tell who it was or even if it was a man or a woman. The voice was disguised or something. It warned me to stay away from Mark.

It threatened to hurt me if I didn't. Whoever it was made it clear that it would be bad if I saw him again."

Peggy took out a notebook. "When was this?"

"About an hour before I left to see *Oklahoma!*" Ronda answered. "I thought it was stupid at first. But the more I thought about it, the more afraid I got. I didn't even call Mark to tell him I wouldn't be there. Instead, I left the play and got in my car. I drove around for a while, then went back. No man is worth losing your life over."

"Why did you go out at all?"

"Because I didn't want my friends to know I chickened out. I didn't tell them about the call. I wasn't planning on telling anyone."

Peggy closed her notebook. Ronda didn't have any more of an alibi than Angela, Keeley, or Mr. Cheever. Any of them could have killed Mark. Ronda and Angela seemed to have less motivation than Keeley. It sounded like their affair was all fun and games. Unless Mark threatened to tell her husband. But he seemed to have as much to lose by that as she did since Bob McGee was his boss.

It was possible whoever called to warn her off was the killer. Maybe somehow the killer knew if Ronda didn't show up at the Omni, Mark would go to the Potting Shed. That made it sound like Keeley.

"Peggy? What are you thinking? I swear I didn't kill Mark. I know we went to your shop sometimes, but I wouldn't meet him there to have sex! I always thought Mark was a little conspicuous about the whole thing. Everyone I know is really careful not to get caught. It was like Mark *wanted* Julie to know. I know that sounds crazy. But he insisted on meeting places where people would notice us."

"Did he ever say anything about his marriage? Any possible reason he might want Julie to know he was cheating?"

"No. We never talked about her. She and I have lunch once in a while. I tried not to think about it."

That was all Peggy could think to ask. "If the case goes to trial for my friend, his lawyer might contact you. The only way to help him might be to prove other people who were involved with Mark could've done the deed as well."

Ronda didn't have much choice. "Isn't it enough that college girl was having sex with him? Doesn't that prove anyone could do it?"

"I don't know yet."

"It's bad enough I have to go and be tested for STDs after finding out he was having sex with that girl. I don't want to lose my marriage over it. I hope you'll take that into consideration."

Peggy bristled at hearing Keeley referred to as "that girl," but reassured Ronda, "I hope the police find the real killer before Mr. Cheever ever goes to trial, for your sake as well as everyone else's."

"Thanks. I really didn't kill Mark." She put on her sunglasses and picked up her pocketbook. "Good luck finding who did."

Mark's death was getting more complicated. Every conversation she had with the many women in his life ended up with another suspect. Any of them could be responsible. She wasn't sure how to tell the killer out of the group of suspects. But someone killed him, and she was sure it wasn't Mr. Cheever or Keeley.

Selena was glad to see Peggy, especially without the big dog. "Sorry you lost him. I guess he would've been some company for you. I hate to think of you locking up by yourself and going home to that big, empty house."

"You know, I never felt sorry for myself until you put it like *that*."

"I didn't mean it that way. You have a busy life and all. I just meant . . . never mind. Tell me about Keeley."

Peggy told her what she knew. "It sounds bad for Keeley. If the police hadn't already built a case against Mr. Cheever, I'm sure they would've taken her into custody."

"Wow!" Selena's eyes were wide with wonder. "Imagine Keeley and that rich *old* banking dude. Who would've guessed?"

"He wasn't that old. He was only thirty-nine."

"That's almost old enough to be her *father*! People that old shouldn't have sex anymore."

Peggy put on her apron and stood beside her. "Did I tell you that I might be dating again?"

Selena smacked herself in the head. "I know. But I didn't mean *you*. And besides, that's different. You wouldn't date someone younger than you."

"He's forty-five. I was fifty-two in September."

"I think I'm leaving now before I say anything else." She picked up her book bag. "I'll see you tomorrow, Peggy. Let me know if there's anything I can do to help Keeley."

Peggy laughed at her. "Bye, sweetie. Don't worry. The old people of the world who are still having sex aren't going to come after you. You're young, and you don't know any better. We make allowances for that."

It was only two hours until closing when Selena left. Sam called in, and Peggy told him everything that had happened. They were due for another shipment of pansies that would be planted outside the uptown library building. With Keeley gone, other arrangements would have to be made.

"I'll call Dawn or Brenda," Peggy told him. "One of them might be able to help with the planting. Do you have a design in mind?"

"Yeah. I had this swirly kind of universe-in-motion idea. But the library board didn't like it. They want straight rows. No imagination."

"I guess that says it all. What time is the shipment due tonight?"

"It shouldn't be too late. Maybe you could go and get supper, then come back. I'm sorry I can't be there."

"That's okay, Sam. I'll be fine. I'll talk to you later."

Peggy decided not to go out for dinner. She ran to Emil's shop and picked up some tea and a bagel. She didn't need any rich, French food or spicy Caribbean. What she really needed was some time to mull over everything that had happened. Somewhere, all of it made sense.

She set up her portable radio, changing the station to NPR. Then she put her legs up on the garden bench and ate her bagel sandwich while she looked through some new gardening catalogs. There was a lovely new miniature blackberry bush she marked to buy. Also some antique-looking garden implements she thought might go over well in her market. In Charlotte, the next best thing to real antiques were faux ones.

She called Hunter when she finished eating. She was out; Peggy left her voice mail. She glanced at the big clock on the wall. It was almost seven-thirty. She was wondering when the delivery truck would come when she heard it make the turn into the back. Putting on her jacket, she walked to the loading dock.

The back light still wasn't working. She went inside for a flashlight, worried that the truck driver would back right through her storage area if he didn't have *some* light. The truck was moving into place when she emerged again. She switched on the flashlight and went to stand at the end of the dock. Not sure how to signal the driver, she tried waving the flashlight back and forth like they did at the airport.

It was cold despite the sunny warmth of the day. Sunset brought a biting wind and a clear, starlit sky. She could smell the Dumpsters behind the shops around hers. The sweet aromas of baking bread and cinnamon were long gone from the bakery a few doors down. Everything was shut tight in the courtyard.

As she was looking up into the sky, a hand came out of the darkness behind her and pushed her off the dock into the path of the truck. It was so startling, so fast, it took her a moment to realize what happened.

Her knees and hands stung from hitting the gravel. She couldn't catch her breath. The truck kept coming, not seeing her. The flashlight had rolled to the other side of the dock. Red taillights coming closer pushed her to her feet. She had to get out of the way.

Reeling from shock and pain, she limped to the stairs and collapsed. The wood was hard and real under her. As hard and real as the hand that pushed her off the dock.

She glanced back into the shadows and took out her cell

phone. Her hands were shaking so badly, she could barely push the numbers. When the 911 operator came on, she gave the address and explained what happened. Her voice sounded weak and pathetic to her ears.

The truck was in position at the dock. The cab door squeaked open and slammed shut. Footsteps started toward her. "Hey! Whatcha doin' down there? I coulda hit you. It's dark back here. Ain't you got no light?"

She couldn't find words to explain to him. She still couldn't believe someone had tried to kill her. She couldn't see another way to say it. And that's what she told the police officer who came right after the paramedics.

"So you say someone pushed you off the loading dock?"

"That's right. I couldn't see anyone because it was dark. The light isn't working. The truck was backing up, and someone pushed me." She winced as the paramedic cleaned the scrapes on her hands and knees.

"You should probably go in for some X rays on your wrist and knee," the technician told her. "You've got some swelling. I don't think either one is broken, but it wouldn't hurt to check on it. You're lucky you didn't fall on any glass back here."

The officer looked skeptical. "Are you sure you didn't take an extra step off the dock?"

"I know what I felt," Peggy insisted. "Someone *pushed* me."

He shrugged and took out his notebook. "Okay. I'll write it up as an assault. We'll take a look around and see if we can find anybody. You should probably go with the ambulance. These people know what they're talking about."

Peggy knew they were right. Her knee felt tight and swollen. She asked the truck driver if he'd unload the pansies for some extra money. He agreed, and she waited to leave in the ambulance until she could lock up behind him.

SHE WAS STILL WAITING to be X-rayed at Carolinas Medical Center when Al and Paul found her. A nurse had left her in a wheelchair in the drafty hallway about an hour before. She was starting to get impatient and thinking about leaving.

Paul crouched down beside her. "Are you okay? Al caught what happened on the police scanner and called me. Why didn't *you* call me?"

"It's not that serious. I think the knee is wrenched. I'm pretty sure my wrist isn't broken either."

"That doesn't matter, Mom. You should've called me. I feel like some kind of moron that I had to hear about it this way."

Peggy sighed. "I tripped going up the stairs at the house two weeks ago. I didn't call you then either."

"This is different," Paul insisted. "You were assaulted. What happened?"

She explained everything. Al wrote as she spoke. "I already told the officer at the scene. I didn't think homicide detectives had time to investigate assaults."

"This homicide detective has time to check out anything that happens to an old friend. Who do you think did this to you?"

"I'm not sure. I don't even want to think there's someone lurking around my shop who wants to kill me."

"Maybe it's involved with the murder somehow," Al suggested. "Maybe questioning people around town has hit someone the wrong way."

Peggy didn't have time to answer. The X-ray technician came for her, and she spent the next twenty minutes with him. By the time she came out, Al was gone, but Paul was waiting for her.

When a nurse didn't come for her, he pushed her wheelchair back up to the emergency room. "You know, you might be right about your homeless friend not being responsible for Warner's death. If someone came after you, there might be something else to hide. They must want you out of the way."

She waited to answer while the nurse told them it would be another hour until the X rays came back. "I've talked to a lot of people, Paul. I don't think I could zero in on any one suspect who seems more likely than another."

"I wish you'd leave this alone. If the killer is out there and worried about you finding out about him, this may only be the beginning. Al is taking a forensics team to check out the loading dock. Hopefully, whoever did this left something behind."

The fall had rattled Peggy, but the idea that someone thought she was on the right track kept her focused. It also made her angry. Did they think it would all go away if she stopped asking questions?

"I'm going to get a Coke from the machine," Paul said. "Do you want something?"

"I'll take the same. I don't think I have to worry about the caffeine keeping me awake. Thanks."

He started to walk away, then turned back. His thin, young face was anxious. "Will you be okay by yourself? I don't have to go, if you need me to stay."

She held his hand a moment. "I'll be fine with all the nurses and orderlies walking around through here. Thank you for coming, honey."

"All you had to do was call. I love you, Mom." He squeezed her hand, then went out the door that led to the hallway.

A moment after he was gone, Peggy pulled her cell phone out of her pocketbook to check the time. It was almost one in the morning. She knew she wasn't supposed to have the phone. She'd turned off the ringer, hoping no one would notice. Before she could put it away, it started to vibrate. Glancing around, she opened it. "Hello?"

"I was wondering where you were." The voice on the other end of the line was husky, unfamiliar.

"Who is this?" she whispered back, knowing the answer before she asked the question.

"How many times are you going to ask me that, Nightrose?"

The same odd feeling of being watched brought a chill

to her spine. She looked around the crowded emergency room. "Where are you? How did you get this number?"

"Where I am doesn't matter. I was worried about you. Are you all right?"

"If you won't tell me where you are, then tell me how you got my cell phone number."

A throaty laugh followed. "I'll be glad to exchange information with you. You tell me how serious your injuries are, and I'll tell you how I got your number."

Peggy looked at every man in the emergency room. "I'm bruised and battered, but otherwise, I'm fine. Your turn."

"There are several companies who will research cell phone numbers and call records. I use one out of Atlanta."

"Is that legal?" Peggy wheeled her chair around a corner to look for anyone else using a cell phone. He had to be close by.

"Probably not. But for the right price, you can get anything, legal or not," he responded. "How did this happen?"

"Since you know so much, Nightflyer, you should be able to pay someone to tell you that, too. Don't call me again."

"I'm sure you'll change your number. Tiresome and expensive for me since I'll have to look it up again. Rest well."

Peggy looked up as the phone went dead. A big nurse was looking back at her.

"You can't use that in here. Turn it off."

"I was just checking the time," Peggy lied. "But I'll put it away."

"What are you doing over here, Mom?" Paul found her. "Are they moving you to a room?"

"No. I was looking around." She closed the cell phone and tucked it away. She couldn't believe Nightflyer tracked her down. She'd heard stories about being stalked by people on the Internet. She didn't think it could happen to her. And she wasn't sure what to do about it. Suppose Nightflyer was the one who pushed her off the loading dock. Al and Paul would be looking in the wrong direction for her assailant.

She thanked Paul for the Coke, and he sat beside her in a dark green chair. She wanted to tell him about Nightflyer but couldn't find the words. If he knew about that, too, he might actually move back home. She needed to talk to someone besides her son about the problem.

An hour later, a doctor approached and showed them Peggy's X rays. Her knee and wrist were sprained. He gave her a brace for each of them and told her to visit her family doctor the next day for further care instructions.

Paul drove her home and insisted on spending the night. Peggy couldn't climb the stairs and refused to let him carry her. They bunked down together in the family room, talking and watching CNN.

Peggy looked at her son after he'd fallen asleep. He didn't look so different from when she'd watched him sleep in the nursery upstairs. She hoped everything that happened was going to bring them closer together. She missed him.

THERE WAS A LOUD banging noise at the front door. Peggy yawned and looked at the sunlight streaming in through the windows. Not wanting to wake Paul, she limped to the door. She couldn't see anyone through the peephole. Cautiously, she opened the door. A moment later she was flat on her back with a Great Dane sitting on top of her, licking her face.

A car pulled up in the drive. Jo-Jo's master was yelling for him. She took a deep breath and wished someone would tell her how to stop the merry-go-round. She was ready to get off.

10

Primrose

Botanical: *Primula vulgaris*
Family: Primulaceae
Common Name: Cowslip

The goddess Bertha is supposed to entice children into her enchanted halls by offering them beautiful primroses. The mysterious number of primrose petals represents woman. The five petals represent birth, initiation, consummation, repose, and death.

"WHAT DID YOU DO to make him come here? Do you have a secret dog whistle or something?" Jo-Jo's owner stood over Peggy as the dog joyously licked her.

Paul rushed out of the family room. "What's going on?"

"I'm here to take my dog back! She can't keep him. I'll call the police!"

"I *am* the police." Paul fumbled in his pocket for his badge.

Peggy put her hands up on either side of the dog's head. "It's okay, boy. You have to get off of me." The dog finally moved away from her, but her hands came away bloody. "What in the world?"

Both men looked at her as she carefully examined Jo-Jo's neck. Some kind of spiked collar had dug into the skin, leaving open sores behind. As she ran her hand down his back, she found other abrasions that were new.

"What's wrong?" Paul asked when he saw her face.

She held up her hands so he could see the blood, then turned on Jo-Jo's owner. "What did you do to him?"

"I had to make him listen," he defended. "He's a damn big dog. He doesn't listen worth a crap. He broke his collar and ran off. I followed him here. But he's *my* dog. I can do what I want with him."

"That's not true," Peggy said. "There are laws against animal cruelty. I'm going to press charges against you for abusing this dog!"

The man grimaced and looked at Paul. "If you're really a cop, I want to press charges against her first. I don't know how she did it, but she enticed my dog to come here. She wants to kidnap him. Book her!"

Paul ran his hand around the back of his neck. He was still half asleep. "I'm sorry, sir. There are no laws to cover dog enticement. But from what I saw, she *could* press charges against you for assault as well as animal cruelty. Your dog wasn't leashed, and he viciously attacked her when she opened the door. We do have laws for *that*."

Peggy smiled at him. That was her son. Then she faced down the other man. "We can solve the whole problem without anyone getting arrested. I'll give you whatever you paid for the dog. You give me his papers and a sworn affidavit stating that you won't ever bother him or me again."

"That's illegal!" Jo-Jo's owner turned to Paul. "You heard her. You're my witness. She's trying to blackmail me."

"All I heard was an offer to buy the dog from you," Paul answered. "If you're not interested, I'll get my shoes and jacket. I can take you into the station so she can press charges against you." Paul walked toward the family room.

"Wait!" The man shuffled his feet, glanced at the dog, and glared at Peggy. "Fine. I paid five hundred dollars for him. I've only had him a month. I still have his papers in the car. I'll take a check. But it better be good!"

Paul smiled at him. "I'll need to see proof you paid that much for him."

"Okay, three hundred," he compromised, "and I have a receipt for it."

"Then I suggest you get it and his papers and get the hell out of here. I patrol this area. If I see your car anywhere near my mother's house again, I'll arrest you for stalking."

The man slammed the door behind him as he went to get what Paul demanded.

Peggy hugged her son. "You were *awesome*! I can't believe you handled that so well."

"Thanks, Mom. Now I feel like a complete moron. When haven't I backed you up? All you ever have to do is include me. You just hate asking for my help." He looked at the dog. "What are you going to do with him now?"

"You aren't a moron. But I wasn't sure if you could bend enough to follow my lead. I love you, Paul." She kissed his cheek. "As for the dog, I guess I'll have to keep him. But he needs a better name than Jo-Jo."

"How about Shakespeare? He's a giant among writers."

"Good choice. Do you remember how many times I read *A Midsummer Night's Dream* to you when you were little?"

"Yeah, I remember. But my favorite was always *Macbeth*. All those ghosts and swords."

She laughed and patted the dog's head tenderly. "I think Shakespeare suits him. Thank you." She reached for the phone. "I think I'll give Steve a call. I hate to leave Shakespeare like this too long. He's still nothing but skin and bones. An infection might kill him."

"Steve must *really* like you if you're thinking about calling him this early in the morning." Paul shrugged. "I think I can handle my mother dating *after* I do a complete background check on the guy."

"I can handle you dating, too, you know. I think Mai Sato in forensics likes you."

He frowned. "Don't go there. Just call your private vet and let me get my shoes on."

SHAKESPEARE'S FORMER OWNER returned with the papers, but Paul didn't let him in the house. He took the papers from him and handed him Peggy's check. The door closed quickly behind him.

Steve arrived shortly after and examined the dog. He told Paul he was disappointed everything went so smoothly. "I was hoping you might have to shoot him. This dog has been through hell."

Paul gave his mother the receipt for the dog. "Yeah, well at least he's safe now. My captain frowns on off-duty altercations between officers and civilians."

Peggy put the paperwork into the side table drawer in the foyer. She smiled as she looked at the two men who had moved on and were talking about football. *All's well that ends well.* "I'm going to make some strawberry pancakes for breakfast. Can you both stay?"

"I don't think you should try to use your hands or stand up for too long on your hurt knee," Paul told her. "I'll make the strawberry pancakes."

Steve looked at the brace on her wrist. "What happened?"

She shook her head, glad she'd taken a moment to brush her hair before he got there. It was painful and silly, but she wanted to look her best for him. "It's a long story."

"I think I have time to hear it over breakfast."

Peggy told him what happened as she sat down in the kitchen. She directed him to the plates, forks, and cups. Paul made coffee and pancakes. Shakespeare wrapped himself around her feet on the floor.

"So you think whoever killed Mark Warner wanted to kill you?" Steve asked when she was finished.

"I don't know." She wanted to tell Steve or Paul about Nightflyer but couldn't think how to start. "I don't know whose feathers I ruffled to receive that kind of response."

"But you admit any of those women you talked to could've killed Warner," Paul reminded her, using the spatula to punctuate his remark. "They all had motive and opportunity. Maybe you got too close to the truth without realizing it."

A knock at the door brought Sam in with a blast of cold morning air. His handsome young face was stricken with remorse. "God, Peggy, I can't believe this happened to you. I heard about it on the news this morning. Are you okay? Who do you think did it? Are there any extra pancakes?"

Paul poured more batter into the skillet, and Steve took out another place setting.

Peggy went over the story again as they sat down to eat. She'd barely finished explaining what happened when there was another knock on the door.

"I can smell those pancakes outside." Al didn't wait for anyone to let him in. He looked around the crowded kitchen. "I thought you'd need some company, Peggy. I didn't know you were cooking up breakfast for everyone. Where's the syrup?"

He grabbed a cup and filled it with coffee, then snagged three pancakes from the serving plate before he hefted himself into the chair beside her. "I wanted to tell you that we didn't find anything on the loading dock. Nothing unusual anyway. All the fingerprints we came up with belong to the people who work for you. Sorry."

"What are the chances whoever pushed me wasn't wearing gloves?" She passed him cream for his coffee. "It was cold. Even if you didn't think about leaving prints behind, you'd want to protect your hands."

"Good point!" Sam said around a mouthful of pancake. "But whoever did this has to be tied to the Warner murder. Maybe the killer left something behind. Or maybe you were his real target. Maybe Warner just got in the way."

Peggy laughed. "There are better places to try to kill me than waiting at the shop."

"What about Keeley, your assistant?" Paul asked. "It seems to me she's a better suspect than Cheever. She seems like a nice girl, but she had every reason to kill Warner *and* she admitted to being there."

"But why admit she was there if she was the killer?" Steve wondered as he passed the nearly empty syrup bottle to Sam. "Wouldn't she want to keep it to herself? The police already have someone in custody. She could sit on the information instead of putting it in the spotlight."

"Unless she *wants* us to think that was her reasoning," Al argued. "She seems like a pretty sharp cookie to me."

Sam was quick to come to Keeley's defense. "She's smart but not devious. She can't keep a secret worth a damn. I know. I work with her. Look how she confessed about those old pansies, Peggy."

"Did she tell you she was pregnant?" Al demanded. "Did she even tell you she was dating Warner?" He used his tongue to catch a bit of syrup at the corner of his mouth, ruining his tough-cop attitude. "I rest my case."

"Does that mean you like Keeley for the killing instead of Cheever?" Paul asked him as he wiped his mouth carefully.

"No. Rimer and I reviewed the case with the DA last night. He still wants to prosecute Cheever. He feels like Ms. Prinz had nothing to gain by killing Warner. We agree. She could've ruined him by suing for paternity in open court."

Steve leaned back in his chair. "I'm not a police detective, but couldn't the killing be construed as a crime of passion? She used the first weapon that came to her hand when he refused to acknowledge the baby. Maybe she didn't have time to think about it."

Al nodded, his mouth too full of pancake to respond right away. When he was done chewing he said, "We talked about that. The DA doesn't think that story will fly with a jury. He thinks they're more likely to buy a drunken homeless man killing for shoes and money."

Steve smiled. "My tax dollars at work."

"Take it up with the DA." Al shrugged. "I'm not saying either story is more likely. The point is that Warner was an important man in the community. People want to see justice."

"Justice or retribution?" Sam suggested. "I don't think Keeley did it either. But just because the man is homeless doesn't make him a killer."

"Not even if he took the man's shoes?" Al debated. "Come on, kid! If you could stoop that low, you could stoop to killing to get them."

"Mr. Cheever wouldn't kill anyone!" Sam's face turned red as he exploded.

Al shrugged. "I didn't make the system the way it is. I just enforce the rules."

Sam sighed and turned to Peggy, changing the subject. "Are you going to keep the dog after all?"

"Yes. He and his owner parted company this morning." Peggy thought about something else. "You know, the other night when we were leaving the store, Shakespeare growled at something in the shadows behind the shop. Maybe someone was there that night but was scared of the dog. I thought it was probably rats, but after last night, I'm not so sure."

"We'll go over everything," Al promised. "You don't have to worry about it."

Paul and Steve decided it was time for them to leave. Al stood with his mouth open as Steve kissed Peggy good-bye. Sam snickered and took the dog out for a walk.

Paul sighed and kissed Peggy's forehead, reminding her to call him if she needed anything.

When they were gone, Al took a deep breath. "I must be out of the loop more than I realize. When did that happen?"

"Nothing happened," she denied, not wanting to talk about Steve yet. "But there *is* something I'd like to talk to you about." She told him about her cyber stalker. "I didn't want to mention this to Paul. But I'm wondering if my fall from the loading dock might be part of that problem rather than anything to do with the murder."

Al took it seriously. "We have an officer who specializes in matters like this. Let me give him a heads up. I don't know exactly what he does to track this kind of thing. It's all I can do to get my reports into the computer every day without erasing them."

"Thanks. Do you know about places where they can track your cell phone?"

"This is America, Peggy. Anything is possible. Until we clear this up, keep your head down and stay out of dark places. Don't encourage this man by talking to him again on the Internet."

"I won't. I'm going to ask Sam to haul me around today. I have a class, and I'll be at the Potting Shed. Let me know what I need to do for your cyber detective."

"I'll have him call you." Al lumbered to his feet. "Good pancakes. I hope I can stay awake through our briefing this morning after all those carbs."

"What about Mr. Cheever?"

"The wheels of justice turn. He'll have his day in court like everybody else. I'm sure you've told that pretty, young lawyer everything you know. If she can create doubts in the minds of the jury, your friend will get off. If not, he'll do his time. It's the way the system works. You know that."

"Can you investigate other possibilities?"

"I'd like to help you, Peggy, but I've got unsolved homicides on my desk that don't have any suspects at all. It's all I can do to keep up with those. You should hire a private detective. There are a few who work with the police. I can give you their names, if you like. At least you'd know they're reputable."

"I don't have the money for that. And Mr. Cheever's daughter has even less. But thanks anyway."

Al squeezed her shoulder gently. His big, dark hand rested lightly on her for an extra moment. "As for your new beau, I think it's great. You need someone in your life besides Paul. I know you think your plants are enough company. But John wouldn't want you to be alone."

She thought about what he said, grateful for his kindness and friendship. The legal system made her angry, but that wasn't anything new. She and John had talked many times about police detectives being overworked and underappreciated.

After Al left, Sam managed to open the back door before Shakespeare pulled him through it. "Nice dog." He was panting, glad to drop the leash. "But I think something this big should be running free in a pasture somewhere."

"Thanks for walking him. If you wouldn't mind, I could use your help getting around today. I don't think I'm going to be able to ride my bike."

"Whatever you need, you know that. I'll have another cup of coffee while you get ready. Could you believe those pancake-eating animals? They didn't leave any behind for me. I only had a few stacks. Got any cookies?"

"Check the cabinet." She laughed. "But you'd better be careful. You don't want to grow sideways now that you've grown up."

Taking her time, Peggy negotiated the long stairway. Shakespeare bounded up, then waited at the top for her with his tongue hanging out of his mouth. He looked like a distorted version of Scooby-Doo. She smiled and stroked his big head. "I guess it's up to us. If we want to help Mr. Cheever, no push off the loading dock can slow us down. Besides, I'll have you with me, won't I? I bet if you'd been there last night, this wouldn't have happened."

As if to reassure her, the dog followed her to her bedroom. He curled up on the floor in front of the door while she showered and dressed. Peggy told herself that the look on his face dared anyone to enter her room. But really, he was comical with his floppy ears and long tongue.

Feeling decidedly defiant, she wore jeans and a No Fear sweatshirt that Selena gave her for Christmas last year. Her knee was still swollen and sore, but she realized it could've been much worse.

She took the bandages off her palms. The scratches weren't too bad and didn't hurt at all. They needed some airing, as her mother called it. She always said things couldn't heal right closed off. As old as she was, getting hurt still made her want to run home and be comforted by her mama and daddy. Of course they were too far away, and she wouldn't want to worry them, but she promised herself a weekend in Charleston soon.

She brushed her hair and used two antique pearl clasps

to hold it back from her face. There was a spark of emerald in her eyes. John always teased that it meant trouble for anyone trying to stand in her way. She wasn't sure how much trouble one botany professor/garden shop owner could cause. But she was about to find out.

"You look great," Sam said when she hobbled back downstairs. "Are you bringing the horse with you?"

"Shakespeare," she corrected him. "And yes, I think we can fit him in your truck."

He laughed and patted the dog's head. "Yeah, if me and you ride in the back. Have you taught him to drive yet?"

Peggy's first stop was the university. Everyone in her class had heard about what happened to her. They talked about it for a few minutes. She didn't explain more than she had to. As she finished and opened her textbook, the dean came in. She took a deep breath and went through the whole story again.

Class went quickly since there were only about twenty minutes left when she was done answering questions about her experience. Sam was waiting when she got outside. They drove through the busy streets toward the heart of the city. Shakespeare rode between them, sitting on the seat with his head up and his chocolate-brown eyes alert.

"What's next?" Sam asked her. "Do you have anything else up your sleeve?"

"I don't know. As far as I can tell, Ronda and Angela had fewer motives for killing Mark than Keeley. I'm not sure where to go from here. I know any of them could have done it. At least physically. All three of them are fine, strapping young women. Any of them could've hit him in the head with the shovel."

"But how do you decide which one actually did the deed? Maybe you could convince one of them to confess."

"That would be nice. But another thing they have in common is brains. I think they're all too smart for something like that. There must be something we're missing. John always said there was no such thing as a perfect murder. Everyone makes mistakes. We have to find what those mistakes were."

He turned the truck into the parking lot behind the Potting Shed. "One of my professors says we should listen carefully to our patients and make sure we write down everything they say to us. That way, we can look back at our notes and come to a better understanding of the problem. Maybe you should try that."

Peggy nodded as he jumped out and helped her from the truck. "Thanks, Sam. For the ride and the suggestion. I'll do that this afternoon."

He glanced at his watch. "I have a class, then I'm supposed to help Dawn plant primroses at Mrs. Margate's house over on Providence Road."

"Outside?"

"That's what she wanted."

"You told her they couldn't survive the winter, right?"

Sam shrugged. "The woman wanted primroses planted on the west wall of her house. She says they can survive there because her eaves will protect them. What was I supposed to say?"

"That you'd plant them, I suppose. Where in the world did you find primroses at this time of year?"

"They grew them for me at that new greenhouse over by UNCC. They cost a fortune, but Mrs. Margate didn't care."

Peggy wasn't completely surprised. Sometimes they got strange requests. Last year, one of the wealthiest families in the city asked her to plant a thousand brown-eyed Susans for their brown-eyed daughter named Susan. Her birthday was in January. The family had a wonderful party, then she went back and ripped out the plants that had frozen overnight.

Selena hugged Peggy when she saw her. "I'm never going to leave again before closing. I can't believe anybody would want to hurt you."

"Thanks, sweetie. We both know you can't always be here. But Shakespeare can be." The big dog came bounding in with Sam. "It looks like it might be just as well that I'm going to keep him."

Shakespeare walked through the shop, sniffing everything. He finally curled up on the big rag rug in the middle of the autumn scene. Garden implements and plants flew out of the way as he made room for himself.

"I guess he's made himself at home," Selena said hesitantly. "If it helps *you,* it's a good thing. Someone would have to be crazy to get near you with *that* in the way."

"I'll be back to take you home," Sam told Peggy. "Wait for me."

Peggy promised not to hobble anywhere without him. She took off her coat and put on her green shop apron. The lunchtime crowd was starting to mill through the Arcade and Brevard Court. For the next two hours, she and Selena were too busy to talk.

They sold out of red tulip bulbs and had to order more. Jumbo elephant ears were almost gone as well. They seemed to be a favorite of the new uptown urban dwellers who were bringing weekend life to the city.

"I think we're going to need more of those antique-looking watering cans," Selena told Peggy after she rang up a sale and thanked her customer. "They're really popular."

Peggy noted it on her supply list. "I'll have some brought in with the next shipment Thursday." She told Selena about the faux antique garden implements she'd seen in her catalog the night before. "I think they'll go over big, too."

Selena laughed as she went to help a man pick out a new brass sundial for his garden. "You know what we say around here. If you can't get real antiques . . ."

". . . get new ones that look old," Peggy finished.

When the rush was starting to become a trickle, Sofia brought lunch from the Kozy Kettle. "I can't believe what a hellhole this place has become! You'd think we were living in a big city. Guns. Drugs. People pushing old ladies off of loading docks."

Peggy took exception to the "old lady" part. "It could've happened to anyone. I don't think age was a factor."

Sofia handed her a cup of peach tea. "At least the animal didn't try to rape you. God forbid any woman should have to suffer the fate of my Aunt Bibi. Did I ever tell you about her?

She was trapped by a group of Nazis in the forest outside her home in Warsaw. She was a brave woman, but she was no match for that many filthy pigs."

Selena looked at Peggy. They'd heard the terrible tale of Aunt Bibi at least a hundred times. It was a cautionary tale of the worst thing that could ever happen to a woman. It always ended the same way.

"The best thing to do is carry a knife. Aunt Bibi always carried a knife after that. She said if a drunken man ever tried to have his way with her again, she'd slit his throat. She was a brave woman."

Peggy was mouthing the last few words with Sofia as the tale finished. She took a sip of her tea and sputtered liquid out as she realized that she'd missed something in her interviews with Mark's women. Quickly, she took out a small notebook and wrote it down. "Selena, can you close up for me if I'm not back in time? I just remembered something important."

"Sure." Selena shrugged. "Where are you going?"

"I have to see a friend about some blood."

Sofia crossed herself. "God forbid! Peggy Lee, you're going to get yourself killed if you don't watch out. I see the evil eye looking down on you."

Peggy clipped the leash to Shakespeare's collar. "It better be careful. I have a big dog."

Sofia crossed herself again and went back to the Kozy Kettle. Selena went to help a woman who wanted to set up a small fountain and pond on the balcony of her condominium.

Peggy walked Shakespeare out of the courtyard, noticing when people made a wide path for him. She yanked on his collar to no avail when he lifted his leg and wet on a large evergreen in a pot. "Bad dog! You shouldn't go to the bathroom there. Where are your manners?"

She used her cell phone to call a taxi, then sat on a bench outside the courtyard waiting for it. Her whole body thrummed with the excitement of realizing she might have found something the police missed. The only way to know for sure was to talk to Mai. It was too important to trust to a phone call.

But the taxi driver was wary of letting the dog into his car. "I don't allow animals."

"We're not going far. I'll pay an extra fare for him."

The man stubbornly refused. "Only those dogs that help blind people."

She pushed the dog into the back of the cab and followed him slowly, mindful of her injured knee. "Well, this is my Seeing Eye dog."

"But you're not blind."

"Not yet. But I had an aunt who was blind. Who knows when it might happen to me?" She closed the door. The driver shrugged, unable to argue with her logic, and they left the courtyard.

MAI WAS COMING BACK from a meeting when she saw Peggy waiting for her in the lobby of the precinct. "Hey Peggy! This is becoming like your home, too. You're here almost as much as I am."

Peggy winced a little as she got to her feet. Her knee got stiff when she sat down for too long.

"Oh, I'm so sorry." Mai took her arm. "I heard about what happened to you. Are you okay?"

"I'm fine, thanks. Just a little bruised."

"Is this your dog?" Mai's eyes grew wide as Shakespeare stretched and got to his feet. "Is this a dog?"

"He's a Great Dane. His name is Shakespeare."

"He looks strange. He's a weird color, isn't he? And his ears don't stand up. I thought Scooby-Doo was a Great Dane. He doesn't look anything like him."

Peggy smiled. "He's been abused and neglected. I rescued him. But I think he'll fill out nicely. I don't think I have the heart to crop his ears since he's not a puppy anymore."

"I think he's filled out pretty well already, Peggy. But I

know you didn't come here to show me your dog. What can I do for you?"

"If I could have a few moments of your time, something has come to my attention. I need to talk to you about it."

"It's about the Warner case, isn't it?" Mai folded her arms across her chest. "I have some time. Although I don't know if it will do any good to talk about it."

"I enjoy talking to you, no matter what. If you don't mind listening, where's the harm?"

Mai put her hand on Peggy's arm. "Let's go back then. Do you need any help?"

"Thank you. Just a little guidance is fine."

The sergeant at the desk looked up. "Watch out for that first step going in, Mrs. Lee. Somebody should take care of that bump in the floor before someone gets hurt. Nice dog."

Peggy sat down in Mai's crowded office. Shakespeare sat beside her, his head almost level with hers.

"What can I do for you?" Mai asked.

"I'd like to see the tox screen results for Mark Warner."

Mai looked hesitant. "Peggy, you know I want to help you . . ."

"All right. If you can't do that, you could look at them and answer a question for me."

"I can do that. I don't see where that would give anybody a wedgie." Mai searched through her files until she found the one she needed. "Okay."

"What were the results of the tox screen?" Peggy waited for the answer on the edge of her chair.

Mai searched through the file. "Nothing."

Peggy's enthusiasm waned. "Nothing unusual?"

"Nothing at all. There *was* no tox screen."

11

Heather

Botanical: *Calluna vulgaris*
Family: Ericaceae
Common Name: Scotch heather

Calluna *comes from the Greek word* kallunein, *which means to* cleanse. *The name was appropriate because heather twigs were used as brooms, and the plant contains properties that can help internal disorders.*

"ISN'T *THAT* UNUSUAL?" Peggy asked.

"Not necessarily. Cause of death was apparent. We knew it was from a blow to the base of the skull." Mai shrugged. "I suppose the ME didn't see any reason to do a tox screen. We're very cost conscious right now. They won't even put in an extra roll of toilet paper in the ladies' room."

"Suppose I could give you a reason to do a tox screen. Do you think the ME would consider it?"

"I could ask him, Peggy. But it's unlikely. They're scheduled to release Warner's body tomorrow. I don't think they'll add any new tests to hold that up. The widow and her lawyer have been giving them fits as it is."

"But Mai, this could be crucial to the case. There must be something you can do."

"I appreciate your faith in me. But I'm only a peanut in

the food chain around here. My opinions don't matter much. Mostly, I go-for."

Peggy tapped her fingers on the desk. "Once the body is buried, it will be impossible to exhume. We have to do that tox screen *now*."

"Tell me what you know." Mai sighed. "I'll see what I can do."

Peggy explained several pieces of information she'd picked up in conversation. "Mr. Cheever didn't have any of Mark's blood on him, even though he handled his body to remove his watch and wallet. He said he thought Mark was sleeping."

"But that could just be coincidence."

"Then there's Keeley. She told me that Warner was slurring his words, staggering, acting like he was drunk. I didn't think much about it until Warner's other lady friend told me he was allergic to alcohol. He never drank."

"So, what are we looking for? Checking to see if he had a drink? Checking for drugs?"

"If he accidentally imbibed, it would go right to his head. Allergic reaction. It would make him an easier target. Don't you see? If someone purposely gave him alcohol, someone who knew he couldn't have it, it would change the dynamics of the crime. The murder may have been set up before Mark ever got to the shop."

Mai nodded. "Which would take your friend out of the picture. At least one of them, anyway. You realize it could be worse for Ms. Prinz?"

Peggy nodded. "One thing at a time, I suppose."

"Okay. Stay here for a few minutes. I'll talk to the ME's chief assistant."

Peggy waited impatiently in Mai's office for about twenty minutes until the younger woman returned. "Well?"

Mai closed her door. "The chief assistant ME doesn't see where a tox screen is appropriate or warranted at this time. He appreciates your concerns, but the case is closed."

"It must be nice not to second-guess yourself," Peggy muttered. "What can we do now?"

"Nothing really. The chief assistant ME is the only one who speaks directly to the medical examiner. There's a chain of command. I have to live by it. In this case, so do you."

Limping a little, Peggy put her arm around Mai's thin shoulders. "Have you ever heard the expression, 'Nothing ventured, nothing gained'?"

"Have you ever seen my landlord? If my rent isn't there by six the night before it's due, he starts auctioning my stuff. If I don't have a job, I can't pay my rent. Then I'd have to move back home with my parents." Mai paused for breath. "Nothing is worth that."

"Don't worry. What I have in mind will work, and we probably won't get caught."

"Probably?"

"And if the worst happens, you can move in with me. I have a very large house."

"Peggy, I don't like the sound of this. What do you want me to do?"

ONCE SHE AGREED to the plan, Mai insisted it had to be done at night. They agreed to meet at the precinct parking lot at midnight. Peggy took Shakespeare home before going back to the Potting Shed and gave him free roam of the house after he'd taken a long walk in the yard. "I'm going to trust you not to break too many things and not to howl. I'll be back as soon as I can. Your food and water are in the kitchen. If someone tries to break in, I expect you to bite him. And keep an eye out for Nightflyer. We *really* don't want him around."

The dog sat and looked at her with his head cocked to one side. When she finished speaking, he barked once, then padded toward the kitchen. Peggy shook her head. Of course he didn't understand a word she said. But at least he didn't jump up on her or drag the china cabinet into the kitchen with him. Maybe everything would work out. Maybe having a dog wouldn't be so bad after all.

She listened to her messages while she changed clothes.

There was a sweet phone call from Steve who asked her how Shakespeare was doing. Paul called to see how she was doing. The other two messages were telemarketers. She pressed Erase, then finished dressing.

The taxi driver who brought her from the downtown precinct was the same one who came to pick her up when she called. He was relieved that she left her dog at home. There was an overturned truck that was blocking College Street. The driver swore and honked his horn. Peggy suggested an alternate route . . . and some Saint-John's-wort. Really, people were too tense.

Selena was ready to go when she reached the Potting Shed. "I have to run, Peggy. I hope you can handle closing up. If not, Sam says to call him. He said he'll be here to pick you up."

"Thanks. Late class?"

"Nope. Date!"

"Good luck. I hope he's Mr. Right."

Customers walked through the shop fitfully, looking but not buying. Peggy kept a close eye on a toddler whose mother was too absorbed in a catalog to notice what he was doing. He finally managed to pull a bag of fertilizer over on himself and started howling. That got his mother's attention. She muttered something about stores not being childproofed and dragged the child out.

A distinguished-looking gentleman with a sheaf of flowers on his arm approached her. "Peggy Lee?"

"Yes."

He handed her the flowers. "These are for you. I hope you enjoy them."

She smelled the heather. "Where did they come from?"

"I'm just the delivery boy. There's a card attached."

Peggy waited until she was alone to sit down and read the card. She looked at the heather, pink, white, and purple, wrapped in green tissue paper. Heather like this would be difficult to get. The card read: *"Pink heather for good luck. White heather to protect you from danger. Purple heather to express my admiration for you. Nightflyer."*

The lights were coming on in the courtyard. It was so quiet she could hear the big clock on the wall ticking. The scent of heather wafted sweetly around her. She had to admit that he knew his flowers. He'd given some thought to his gift. In a way, that made it even more frightening. It was like he *knew* her. She didn't want to think how that was possible.

"Ready to go?" Sam asked as he bounced in from the back around 9 P.M., after a late delivery. "Nice flowers. Going to a funeral?"

"No. The flowers are from an admirer."

He grinned. "That Steve knows his way around, doesn't he? I wonder if he has a brother?"

"No. They aren't from Steve." She told him a little about her cyber stalker. "It sounds silly, but the idea that he's looking over my shoulder gives me a chill."

"It's probably nothing. You know, it's not easy to meet someone face-to-face nowadays. You have to worry about how your hair looks and whether or not your teeth are as white as Tom Cruise's. Then there's the whole smell dilemma. Do you wear Giorgio or go natural with some good soap and deodorant? Who knows what people are looking for?"

She smiled at him. "It sounds terrible. How do you survive?"

"By coming up with great ideas like these flowers." He sniffed the heather. "You meet someone on-line. Talk to him a little bit. Get a feel for what he's into. Check him out with the police and FBI to make sure he isn't a terrorist. Then you send him something pretty. That way, when you meet in the real world, if you're lucky, he won't notice that your hair never lays down smooth on top because you have a double crown."

"So you've done this before?"

"No. But it sounds like a good idea. I might try it." He grabbed a Coke from the minifridge behind the counter. "I'm starving! Have you eaten? What's with the black clothes? Do you have ninja class or something tonight?"

"Let's grab some food." She explained her plan to him. "Then you could drop me at the uptown precinct. I can go with Mai from there."

He whistled through teeth that made Tom Cruise's look dingy. "That sounds wild. Need any help?"

"You're my most experienced assistant," she told him. "I can't afford for both of us to be in jail."

Sam couldn't argue with that logic. He didn't seem eager to try. They locked up the shop, and went for pizza before he drove her to meet Mai.

"Can I leave the heather in your truck?" Peggy asked him.

"Sure. Want me to take it to your house?"

She looked at the flowers, thinking about what they meant. "No, that's okay."

"So much for *that* way of meeting someone. Guess I won't try it," he quipped. "Call me when you're done spying. I'd like to hear all about it."

Mai was waiting nervously in the parking lot by her car. She crouched down when she saw the truck's headlights. "Maybe we shouldn't do this, Peggy."

"How else will we know what really happened to Mark and who was responsible?"

"I don't know. But I'm feeling kind of queasy. I might be coming down with something. I think I should go home."

"You'll be fine. Have some chewable zinc. This won't take long. Where do we go from here?"

Mai drove them to the medical examiner's office on College Street. She used her police pass to park in the lot next to the building. She turned off the car but didn't move. "Are you *sure* we should do this?"

"I've only seen a few dead bodies in my life, sweetie," Peggy told her. "I'm not anxious to see any more. But I know this might be the only way to prove what really happened. We can't let the opportunity go by, can we?"

"No. I suppose not." Mai straightened her spine, then got out of the car. "Let's go."

It wasn't exactly stealthy. Mai had to show her ID and

tell the security guard that Peggy was there to identify her
dead uncle. Once they got past the front desk, they followed
the spotless corridor to a set of double doors that opened
into the morgue.

"Put these on." Mai gave Peggy a mask and a pair of latex
gloves. "You never know what could be up here. And for
goodness sake, don't touch *anything*."

They walked into an area where the walls were lined
with handles. They almost looked like recessed file cabinets. Then Mai picked a drawer with a case number on it. It
slid open with a little squeak. The body was covered by a
paper sheet. Peggy felt the blood drain from her face.

"Are you okay?" Mai asked her.

"I'm fine, thanks. I told you I haven't seen many of these."

"We'll all be one someday." Mai took out a syringe. "I
just don't want you to faint. I don't want to do anything to
draw attention to us. We've been lucky so far. Getting out
could be more difficult."

Peggy watched carefully as Mai filled three syringes
with blood from Mark's body. She didn't think she'd be
able to. Her plan had been to get Mai in there, then look
away. But she found that she couldn't. Mark looked far
worse than when she found him in her shop. Deterioration
was starting to set in. His gray skin looked like rubber. She
couldn't see his face and thought she should probably be
glad.

"Almost through. I might need a tissue sample. This is
definitely our last chance to get it." Mai replaced the cap on
the syringe and took out a plastic bottle. She unscrewed the
lid and handed the bottle to Peggy. "Hold this."

Peggy held it out for Mai's sample. She noticed the
other woman's hands were shaking. "Are you all right?"

"Just nervous. I like my job. I plan to be chief medical
officer someday. I don't want to end up in that little office
forever."

"I can understand that. And just think of the top marks
the medical examiner will give you when you prove my
theory."

Mai laughed. "Or when my landlord throws me out because I've lost my job. I don't think the ME will be too pleased if I prove he was wrong. People are funny that way."

"You must think there's some merit in what I told you," Peggy reasoned, "or you wouldn't be here risking so much to help me."

"You must be right." She put the top back on the bottle. "Or I'm crazy. There we go. Now all we have to do is get out of here without getting caught."

No sooner were the words out of her mouth than they heard voices coming toward them.

"Quick! Behind this door!" Mai closed the body drawer, then shoved Peggy and herself into the next room through a set of swinging metal doors.

Peggy put her hand out to stop the motion of the doors after they were out of the way. The two women stood quietly together in the dark room. The two men were still talking as they entered the room. One of the body drawers slid open and closed. The techs talked about the Panthers' game and getting season tickets for the Bobcats, the new basketball team.

The drawer the techs opened didn't squeak. Peggy hoped that meant it wasn't the one Mark was in. There wasn't time to put the paper sheet back across him. Maybe they wouldn't notice.

"I forgot to fix the sheet," Mai whispered, echoing her companion's thoughts.

"Different drawer, I think." Peggy glanced at her lighted watch. It was almost one A.M.

After a few minutes, they heard another drawer open and close again. The voices moved toward the door that led to the hallway, and the light clicked off.

Mai took a deep, shaky breath. "That was close."

"Let's take care of that sheet and get out of here." Peggy pushed open the door.

It seemed so simple. They had what they needed. Even if someone noticed they signed in, no one would ever know what they were doing there. If Peggy's theory was correct,

even Jonas would have to admit they'd done a good thing.
If not, no one would be the wiser. They didn't talk about
how Mai would present the evidence. There was no point
in debating that until they knew if what they had made a
difference.

She and Mai hurried down the corridor toward the front
desk to sign out. They were only a few steps away from
walking out of the building.

Paul pushed open the front door and walked in. "Mom?"
He swiveled his gaze to the right. "Mai? What are you doing here?"

"We're working, of course." Mai's gaze narrowed, and
her pointed chin came up defiantly. "What are *you* doing
here?"

"I came for some documents the captain wants. That's
not the point. What's my mother doing here? Last time I
checked, she didn't work for the city or the county."

Mai glanced at Peggy. "She's helping me do some research."

"With *what?* What are either one of you doing here at
this time of the night?"

"I don't think that concerns you, Officer Lee. Your
mother and I had business here. Now we're leaving. Good-
bye."

Paul put one hand on Mai's shoulder as she started to
move away. "Hold on a minute—"

"I'm a thirty-second-degree black belt," she warned
with a laser glance at his hand. "Don't invade my personal
space unless you want to lose a hand."

Paul's green gaze clashed with Mai's infuriated brown
eyes. "Yeah?"

"Is there a problem, Officer?" a short security guard
with bulldog features asked him.

"No problem." Paul took his hand away from Mai's
shoulder. He waited for the security guard to walk away,
then turned back to the two women. "Unless you want me
to mention this to Lieutenant Rimer, the two of you better
wait outside for me. I'll only be a minute."

Mai ignored him and walked outside. Peggy smiled and followed her. Paul shook his head and went to the front desk.

"Do you think he means it?" Mai asked his mother when they were alone.

"I think we should tell him what we're doing. The best way to keep someone quiet is to make them an accomplice."

"You're pretty sharp, Peggy. Paul can't report us if he's guilty, too." Mai shivered. "But I think we should wait in the car. It's freezing out here."

When Paul came out, he told them his shift was over. "Let's not draw any more attention to this, whatever it is. I'll meet you at your house, Mom."

"I'll put some coffee on," Peggy agreed before he went back to his squad car.

Mai shifted the small freezer chest she was using to protect and transport the blood and tissue sample they collected. "I suppose he means me, too."

"I'm sure he does. But don't worry, we'll talk to him, and everything will be fine." Peggy looked at Mai as she started the car. "Do you really have a black belt?"

"No. But everyone thinks I do because I'm Asian. It comes in handy sometimes. Bruce Lee made all of us masters of the martial arts."

Paul followed them back to Queens Road. With the cold and the light drizzle, the streets were nearly deserted. It was unusual for Peggy to be out in the city late at night. She admired the lights and the shimmering lines of glossy black pavement. Especially because it gave her something to think about instead of what they'd just done.

Mai slapped her hand on the steering wheel. "I can't believe he's escorting us to your house! What does he think we are? Incompetent teenagers?"

Peggy didn't comment. There was enough friction between those two to light up a house. Someday they'd realize what it was all about. It would be nice to have grandchildren before she was too old to appreciate them. Or before she went to jail for all the laws she'd broken tonight.

She was pleased not to find anything damaged in her

house. Shakespeare galloped to the door, letting out long, low woofs as he came. He wagged his tail so hard that it contorted his body left and right. Then he licked Mai and Peggy, grinning at them.

"It's a good thing you have such a big place," Mai remarked, her eyes following up the side of the blue spruce. "You couldn't keep a dog this big in my apartment."

Peggy put on the coffeepot. "Until I was coerced into it, I would've sworn this house wasn't big enough for both of us. But I think it's going to work out."

Mai was asking about the history of the house when Paul came into the kitchen. She stopped speaking midsentence and sat down at the kitchen table.

"Okay." Paul glared at them both. "Who's going to tell me what's going on?"

He was grim-faced through the entire explanation. He shook his head, rolled his eyes, and sat back in his chair, purposely not looking at his mother. "Besides the laws you've broken doing this, did it ever occur to you that whatever you find will be useless?"

Peggy stirred sugar into her coffee. "Why is that?"

"Because the district attorney will immediately have the evidence we found as well as anything that extends from its discovery declared not admissible." Mai looked at Paul. "Does that about cover it?"

"You should've thought of that before you took a chance on your career," he answered. "The best thing to do is get rid of whatever you took out of there. Forget about it. Chances are, no one will call you on it."

"But if we discover there was alcohol in Mark's body, that might be enough to reopen the investigation," Peggy disagreed. "Even if the evidence isn't admissible in court, it would at least lead the police to someone besides Mr. Cheever."

"You're not a lawyer, Mom. And the lieutenant is gonna be pissed when he finds out you were involved with this again. It's against the law to impede an investigation."

"But that's the problem. There *is* no investigation."

"Let's say there is alcohol in Warner's body. What does that prove?" Paul argued. "Alcohol didn't kill him. A shovel did."

"Yes, and alcohol doesn't kill a drunk driver," Peggy persisted, "the car does. But alcohol is a contributing factor. Someone may have given him a drink without his knowledge to make it easier to kill him."

"That isn't police thinking. You aren't a police officer or a homicide detective." He put down his coffee mug and got to his feet. "It's late. I'm exhausted. Promise me you'll throw this stuff away and not go any further with this."

Peggy's eyes were like shards of bright green glass. "I can't do that, Paul. If there's a chance I can help Mr. Cheever with this, I will. You could be more useful, since *you* think like a police officer."

"I'm going home." He glanced at Mai. "I'd like to talk to you outside for a minute."

Mai stood up. "Sure. I'm on my way out anyway."

Peggy waited until her son stepped outside, then faced Mai. "I won't blame you if you don't want to go any further with this. I probably had no right to ask you in the first place."

"Whatever! Like I'm going to let him tell me what to do! He's a badass rookie cop. I have three years of experience in forensics. I outrank him technically. Don't worry about it. I have a day off and a friend at the state crime lab in Raleigh. I'll run this up to him, and we'll see what happens. It might not be anything."

"I realize that." Peggy hugged her. "Thanks for trying. And don't let that blowhard intimidate you."

Mai made a strange whooping sound in the back of her throat and assumed a martial arts stance. "I saw this on TV the other night. Impressive, huh?"

Peggy laughed and saw her to the door. She started clearing away the coffee cups when she noticed that Mai left her gloves behind. She hurried to the kitchen door and poked her head out into the frosty night to see if the other woman was gone.

Instead, she found Mai and Paul engaged in a passionate kiss against the brick wall. Mai's boots were barely touching the frozen ground, and Paul's face was hidden by her hair. Neither one of them noticed when Peggy opened and closed the door.

"That's interesting," she told Shakespeare. "I think we'll leave them alone. It would be good for both of them to have something besides their work."

Shakespeare looked like he understood. He waited for Peggy to put the cups in the dishwasher, then followed her into the basement.

Peggy's first attempt at a night-blooming rose was a dismal failure. The graft wouldn't take, and the plant died. She noted it and tried again. The water lily was doing very well. It seemed to like her little pond. Her six-foot angel's trumpet was blooming, six, waxy white hanging flowers perfuming the air.

She put on gloves to gather pollen from the stamen and harvest a few seeds. She was working on a fast-acting antidote to angel's trumpet poison she hoped would someday find its way to pet store shelves. Thousands of animals were attracted to the plants and died from its toxin.

After watering the plants that were dry and logging in her results from all of her work, she crept slowly up the basement stairs. She'd never considered an elevator for the old house. But necessity might make her think about it. Someday. Not right now. Her knee was feeling better. She wasn't old enough or dysfunctional enough to need help yet.

She went up to her bedroom with the dog at her heels. He jumped on the bed as she changed clothes. "I don't think that's going to work." She grabbed a couple of large floor pillows she used for decoration and threw them on the carpet next to her bed. "There you go. Down boy. Down Shakespeare. Come on. On the pillows. Get down."

The big mouth was grinning and slobbering. The tail was thumping the mattress. The more she called him, the more excited he got. Finally, she gave up and promised she was going to buy a book about dog training.

Peggy glanced at her computer. She hated not to log on and collect her messages. One of them might be from Nightflyer. Not that she wanted to answer it. She lost the debate with herself, sat down in the chair, and booted up her computer.

There were 215 messages. Some of them were spam, but she'd installed a good spam blocker a few months ago, so it caught most of them. Only one message asked her if she was ready to refinance her mortgage. Then there were the obligatory ads that either wanted to enlarge her penis or her breasts. She trashed those and went on.

The rest of the raw autopsy data from Hal Samson was waiting for her. She didn't want to look at it until morning. Unlike the Warner case, there was no suspect in the Columbia poisoning. No one's life was at stake since the poor girl was already dead. She could relax and go through the details later.

There was one message from Nightflyer. He wanted to meet her for chess at midnight. She glanced at her watch. It was almost two A.M. Surely he wouldn't wait that long for her.

She logged on at the site and waited for a partner. Since the players were located all over the world, there were always people waiting to play. The chat box showed two of them from New Guinea who were already engaged.

Nightflyer has accepted your game.

The statement always meant a clearing of the screen and insertion of the chessboard. She tapped her fingers on the desk and bit her lip. She knew she shouldn't stay. Wasn't she worried enough yesterday to ask for Al's help?

"You've been busy."

"I have to go."

"You just got here. Are you feeling all right?"

She looked at the words in the chat box and answered. *"I should warn you, I reported you to a police friend of mine. It's illegal to stalk people."*

He put in the symbol for smiling. *"So you're worried about me stalking you? How ridiculous. I suppose you're worried I'm the one who threw you off the dock then."*

"If you're smart, you won't pursue this." She typed with a shaky hand.

"How can you ask me to give up our relationship? It's the only bright spot in my night."

Peggy moved her cursor to hit End Game.

"I could help you solve the murders. Trust me, Nightrose. I won't hurt you."

She didn't reply. She watched the screen clear, then shut down her computer. She half expected the phone to ring. Nothing happened. Maybe he'd take the hint. Maybe he didn't realize how much he was bothering her.

She climbed into bed, pulling the blanket and sheet from the dog. Lying back against her pillow, she stared at the ceiling. The old house groaned and creaked around her. She loved the sounds. They represented the peace and security the house provided her. Sometimes it almost felt alive and caring, nestling her inside its wood timbers and mellowed bricks.

Peggy didn't want to think about Nightflyer or the pang she felt leaving him there alone. It was too desperate, too pathetic that part of her enjoyed his attentions. The logical, sensible part of her was the one who told Al. It argued with the romantic, emotional side that she didn't know this man. Anyone who went to such lengths to stay in touch with a stranger had a problem.

Sam's theory about Nightflyer being too shy to approach her in real life set up the debate again. She was right to consult Al. The idea that Nightflyer was some love-starved recluse might fit in with her teenage readings of *Jane Eyre* or *Wuthering Heights*. But this was the real world. There were wacky people out there. The chances were that Nightflyer was one of them.

She convinced herself and was almost asleep with the dog snoring next to her when the phone rang. The noise jerked her out of bed, trailing the sheet behind her as the pillow fell to the floor. "Hello?"

His voice was raspy and deep. "Good night, Peggy. Sleep well."

The phone went dead in her hand before she could reply. Wide awake now, she knew there wouldn't be any sleep for her that night.

12

Angelica

Botanical: *Angelica archangelica*
Family: N. O. Umbelliferae
Common Names: Angel plant, dead nettle, holy herb,
wild celery

*According to legend, angelica was a gift to man from the
Archangel Michael. It is said to have protected whole villages
during the plague. It will protect against witchcraft. Angelica
was planted at all four corners of a house to ward off lightning,
witches, spells, evil spirits, and evil of all kinds.*

SERGEANT ANDY JONES of the Charlotte-Mecklenburg
PD Cyber Unit arrived bright and early the next morning.
After tea and toast, Peggy led him upstairs to her bedroom. She bit her lip when she looked at the sheets and
pillows all over the floor. "I'm sorry for the mess. My dog
sleeps with me."

He laughed. "Yeah, I got a crazy poodle that'd be a
snack for your big boy downstairs. Don't worry about it.
Log on and show me where you go to play chess with this
man."

Peggy showed him, very conscious of her moves, knowing this man was an expert. "What will you do to catch
him? Do you have some gizmo that will detect when he
challenges me to a game of chess?"

"Bill Gates might have something sophisticated like that," he answered. "I take down the name of the site and set up a monitor to look for his login. As soon as he gets into the system, we got him. I can trace him back to his source. Every IP keeps information on their clients nowadays. Depending on where he is, we can have someone pay him a visit that day."

"Thanks, Andy. I feel much better now." She glanced at her watch. "And I'm sorry, but I'm late for a class. If you'll excuse me, I have to run!"

"Sure thing. I'll let you know when we pick up on anything. Nice to meet you. Thanks for the tea. What kind did you say it was?"

"Orange peach with a hint of lemon." She handed him a slip of paper with the name on it and walked with him to the front door. "Give my best to your wife. Have her try that feverfew for her migraines. It can make a world of difference."

By the time she walked Shakespeare and got everything together, the taxi she called was waiting in the driveway. She sighed as she glanced at her bike but knew it would be a few more days before she could ride again.

She needed to find time to work on the hydrogen conversion for the Rolls. It wasn't so difficult as it was time consuming. If she wasn't so stubborn, she'd hire someone else to do it. But where would the fun be in that?

She was lecturing to both of her classes as well as a group of undergrads at Queens that morning. The auditorium was packed as she limped to the speaker's platform. Fortunately, she could give the lecture in her sleep if she had to. After last night, that's exactly what she felt like she was doing. Maybe Nightflyer would log on to the game room looking for her and find Andy waiting instead.

She didn't think she'd prosecute him. Just knowing who and where he was would make her feel better. He was obviously in Charlotte somewhere to be able to track her movements so closely. Right now, he could be anyone she passed on the street or worked with at the university. She needed a name and a face to have some peace of mind.

At the conclusion of the lecture on collecting and preserving sample pollens, Peggy answered questions from the group. She wondered if Nightflyer was in that sea of faces. Would she know his voice in person? From his previous behavior patterns, she felt sure he'd give himself away to let her know he was there. He definitely wanted her attention.

But the students were leaving, and the lecture was over. There was no sign of Nightflyer. She gathered her notes and ruminated over becoming a worried old woman who jumped at sounds in the night.

"Hi, Peggy." Sam's cheerful face appeared in her line of vision. "I was over here mulching some gardenias for the Bostics and noticed it was about time for your class to be over. Need a ride to the shop?"

She hugged him. "Yes, I do. Thanks for thinking of it."

His face turned red, and he glanced around at the group of rapidly retreating students. "It's only a ride. You even paid for the gas."

"Sometimes it's the little things that matter, Sam. Let's go."

Shakespeare was waiting in the truck. "Thought I might as well pick him up." Sam helped her into the truck and shut the door behind her. "How did it go last night?"

While the dog licked her face, she described the whole experience in dramatic detail for him. She knew he liked it that way. "The big surprise was walking out into Paul. But I think Mai took care of that problem."

"She somehow managed to take the oak tree out of his butt?"

"No." She laughed. "She kissed him. *Really* kissed him."

"Wow! That was above and beyond. I wouldn't have gone that far." He considered the matter. "Well, probably not anyway. So little Paul finally has a girlfriend. I hope you got pictures."

"I barely got to see it. They were outside. But it looked pretty hot and heavy. I knew they had a thing for each other. I guess we'll have to see what develops."

"What happens now?" Sam pulled the truck behind the shop. "We find out someone slipped Warner some alcohol, and then what? How do we find out which one of his many women did him in?"

"Don't count out the men in those women's lives," she replied. "It could've been one of them."

Sam stroked his chin. "Hmmm, Keeley didn't have a man in her life besides Mark. You said he broke up with his personal assistant a while before. Unless you're thinking the man who replaced him . . ."

"No, not really. I think that's a dead end altogether. Excuse the pun."

"Excused. That only leaves one man who might have been jealous enough to do something to Mark for sleeping with his wife: Bob McGee."

"That's right. Ronda said he was out of town that night. But suppose he set the whole thing up to make it look that way. Maybe he wasn't out of town at all."

Sam laughed. "And you're going to prove that *how*?"

"Don't ask me." Peggy shook herself. "I'm new at this detective thing. I suppose I'll walk up and confront him. That seems to work best for me."

"Has it occurred to you that your style might be what got you thrown off the dock? Or that it could happen again if you confront the wrong person?"

"You mean the *right* person? Don't worry. I'll be careful. I'll either have Shakespeare with me, or I'll make sure I do it in a crowd. Then I'll have Shakespeare with me afterward."

"I don't know if that dog would do anything more than wag his tail and bark a lot, Peggy. Maybe you should get a gun."

"And shoot myself in the foot? No, thanks. I appreciate your input though. Where are you off to now?"

"I'm going to talk to a buddy of mine who's working for the new arena group. He promised us a shot at bidding for the plant work."

Peggy raised her eyebrows. "That's a big contract! Is that interior or exterior work?"

"Both. And whether we get it or not, you need to start thinking about hiring someone to take Keeley's place. I talked to Dawn, but she's not interested in doing fieldwork all the time. I need some help. I can't keep going with school and work without someone else helping out."

She patted his hand. "I know, and I'm sorry. I should've already seen to that. There's been so much going on that I forgot. Or maybe I was hoping Keeley would come back. But I'll get some ads out today. Thanks, Sam."

He cleared his throat. "I can manage for a while. Just don't forget about me."

She promised not to and got out of the truck. She walked up the back steps, her eyes torturing themselves by going over the ground where she'd fallen from the dock. She knew if there was anything left behind, Al would've found it. Resolutely, she turned away from the area and went inside.

The extreme warmth from the shop hit her as she walked in. Keeley and Selena were sitting behind the counter talking. The front door was open into the courtyard.

"I hope you called maintenance," Peggy said to Selena as Shakespeare ran into the shop and found his familiar spot. "It must be a hundred degrees in here!"

"I called when I first got here," Selena answered. "No one was there yet. I left a message. It's the same at the Kozy Kettle. Probably the same at all the shops."

"Hi, Peggy," Keeley said quietly. "I thought I'd stop by for some tea."

Peggy took off her cape and hugged her. "I'm glad you did. How are you feeling?"

"Ready to go back to work. Light duty for a few weeks. But I'd really like to have something to do."

"What about school?"

"I've decided to drop the rest of this semester. My

brain needs some time off. But the rest of me needs to be busy."

Selena went to help a customer. Peggy faced Keeley. "You know I'd like to have you back, and Sam is crying for some help, but I don't want you to come back too soon."

"Are you worried about the Warner thing?" Keeley suggested. "Because I don't think it's going to be a problem. Even if they decide not to prosecute Mr. Cheever, I think I'll be fine."

"I'm not worried about that. I know you've been through a strain, and I want you to have plenty of time to get better."

"So you don't want me back." Keeley's voice was flat. "Okay. I understand."

Peggy laughed. "I think we're talking, but we're not communicating. Of course I want you back. You can start on light duty whenever you're ready. But if you start back too soon and your mother comes after me, I'm going to tell her it was your idea."

Keeley hugged her. "Thanks, Peggy. I won't do more than I can handle. Don't worry. Besides, I'll be with Sam. He's close enough to being a doctor that he can take care of me if I try to do too much. And no matter what, I won't tell Mom. I'd appreciate it if you didn't mention to her that I'm skipping this semester. I haven't told her about that yet."

"You've got a deal." Peggy consulted her workbook. "Sam's trying to get us a bid on the new arena. But I could use your help counting supplies before we order at the end of the month."

"Sounds great. I don't think counting supplies should be too strenuous."

The shop was busy for a Wednesday. Peggy was hoping to get her presentation for the Thursday morning garden club ready while she manned the cash register, but it was going to have to wait. Between getting ready to order supplies and the steady stream of customers, it was all she could do to keep up. She was glad to have Keeley there. Maybe she needed to consider another assistant for the shop.

Just after the lunchtime crowd began to dissipate,

Hunter and Jane Cheever arrived at the shop. Keeley and Selena took over so Peggy could have lunch with the two women.

"The judge postponed the trial indefinitely while the doctors try to make some kind of judgment about Mr. Cheever's medical condition," Hunter told her as they sat down inside Anthony's Caribbean Café.

"That's good news." Peggy waved to Anthony, who hurried over to her table.

"I was beginning to wonder if you'd taken a strong dislike to my food, Miss Peggy." The tall, thin Jamaican man hugged her. "But here you are, and you brought some friends."

Peggy introduced him to Hunter and Jane. "I don't know what they'd like, Anthony, but I want my usual. Rice 'n' peas, candied yams, fried plantain, and red sorrell tea."

Hunter shrugged. "Sounds good to me, too."

Jane agreed, and Anthony took their order back to the kitchen. The colorful café was crowded with shoppers who were taking a late lunch. Flags from the island nations hung from the ceiling, and palm trees decorated the walls. A huge mural of the ocean covered one whole side of the café, while a thatched roof covered the kitchen and the bar areas.

"This is good news," Hunter continued with their conversation. "It gives all of us time to do what we can for Mr. Cheever. If there's any information out there to support the possibility of his innocence, now's the time to bring it forward."

Peggy didn't respond. She knew Hunter wanted what she knew about Ronda McGee. But after talking with Mark's lover in the courtyard, she agreed that it wouldn't make sense for Ronda to kill him. Maybe Ronda made a mistake by having an affair with Mark, but that didn't make her a killer.

"Dad's doing much better." Jane thanked the waiter for her iced tea. "The doctor isn't sure how much he'll recover from the stroke. He may never really remember that night."

"I believe he remembers the important part." Peggy

explained her theory about Mark's alcohol allergy to them. She didn't go into detail about what she and Mai had done to discover the truth.

Hunter put more sugar in her tea. "Didn't they release his body today?"

"I heard something about that," Peggy agreed.

"How are the police going to run tests on him if they don't have the body?"

Peggy smiled at her. "It's already been taken care of."

"Then why haven't I been informed of any changes in the case? If they found alcohol in Warner and he was allergic, it would change everything. There was no way for Mr. Cheever to know he was allergic or to administer the alcohol."

"There haven't been any changes *yet*." Peggy thanked the waiter for her plantain. "When there are, I'm sure you'll be the first to know."

Hunter leaned closer to her, her bright eyes flashing. "What's going on? What aren't you telling me? You hired me to save Mr. Cheever. Whatever you know that could help—"

"When I know something I can share, I'll tell you," Peggy said. "Right now, all I have is theory and specula-tion. We need proof."

The lawyer sat back in her chair. "You're sure you're not trying to protect Keeley now that she's been implicated?"

"I wouldn't know how to make that choice. I just don't have all the answers yet."

The three women ate their peas 'n' rice in silence. The funky island music played around them, and the waiter kept their drinks filled.

"I'm really going to push Dad to come home with me again, if he gets out," Jane interrupted the silence. "This wouldn't have happened if he'd been at home where he be-longs."

Hunter and Peggy agreed with her. The conversation picked up involving elderly relatives and their care. None of them mentioned the trial again.

"Well, I have to go." Hunter glanced at her watch. "I'll

let you know if I hear anything new. I assume you'll do the same."

"I will," Peggy promised. "Thanks again for taking the case."

Jane lingered a little longer, talking about the way her father was when she was a child. "It's terrible to see this stranger. I don't know what to do about it. He doesn't think rationally, but he's not a child. I can't send him to his room."

"He's one of the most rational men I've ever met," Peggy disagreed. "I don't understand why he prefers to live on the street. But it's certainly not because he's a half-wit."

"You think it's me, don't you?" Jane wrung her hands.

Peggy squeezed her arm. "Of course not! It's him. Something inside of him won't let him rest. I wish I understood it more, and I could help. But it's not anything you've done."

Jane thanked her, then gathered up her belongings. "I'd appreciate it if you'd let me know, too, if you hear anything."

"I will." Peggy smiled as she watched the younger woman leave the café. Talking to her made her think about her relationship with Paul. How much was there between them that neither of them understood?

"Your friends eat like rabbits," Anthony told her with a laugh. "Next time bring somebody with an appetite!"

Peggy promised she would and thanked him for lunch. She walked back to the Potting Shed, for once glad to see her customers had thinned out. She sent Keeley home when she saw how tired she looked and had Selena wait to leave until she could take Shakespeare for a short walk.

"You think Keeley's okay?" Selena asked her when she got back.

"I think she'll be fine," Peggy answered. "She needs time to get her strength back. Losing a pregnancy isn't only the physical aspect. It's the emotional one as well."

"I can't believe she was pregnant! Especially with that old guy's baby. What was she thinking?"

"That he wasn't all that old?"

Selena ducked her head. "I guess I should go before I say anything else stupid. See you later, Shakespeare. Bye, Peggy."

When Selena was gone and the shop was empty, Peggy called in her monthly plant order. She included some poinsettias for Christmas as well as a large supply of paper-white narcissus. Besides some decorations and a few gift ideas for gardeners, it was the only consideration she gave the holiday season. Christmas wasn't as big for her as for some other retailers.

Feeling accomplished when the order was in, she sat down behind the counter and put her leg up on a basket. Her knee was feeling a little better, but she might have to give some thought to a few sessions of physical therapy, as the doctor suggested. It was still a little stiff, and she didn't want to give up riding her bike.

She picked up the newspaper and glanced through it, checking out competitors' ads as well as some news stories. A short mention in the society page caught her attention. Ronda McGee had filed for divorce yesterday. Peggy's eyes narrowed and lost focus as she considered what that could mean. It might not have anything to do with Mark's death. But on the other hand . . .

Before she could consider her actions, she looked up the address of the McGee household on the computer. She could empathize, take Ronda some tea and a plant. It was the least she could do. They were passing acquaintances anyway. After her thoughts that morning about Bob McGee, she had to know what happened. The best way was to go to the source.

She waited impatiently for the hands on the big clock to swing to six. A few customers straggled out of the dark courtyard and purchased some bulbs and a few planters. Peggy talked to them about their needs and explained what they had to do to see their plants flourish. All the while she kept glancing at the clock. Impatience made her edgy. She called for a taxi at 5:40 and started shutting down the shop.

The new lights by the loading dock made the whole area bright again. The maintenance crew finally installed them that day after the furnace was repaired. As predicted, no shadows lingered. Satisfied, she shut off the back lights and locked the door. At the same time, she heard the front door open and close. She should've locked it.

Smile fastened firmly in place, even though her heart was pounding, she turned to greet what she determined was going to be her last customer of the day.

"Am I too late? I suppose I should've called." Steve waited by the counter for her. "I finished with a patient and thought about surprising you with a ride home. Surprise!"

Peggy didn't know what to say. "That was . . . thoughtful of you. But I already called for a taxi."

"You can cancel it. We can go out for dinner, and I'll take you home." He studied her face. "Unless you had other plans."

"Not exactly. There's this one thing I need to do. . . ."

"Great! You close up; I'll cancel the taxi." He picked up the phone. "Which company did you call?"

"It might be best if you don't come with me," she suggested, trying not to hurt his feelings.

"What is it? Are you meeting someone else?"

"Not the way you make it sound," she said. "It's something else about the Warner murder. You might not want to get involved."

"I'm already involved. I went to the Warners' with you, and I ate pancakes at your house with all your police friends. What are you going to do? Break into a building? Meet an informant in a dark alley?"

She laughed at him. "I did that last night. Tonight, I'm going to see Ronda McGee to see if it's possible her husband might be involved. You're welcome to come along. But you'll have to wait in the car. I don't think she'll be as open with a man since she lost her lover and now she's divorcing her husband."

"I wouldn't want to be there either," he agreed. "I can be

Kato. You can be the Green Hornet tonight. Are we grilling the suspect before or after dinner?"

"Before. I thought it might be better on an empty stomach." She watched him pick up the phone and cancel the taxi. He was definitely a man after her own heart. "Come on, Shakespeare. Let's go!"

RONDA AND BOB McGEE'S HOME was a two-story Tudor set within an elaborately fenced yard on Providence Road near Myers Park. The wrought-iron gates were open when Peggy and Steve arrived. It looked like every interior and exterior light was turned on. As Steve started to turn into the drive, a fast-moving gray Jaguar squealed past them and into the street.

"Do you think that was the suspect, and he got tipped you were coming?" Steve asked as he pulled through the gate.

"It's possible," she quipped. "My reputation may have preceded me."

"Or he heard you had a big dog."

She opened the car door. "Stay!" Shakespeare subsided with a groan. "Have a good time, you two. I'll be out as soon as I can."

"I'll be practicing my karate moves."

Peggy rang the doorbell and waited, juggling her gifts of angelica and lemon balm tea. The dried leaves from the plant made a lovely sachet to relieve stress and insomnia. The lemon balm tea tasted good and was soothing. Ronda's housekeeper opened the door, looking frazzled. Without a word, she walked back into the house, leaving the door open. Not sure what to do, Peggy followed her.

Ronda was in what looked like the library. Huge, oak shelves lined the walls surrounding a stone fireplace. The room was a wreck, books and other articles strewn everywhere. The desk looked like it had been looted. Papers and computer parts were scattered across the top.

"Hello, Ronda." Peggy approached her. "I heard about what happened. I wanted to offer my condolences."

Ronda picked up the telephone and threw it across the room. "Can you believe it? That son of a bitch had his girlfriend pick him up!"

"Maybe it was better for him to leave right now." Peggy put the plant and tea on the desk. "What happened?"

Ronda collapsed in one of the high-backed chairs. "I don't know. I had a feeling something was going on. Then he went out of town for another business meeting. They usually cover for each other. I don't know what went wrong. But I found out he was with *her*."

"Who is she?" Peggy sat down opposite her.

"A secretary. Not even his secretary. Some young twit they hired. She looks like she's sixteen. I caught them out at *our* house on Lake Norman. He had her in *our* bed. Can you believe it?"

"It was certainly brazen of him."

Ronda laughed. "I'll say. I mean, it's not like I expected him to be faithful. These things happen. But not in your own house. That's too much."

"So you kicked him out."

"You bet your ass I did! He can have his little bimbo, but he's going to pay for it. It's not like this is the first time either. That night Mark was killed, Bob was out of town. He wasn't working. He was with her that night, too. I had a private detective following him. I have pictures. He's going to pay big time. This may be a no-fault state, but my lawyer says adultery means major property settlement. By the time I get done with him, he and that little slut will have to live in the Tryon Arms!"

Peggy sighed. That brought down her theory about Bob McGee being involved in Mark's murder. It was a long shot anyway. She didn't mention to Ronda that she'd been doing the same thing to Bob. Obviously, in her mind, infidelity had its rules. Bob crossed over them.

As if Ronda suddenly noticed Peggy was there, she wiped her face with a tissue and combed her hair back with her fingers. "I know you didn't come to hear all of this. Did you have something you needed to ask me about Mark?"

Thinking quickly, Peggy answered, "Yes. I was wondering how many people knew about Mark's allergy to alcohol."

"Not many people. Mark felt like it made him seem old. He'd pretend to drink to keep up appearances."

"And he *never* drank liquor?"

"Not that I know of," Ronda replied. "I read the old guy who killed him had a stroke. I guess it was bad luck all the way around. Even for Julie, that spiteful little bitch."

"I'd say especially for Julie, since she lost her husband," Peggy said, not feeling particularly sympathetic toward Ronda.

"You know, the rest of us knew how the game was played. I always knew Bob fooled around. He knew I fooled around. We respected the limits. Julie never got that. She felt like Mark was her own personal property. How realistic is that?"

"You mean Julie never cheated on Mark?"

"Never! Mark was the one and only man for her. We laughed at her behind her back. That kind of marriage is so yesterday. She was nasty about it, too. I really believe she was the one who called and threatened me about seeing Mark. If you could've seen the look in her eyes when I passed her that night leaving Mark's office. If looks could kill, as my mama always said, I'd be stone dead."

Peggy thanked her and showed herself out of the house. It was easier for her to understand Julie's point of view on not sharing her husband with other women. She wasn't sure what she would've done if she'd found out John was cheating on her. Maybe Ronda considered jealousy a thing of the past. But clearly the controlled infidelity she believed in didn't always work either.

She got back in the car with Steve and Shakespeare. The lights that shone on the house picked up the crystals of ice forming in the drops of water as the sprinkler system rained on the yard. It was almost a fairy-tale setting in the beautifully manicured park that surrounded the McGees' unhappy home.

"Did you get what you were looking for?" Steve pushed the dog into the backseat.

"Yes and no." She closed the door and put on her seat belt. "Bob McGee was with his lover the night Mark was killed. Ronda has proof of it. Since they were both unfaithful, it would hardly follow that Bob would kill Mark over his wife anyway. That theory is useless."

Steve started the Saturn. "I'm sure you'll think of something else. Someone killed him. If you don't believe it was either one of your friends, the truth about who was responsible will have to surface at some point."

"We have some extra time anyway." She told him about the postponement of the trial. "I guess it's just as well. This is taking a while."

"While we're waiting, how about dinner? I know this great place for frozen potpies."

Peggy laughed as she patted Shakespeare's head. "Sounds like my kind of place."

WHILE THE POTPIES WERE cooking, Steve showed Peggy around his house. It was very much the same style as her own but on a smaller scale. He was in the midst of remodeling, tearing out the old carpet to reveal the beautiful patina of the old heart-of-pine floors and replacing the worn drapes at the big windows.

"I plan on operating my private practice from here," he told her, flicking on the overhead fluorescent light in a front area of the house. "My uncle did pretty well here. Business is starting to come in for me, too."

She looked around the white and silver exam room, investigating the medical instruments he used. "You must really love animals to want to work with them all the time."

"I guess I could say the same thing about you and plants." He smiled. "And kids, for that matter. Animals have to be better than college students."

"Sometimes there's not much difference," she agreed. "I think you'll do well here."

He crossed the room deliberately and put his arms around her. "You do, do you?"

Peggy stifled the frantic impulse to be embarrassed at his casual embrace. She smiled up at him. "Yes, I do."

He kissed her lips lightly, and the oven timer buzzed. "It's always something. But don't worry. I'm not going anywhere. We have plenty of time."

"Thanks. Those potpies smell delicious!"

They ate their potpies with an Aussie 2001 Annvers Shiraz from Steve's uncle's wine cellar. The conversation was intimate as they tried to learn more about each other. Peggy laughed and enjoyed herself more than she had in a long time. Shakespeare rolled over on his back by the kitchen door and looked totally at ease.

It was nine before she looked up at the clock. "I hate it, but I have to go. I have tests to grade for tomorrow."

Steve laced his fingers through hers. "Why do you work so hard to stay busy? It seems like the garden shop would be enough."

It was difficult to explain how empty her life was after John died. It wasn't something she was willing to try to put into words. Not yet. "I like to be busy. And the kids keep me on my toes. I was worried about the Potting Shed making it to begin with. Then I just enjoyed having something to do."

He nodded and smiled at her in a way that made her feel he understood some of what she didn't explain. The kitchen was quiet around them as they sat together at the table. It was a good, pleasurable silence that drew them together, giving them a few moments of tranquillity from the outside world.

The peace was shattered when Peggy's cell phone rang. She apologized to Steve but answered when she saw the number that came up. "What is it, Mai?"

"I've got the results of the tox screen, Peggy. You aren't going to believe this."

13

Hyacinth

Botanical: *Muscari racemosum*
Family: N. O. Liliaceae
Common Names: Common hyacinth, garden hyacinth

Hyacinthus was Apollo's favorite companion. Zephyr, the west wind, was jealous of the boy's youth and beauty. When Apollo took up the discus and threw it, Zephyr blew the discus over and hit Hyacinthus in the head. When he died, his blood turned into a flower. Apollo put his friend's body into the heavens as a constellation. The legend stands, though the flower is not native to Greece.

MAI WOULD ONLY AGREE to meet her at the Waffle House off of Interstate 85.

Peggy wasn't sure why the younger woman considered the Waffle House a safe place to meet, but she agreed. She took Steve with her since she needed a ride, and taxis were hard to find at night. They dropped Shakespeare off at her house after he had a short romp in the yard.

Mai was waiting in the parking lot when they pulled up. She stared at Steve, then pulled Peggy aside and hissed, "He shouldn't be here. This is too important!"

"He pretty much knows everything about the case," Peggy assured her. "He's okay. I trust him."

"Okay." She glanced at him, still not happy with it. "I don't think you were followed. I didn't see anyone behind you when you pulled in. Did you?"

"Why didn't we meet at my house or your apartment?" Peggy tried to get at the heart of the matter.

"Because Paul or someone else on the job might show up at either place. This has to be kept secret for now. We're the only ones who can know."

They went inside and sat down at a secluded back booth. An irritated waitress took their orders for coffee and hurried off.

"What makes you think someone would follow me?" Peggy asked Mai when the waitress was gone. The whole thing was comical except for the terrible look of anxiety on Mai's face.

"When you know what I know, you'll understand why we have to be careful." She looked at Steve again, sighed, then plunged into her disclosure. "Mark Warner wasn't drinking, he was *poisoned*." Her voice was almost too quiet to be heard across the table.

Peggy sat forward. "Are you sure?"

Mai nodded and glanced uneasily around the restaurant. "My friend in Raleigh finished the tests tonight. Warner had enough pure protoanemonin in his system that he would've died *without* being hit in the head with the shovel."

"Protoanemonin?" Steve asked. "What's that?"

"The poisonous part of the anemone plant," Peggy explained, stunned by the discovery. "In its purest form, anemonin depresses circulation and respiration by paralyzing the motor centers in the brain."

"Right," Mai agreed. "I looked it up. It's rare. Hard to come by. How would Mark Warner have come in contact with it?"

"I imagine someone gave it to him. If it's done right, it's the perfect poison. It's tasteless and odorless. The purer the crystal specimen, the less likely it would cause vomiting if it was swallowed. And no convulsions before death. It would appear as though the person was asleep." Peggy considered what Mr. Cheever told her. "Yet that could account for the odd behavior that made Keeley think Mark had been drinking."

Peggy didn't mention the poisoning in Columbia, though she immediately considered it. How odd to find two rare poisonings with the same substance so close together in time and geography. Unless they were linked somehow. She made a mental note to call Hal Samson and apprise him of the other poisoning.

"This changes everything." Mai gripped her hands together tightly on the table. "But how do I tell anybody? The ME *has* to know. But if I tell him, I have to admit to sneaking into the morgue and conducting my own personal tox screen. He'll fire me so fast, I won't know what happened. And if I don't tell him . . ."

"You sneaked into the morgue?" Steve asked with a glance at Peggy. "Is that legal?"

"There's no point in concentrating on *that*," Peggy answered. "We have to find a way to make the police aware of their mistake without Mai losing her job."

"I've thought of everything." Mai tore her napkin apart. "There's no way to accidentally stumble on these results. I might as well face reality. My career is over. I'll have to get a job at McDonald's or Taco Bell."

Peggy disagreed. "You did what needed to be done. I'll find a way out for you. Has Mark's body been released yet?"

"This evening. I called the funeral home. The body is scheduled for cremation first thing Tuesday morning. His family is holding the memorial service Wednesday. No embalming. At least we don't have to worry about *that*. The ME will have to call the body back for a legal tox screen. The media is bound to pick up on it. That puts the whole office in a bad light. It makes it look like we made a mistake."

"You *did*," Steve reminded her. "But everyone does. At least you caught it before it went too far."

"*Peggy* caught it," Mai corrected him. "I went along with her."

"There has to be some way of undoing this," Peggy whispered to herself as her brain raced for an answer. Like a bolt of lightning, it came to her. "We'll have to steal the body back!"

THE PLAN CAME TOGETHER at ten P.M. in Peggy's kitchen. She sent Mai home after telling her to be ready for anything. She didn't call Keeley. The girl needed her sleep, and she couldn't ask her to be involved with stealing her dead lover's body from the mortuary.

She could and did ask Sam. He was only too glad to oblige. He tapped into his fraternity, who considered the idea as nothing more than a prank. Steve sat through the meeting that created the plan. He shook his head a few times but otherwise didn't voice his disapproval.

Peggy knew she should probably feel the same, but she'd gotten Mai into this mess; she had to get her out. Sometimes, extraordinary measures were required to help a friend.

THE FRANKLIN MORTUARY WAS AT the edge of the county. It was one of only a few places that actually did its own cremations, a fact they cited with pride. The landscaped grounds were well-kept and spacious. Several eternal flames glowed at strategic points throughout the cemetery that surrounded the crematorium.

It was raining at eleven-thirty the next night when the small group banded together to observe their target. The gas flames glowed eerily with heavy fog dripping moisture on the dull brown grass. The building was densely shrouded in fog, only the lights on the outside showing up from the street. Low-hanging clouds embraced skeletal trees and made the night even more ominous. Ghostly white guardian angels watched them.

"We were lucky to get Jeff to help us," Sam whispered. "He worked here a few months last year. He knows the place."

Jeff shook Peggy's hand, his long black hair hanging down in his face. "This is *soo* cool!"

"Uh—thanks." Peggy took back her hand and smiled at him. "Does everyone know what they're doing?"

"Obviously *not*, or we wouldn't be here," Steve whispered beside her.

Peggy frowned. "You didn't have to come."

"I didn't want you to go alone."

"*We're* here. You don't have to worry about it." Sam sounded a little annoyed at Steve's remark. "Peggy's fine with us."

"Thanks," Steve said. "I'll stay."

Before they could get off on that tangent, Peggy reminded them of their jobs. "We only have a few minutes to do this. It's the only chance we'll have."

Everyone sobered and nodded at her. Sam and Jeff and the other five frat boys piled into Jeff's purple hearse. Steve and Peggy got back in his Saturn.

"I hope you don't think I go around doing this type of thing all the time," Peggy defended.

Steve started his car. "I guess I'm new here and didn't know what to expect. There are some strange things going on in this city."

She sighed. Now he thought she was strange. People usually did, but she was hoping he wouldn't. Oh well, it couldn't be helped. She tried to talk him out of going before they left. He'd insisted. If whatever was between them ended even before it began, she supposed it was for the best. She put it from her mind and focused on her task.

Jeff told them there was no alarm system in the crematorium, a fact they corroborated earlier in the day with a visual scan for alarm signs. The only alarm system was on the building where the expensive urns and caskets were kept. That was about a quarter mile down the single-lane blacktop road that led into the cemetery.

Steve followed the hearse behind the crematorium, and they all climbed out of the vehicles. After a few minutes of standing there, looking at the building, Jeff pulled a key from his dirty shirt pocket. "Let's hope it still works."

No one breathed until the key slid in, the door opened, and no alarm sounded.

"Let's go," Peggy urged when no one moved.

"What now?" Jeff asked her.

"Now we find Mark's body."

It took a few minutes for them to find the file that led them to the refrigerated drawer where his body was being kept. Peggy insisted on all of them putting on gloves and masks as they moved the body into a black plastic bag Jeff had thoughtfully provided for their use.

They wheeled the body out to the hearse and loaded it into the back. Peggy collected the gloves and masks to be sure none were left behind. She asked if anyone closed the file on the desk.

"I did," Steve responded, handing her his mask and gloves. "We should be covered."

"Then let's get out of here," Sam advised. "This place is creeping me out."

Jeff relocked the door, and the two cars slowly drove out of the cemetery. The fog closed in around the crematorium as they got back on the road. Peggy looked out the side window and shivered.

"Cold?" Steve asked.

"No," she replied. "I think I'm in shock. I can't believe what we just did."

AT EIGHT THE NEXT MORNING, a young woman walked into the cafeteria at the University of North Carolina in Charlotte. She got a carton of milk and some cookies from a machine. There were only a few other students half asleep at the tables. She chose to sit at a table with a man who appeared to be reading, his head was bent over a book. His floppy hat hid most of his face.

"You look like you had a worse night than me," the young woman said as she sat down. "Finals?"

The man didn't reply.

The young woman shrugged and opened her breakfast. She glanced at her companion. "Are you sick? My roommate has the flu. I hope I don't get it."

The man didn't reply.

The young woman dropped one of her cookies. When she picked it up off the floor, she noticed her companion was only wearing socks on his feet. She brushed off the cookie. "Five second rule, right? It's pretty cold to go without shoes. Did you lose yours?"

When he didn't reply again, she moved closer and looked at his face. Shaking her head, she removed the man's hat and watched as he slid forward to rest against the table. She raised her voice and said, "Okay. Someone call the dean. The frat boys are at it again."

It only took a cell phone call to 911 to set the wheels in motion. A squad car accompanied an ambulance that picked up the body and tagged it as a John Doe. It was taken to the morgue, where assistant ME Mai Sato began work on identifying the corpse, including a tox screen.

By the time the ME realized they were looking at Mark Warner's body again, the tox screen was being processed.

The Franklin Mortuary and Crematorium filed a breaking and entering report along with theft of a cadaver.

Julie Warner's tearful face was all over the news as she begged the thief to return her husband's body.

Even when the ME's office called the crematorium and the Warner residence to tell them they had the body, it took another forty-eight hours to have the body returned to the mortuary.

Just before the body was scheduled to be released again, Mai went to the ME with the completed tox screen. The ME frowned, took a deep breath, then called the DA's office.

Mark Warner's body wouldn't be released after all. Not until further tests were made.

"They're actually talking about giving me a commendation," Mai told Peggy. "I don't know if I should feel guilty or happy."

"The important part is that the ME knows the truth, and he found out without you losing your job."

Mai thanked her. "I don't know how you did it, and I don't want to know. But I appreciate your help."

"I got you into this mess. I apologize. Sometimes I get a little overexcited about things. I don't always think before I act."

But Peggy was pleased with the outcome. Her knee was feeling so much better, she was going to be able to ride her bike to the shop. It was Saturday, but she was expecting a few special customers in for their orders. Then she was going to tackle a new design for an indoor flower box at an uptown restaurant.

She took Shakespeare for his walk, not noticing a basket of flowers on her front step until they were going back to the house. The flowers were purple hyacinths. She breathed in their springtime fragrance, then looked at the card. "Traditional meaning: I'm sorry. Please forgive me. It would grieve me to lose our friendship. Nightflyer."

Her cell phone rang. Peggy recognized his voice and took a deep breath. "What do you want from me?" She glanced around the yard. Shakespeare was pulling toward the house for his breakfast. A man in an overcoat walked by on the sidewalk. At the same time, a car drove slowly past.

"I want to help." Nightflyer's tone was contrite. "I didn't mean to frighten you."

"Then tell me who you are and how you know so much."

"Do you remember a case John worked with the FBI? It was about ten years ago. He had a contact. A friend from college. It was me. As far as how I knew about these two cases, I suppose you could say I'm interested in what appears to be poisonings. I monitor the Internet, police information, and hospitals. It's not hard if you know how to do it."

Peggy recalled the case. John spent a lot of time on it. She couldn't remember what it was about, but she did remember him mentioning being at school with his FBI contact. "I remember that. But if that's you, why didn't you tell me? Why all the mystery?"

The laugh from the other end was harsh. "I was afraid you wouldn't want me to help."

She wasn't sure what to say. It made sense in some twisted way. Of course, he could've found that information like he knew so many other things. "What kind of gun did John carry?"

There was a brief pause and a chuckle. "You're a cop's wife, Peggy. John was lucky to have you. He carried a Smith and Wesson .45. It wasn't standard to his department. He just liked it."

"You're right," she admitted. "I don't think you could learn that from the Internet. So what now? Do you come out of hiding and have tea with me?"

"I'm afraid not. But I'll be in touch."

The line went dead before Peggy could ask his name. Nightflyer would have to do. For now. But at least she knew she didn't have to worry about him stalking her. Maybe he'd change his mind and tell her the whole story. Something in the tone of his voice when he began to explain who he was tugged at her curiosity.

She took the hyacinths and Shakespeare into the house. The phone was ringing. She grabbed it as she released him from his leash. He bounded into the kitchen for his breakfast, and she breathlessly answered the call.

It was Hal Samson. "Sorry I couldn't get back to you before now. I was testifying at an insurance case for the hospital. What's wrong?"

Peggy told him about Mark's death. She didn't go into detail about everything, but she managed to explain about the similar poisoning.

"You think there's some connection?"

"I don't know. I think it might be worthwhile checking into. I'm free this afternoon. How about you?"

They agreed to meet at the county hospital in Columbia. Peggy called Al and gave him the details she knew about the poisoning in South Carolina.

"I can't go with you officially," Al told her. "But unofficially, I'd like to hear the case. It was pretty amazing what happened with Warner, huh?"

"It was. I can't imagine how it happened, can you?"

THE MORNING PASSED QUICKLY AT the Potting Shed. Peggy's first order of faux antique garden tools came in and sold out to the few customers who were there. She got on-line and ordered two more shipments. She knew the implements would be popular, but she didn't imagine they'd be gone before she had time to advertise them.

She let Dawn close the shop while she hurried over to Ri-Ra's Irish Restaurant and Pub on Tryon Street. The owner was interested in adding flower boxes to the upstairs deck. It was outside, in the shadow of the Hearst building. Not many people were eating out there in the cooler weather, but Peggy could imagine colorful boxes during the warmer parts of the year. Of course, there could always be pansies to liven up the cold months.

The owner also wanted a bid on maintaining the rest of the indoor plants combined with building and maintaining the flower boxes. Peggy promised to have something for him in the next few days. She shook his hand and went to meet Al.

He was waiting outside Latta Arcade in his blue Isuzu Trooper. "Lucky for me Mary was busy today. She doesn't take kindly to me mentioning work on a Saturday."

Peggy fastened her seat belt. "I'm glad you could go with me. Dr. Samson treated the woman who died. He consulted me because of my work with poisons. But he doesn't know anything about police work. You may be able to shed some light on the investigation."

"Did they arrest anyone for the poisoning?" Al turned the car on to Interstate 77 toward Columbia.

"They talked to Mrs. Stone's husband and checked the people she worked with," she answered. "They couldn't find anything to connect her death to him or anyone else."

"But you think there might be some connection to whoever killed Warner."

"Anemonin poisoning is rare. These two incidents might have happened on the same day. I found Mark's body that morning, and Dr. Samson consulted with me about the poisoning in Columbia that night. The woman was still alive when I talked to him."

"So where does this stuff come from?" he asked without taking his eyes off the road.

"The chances are it was home-brewed. Whoever did it knows something about botanical poison and set up a little distillery. It wouldn't take much."

"If that's the case, could forensics tell if the poison was the same on the two cases?"

Peggy shrugged. "Theoretically. I'm not a medical examiner, but I believe the poison would be traceable. I'll have to do some research to verify that."

Al laughed. "Damn, Peggy. Why aren't you working for us?"

"There are thousands of cases of accidental poisoning every year, my friend. There are probably hundreds of intentional poisonings as well. But either medical examiners don't catch them or the symptoms are mistaken for something else. I don't think any police department has a botany professor on staff to look for plant poisonings."

"And here I only thought you had a green thumb! You're full of surprises."

"Thanks." She smiled at him.

"Like it wouldn't surprise me to find out you were somehow involved in the whole fiasco with the Warner case. It has all the earmarks, doesn't it? It involved a college prank, or what looked like a prank, that led to us discover he'd been poisoned with some kind of plant. Couple that with the fact that you found the body and you've been poking your nose in on the investigation. Someone might think you set the whole thing up."

Peggy pulled down the sun visor and opened the mirror before she took out her lipstick. "That sounds like a real stretch of the imagination to me. First of all, if I'd known Mark was poisoned by anemonin, I would've simply told you, wouldn't I?"

"I hope so." He laughed. "I think you're right. I think that might be reaching, even for you."

She laughed with him, but her heart was fluttering in her chest. He was closer to the truth than she hoped he'd ever know. She certainly wouldn't ever tell him.

"You know this puts your little assistant in a bad light." Al took out a pack of gum and offered her a stick. "The chances are the DA will do exactly what you've been wanting him to do and drop the charges on Mr. Cheever. But this new evidence gives us a more complete picture of the killer. Not only did she need opportunity at the shop to use the shovel, she needed prior knowledge about plants and how to use them. She needed to know something about Warner's habits, too."

Peggy thought about his accusations. He was right. She helped prove Mr. Cheever was innocent. But her confession put Keeley in the spotlight. "Keeley doesn't have the kind of information she'd need to poison Mark."

"And how hard would that be to get? She could probably go on the Internet and look it up. You said the killer wouldn't need sophisticated equipment. Ms. Prinz told us she asked Warner to meet her at the shop that night. All she had to do was administer the poison. Forensics should be able to tell us how long it was between when that happened and when he died."

"Is that what Jonas is thinking?"

Al wouldn't commit. "I'm not sure. But it's what *I'm* thinking. So what are the chances?"

Peggy didn't want to speculate on that yet. If the two poisoning cases were related, that could immediately change the picture for Keeley. What were the chances she knew Molly Stone? She changed the subject, and they talked about John and times past as they finished the trip to Columbia.

HAL SAMSON WAS WAITING ANXIOUSLY. He jumped up from his chair when he saw them. "I'm so glad you could come. Maybe there'll be an answer to this."

Al and Peggy sat down beside the doctor's cluttered desk. The office was sparsely furnished with older office equipment. The green-and-white tile floor was clean but worn. The place smelled strongly of disinfectant.

"Peggy told me what she knew about this case," Al said. "How about you filling in the rest, Doctor?"

Samson already had the file out. He passed Al and Peggy pictures of Molly Stone. "I'm sure Peggy told you that her husband brought her here presenting with unusual symptoms. Her skin was cold to the touch. She had almost no pulse. Her respiration was slow, almost failing."

"What made you think about poison?" Al asked as he took notes.

"Blood work showed she had a high level of anemonin in her system. We immediately called poison control as well as the CDC since we weren't sure how she came by the toxin. It wasn't injected. I learned this morning that it was in a bottle of root beer she had at the bank. The police assume someone put it there. They just don't know who."

"What time do they think it happened?" Peggy wondered.

"Her husband brought her the root beer at work right before closing, about five P.M. Apparently, she didn't drink it all. She sipped on it until she left the bank at six when he picked her up and they went out for dinner. It was their anniversary."

Peggy asked, "What bank did she work for?"

Samson looked through his papers. "Bank of America in downtown Columbia."

Al nodded when she looked at him. "It's too big a coincidence that both victims worked for Bank of America."

Samson was astonished. "Do you think there's a plot against Bank of America employees?"

"I guess I may be here in my official capacity after all," Al said. "I'm going to have to speak to the Columbia police. Maybe together we can find out what's going on."

Al used his cell phone to call the detective in charge of Molly Stone's case. Peggy and Dr. Samson accompanied him to the downtown precinct, against his better judgment.

"You'll need us," Peggy argued. "Besides, I didn't come all this way to sit in a cafeteria and wait for you."

"And you wouldn't know there was a link between these two cases without us," Samson agreed with her while he looked through the information she brought about Mark Warner.

Detective Bather Ramsey was less than welcoming when they arrived at the precinct. "I think we can probably figure out who killed Ms. Stone without help from Charlotte, Detective McDonald." His pug face was angry and hostile.

"Look here, Ramsey," Al started, "I don't want to solve your homicide for you. I was hoping to get your help solving *our* case of poisoning. We had one the same day as yours. It also involved a Bank of America employee."

Ramsey's expression changed to astonishment. "Well, I'll be damned." He glanced at Peggy. "Pardon my French, ma'am."

"So you see, we have something in common," Al continued. "But we didn't know our vic was poisoned until yesterday. You have a head start on us. Anything you could tell me about your poisoning could help with ours."

"What did you think happened to your vic if you didn't think he was poisoned?" Ramsey asked, looking at the information Peggy brought about Warner.

Al explained the circumstances of the bank exec's death. "A CSI finally brought the information to light for us. Now I find out you had a poisoning on the same day, same kind of poison."

Ramsey nodded and picked up the phone. "I think I should call in my captain on this. If anyone is going to contact the bank, it should be him."

While Ramsey was on the phone with the captain, Al called Lieutenant Rimer to let him know what was going on.

Peggy and Dr. Samson sat together and compared notes. Peggy wished she had both sets of police files to look at. What she had wasn't complete. She couldn't get the whole picture from partial facts.

"Do you think the poison could be traced?" Samson asked her.

"If there was a random sample to go with," she replied. "We'd need that to compare to the others."

"A conspiracy to kill bank employees in two states is a big deal," Samson considered. "They'll probably call in the FBI."

"I don't think it's that kind of conspiracy. I hope they don't jump to conclusions that way."

But the captain decided to call in a bank liaison who would work with them on the poisonings. The liaison asked them not to call in the FBI until they had more information. He didn't want to start a panic among the bank's employees.

They all got in a large black police van and went to look at the bank branch where Molly worked. They walked through the procedure she would've used for closing the day she worked. They looked through the surveillance video footage between the time when her husband brought the root beer and when she left the bank with him. Only a handful of customers came into the bank during that time. Molly handled three of them at her window. Two women and one man.

"Unless the husband brought the root beer with the poison in it," the captain said, "the drink had to be poisoned here by one of these people."

"What about the people she worked with?" Al asked him.

"We questioned them in depth several times. None of them seem to have any motive to kill her," Ramsey answered.

"And their psychological profiles don't add up that way," the BofA liaison added. "We carefully screen all our employees."

"Which brought us back to the husband." Ramsey stuck his hands in his pockets. "But no matter how we looked at this boy, he didn't fit the pattern for someone who murders his wife. His prints were all over the root beer bottle. There wasn't a life insurance policy. We all felt he just didn't have it in him."

"What about the bottling plant?" Al glanced up from his notes.

"We checked that out. They dumped hundreds of gallons of root beer for us. Not a tainted bottle in them. Except for this one." The captain answered his cell phone as he finished speaking.

"That leaves us with these three people," Ramsey finished. "We identified two of them. These two." He pointed to the man and one woman on the tape. "Neither one of them had any connection to the victim."

"What about this one?" Al asked the tape operator to stop. "What's she doing over there anyway? Nobody needs to lean in that close."

"We think she could be our suspect. Unfortunately, we can't ID her. She came in and asked for change for a twenty. Notice she's wearing gloves, so we can't even get fingerprints from the twenty. Not that it would matter with that much money and that many prints without a comparison. If this is what she really looks like, she's tall, long dark hair, slender build."

Al looked at Peggy. "Could be Ms. Prinz."

"What was your system of delivery on the poison in Charlotte?" The captain finished his phone call and questioned Al.

"We're not sure yet. CSI is still working on it. Could be root beer for all we know. We *do* have a suspect who matches this woman on the tape."

"Does she have some beef with Bank of America?" Ramsey asked.

"No. Her thing was the man." Al's face suddenly lit up. "We need to check out a few facts about this. If our suspect was responsible for Ms. Stone's death as well, maybe they had something else in common."

"Such as . . . the man?" Ramsey followed his thinking.

"Exactly."

"Let's take a look at Ms. Stone's phone calls. See if she had any personal or professional contact with your victim." Ramsey took out his cell phone. "What was his name again?"

"Mark Warner. He was a senior executive vice president in Charlotte."

Peggy didn't like the way the conversation had changed. She thought it was a mistake to consider the two poisonings as a conspiracy against the bank. But she knew it was a mistake to try to pin both of them on Keeley.

She had to admit the woman in the video looked like her assistant, at least from the back. She could only hope they couldn't find any record of Keeley being in Columbia that day. Not that it would take much to make the police feel they had a case against her. Keeley's confession had seen to that.

14

Carnation

Botanical: *Dianthus caryophyllus*
Family: Caryophyllaceae

The name comes from the Greek word di, *meaning of Zeus, and* anthos, *meaning a flower. It was called* dianthus *by the Greek botanist Theopharastus, meaning divine flower. It is believed that carnations can tell fortunes. In Korea, three carnations are placed in a girl's hair. If the bottom flower dies first, she will be miserable her entire life. If the top one dies first, her later years will be hard. Her younger years will be hard if the middle flower dies first.*

THE NEWS HEADLINE in the *Charlotte Observer* on Monday morning told the city a judge had dismissed the charges against Joseph Cheever. He was released into his daughter's custody. Local television news showed the father and daughter leaving the Mecklenburg County Jail hospital facility. Joe Cheever was in a wheelchair, said to be recovering from a stroke. His daughter was tearful and thanked the police for releasing her father.

Peggy watched on a small television set in the faculty lounge at Queens. She was glad for Mr. Cheever but apprehensive about Keeley. She knew the police from Columbia and Charlotte had worked through the weekend to prove her assistant murdered two people.

Obviously, the evidence wasn't forthcoming. Or the police were taking their time, making sure they had the right person. It looked bad when they arrested someone only to find out it was the wrong person. They probably wouldn't let it happen again in this case.

And that was why it was imperative she find out who *really* killed Mark and Molly. If she waited too long, the police would have a case difficult to dispute. She knew Al would do the best he could to find the truth. But the Charlotte police were desperate. Everyone from the mayor down was leaning on them. With the added involvement from South Carolina, they needed the right suspect fast.

By now, the police knew if there was a connection between the dead woman in Columbia and the dead man in Charlotte. Since they were still pursuing Keeley, she guessed they'd found one that involved her.

It wasn't a large stretch of the imagination to link the two deaths. Once the method was discovered, just the fact that the dead woman worked for Bank of America made Peggy suspicious. Mark managed several affairs at once in his home office. It was possible he'd managed to conduct a few with women in other offices. The question for her seemed to be, why Molly? If Keeley or anyone else wanted to kill one of Mark's women, why would it be Molly? The others were closer, simpler to kill.

Keeley called her early Sunday morning to tell her the police were searching the apartment she shared with another girl on campus. They confiscated every piece of glassware and two houseplants they found. Peggy advised her assistant to call Hunter Ollsen.

What needed to be done to create anemonin took equipment and specialized knowledge. Keeley didn't have either. But who did? Besides herself, of course. She finished her blackberry tea and left the lounge to go to her classroom. She gave her freshman class a complex quiz requiring line drawings of plant parts. It took the entire hour and gave her plenty of time to think.

If she couldn't find some clue that would lead to a

search for a workplace or utensils to tie to the making of the poison, she was afraid the circumstantial evidence against Keeley could prove insurmountable.

The class bell rang, startling her from her thoughts. Unhappy faces piled papers on her desk as students grumbled while they left her class.

"That wasn't fair, Dr. Lee," one student protested. "I wasn't ready."

"We've been going over this material for six weeks," Peggy responded. "If you don't know it now, maybe you should do a little more studying."

Gathering up the papers, she put everything into her backpack. The ride over made her knee a little sore but not too bad. It was good to be on the bike again. Taxis were fine for late nights or important meetings. If anything could spur her into getting the work done on the old Rolls, this was it. She hated being dependent on other people to take her places, though she was grateful so many were willing to help her.

She hadn't heard from Steve since the night they'd stolen the body from the crematorium. She wasn't surprised. Something like that would be hard enough to take with a person you knew well. She and Steve would probably never have that opportunity. Still, it was a pleasant experience being with him. In some ways, it gave her hope for the future.

"Hey, Peggy."

She was surprised to see Al standing beside her desk. "Good morning. What brings you by?"

"I wanted to give you an update on our progress. I feel like I owe it to you since you brought the cases together." He smiled at her and picked up her backpack. "Any place around here to get coffee?"

Peggy was a little suspicious that he'd take time away from the investigation to update her on anything, despite her help. When he mentioned coffee, she was immediately on guard. "Sure. We can have coffee in the cafeteria."

They walked together through the halls in awkward

silence. Students rushed by them, and announcements grated over the intercom. The aroma of lunch being prepared heralded the cafeteria before they came to the double doors.

Al filled his cup with coffee and waited for her to find a seat. "I'm glad I had a chance to talk with you about this. I wasn't sure if you'd be here today."

She pulled out a hard plastic chair and sat down at an empty table. "Al, you're the worst liar I've ever known. You can stop feeling bad about whatever it is and tell me why you're here."

He shook his head. "I wasn't lying. I came by to talk to you about the case."

She raised her eyebrow in question.

"I *did*. Not to update you exactly, but to ask for your help. I know you don't work for the department, and I know Ms. Prinz is your friend. But we have to find out what happened to these people. You might be able to help us."

"That's all you had to say. But how will you know any information I give you isn't biased? Even if I knew Keeley was guilty of something, I wouldn't be likely to share it with you."

"I know you better than that, Peggy. You want to know the truth as much as we do. Even if your friend is involved."

She sighed and folded her hands around her cup of tea. "That's true. But what can I tell you that you don't already know?"

"First of all, what I'm going to tell you can't be shared with anyone else. Not your friend or her lawyer. The information is part of the ongoing investigation. It has to stay confidential until we decide whether it will be used as part of the case."

"All right," she agreed.

"It looks like Warner and Molly Stone did have a thing going on. There were calls back and forth from both their homes and offices. Her husband told us she went out of town one weekend a month for business. Her supervisor told us the bank never scheduled those weekends. We have people still checking for receipts and confirmation that the two of them were away together, but it's only a matter of time."

Peggy wasn't surprised. "The husband didn't suspect?"

"No. At least he says he didn't. The problem is, he's already been questioned about the poisoning. The police in Columbia tore his home and office apart looking for proof that he made the poison and gave it to his wife. So far as they can tell, he's clean."

"So that leaves you with Keeley."

He nodded as he swallowed his coffee. "Pretty much. We already know she was at the shop. She had opportunity to administer the poison, wait for it to work, then whack him in the head with the shovel."

"Why bother?" she asked. "If she knew enough to poison him, she had to know he was going to die."

"We figure it was a last-minute thing. It wasn't enough that he was dying. Kind of the way a killer will continue shooting or stabbing a victim even after they're dead. Rage. Frustration. Maybe the poison wasn't hands-on enough for her. I'm not a shrink."

"What do you want me to tell you?"

Al got to the point. "How long before Warner would've felt the effects of the poison?"

"It would all depend on the dosage. Probably an hour or so. A small amount would've taken longer and had less effect. A large dose would've taken him down right away." She finished her tea and waited for him to write down the information. "Has the ME decided what the poison came in?"

"The last thing he ate was a Snickers bar washed down with a bunch of coffee. We're not sure if both were poisoned or just one."

"It seems to me with the time frame involved, the poison had to be given before he got to my shop. If he walked from his office to the Potting Shed, then collapsed after he spoke with Keeley, he probably ingested the poison at his office that night."

"Or she gave it to him when she met him at your shop."

Peggy disagreed. "If we believe Mr. Cheever, he went in right after Keeley ran out and found Mark on the floor. There was no blood yet. If she poisoned him, why wouldn't she wait to be sure he was dead? Or hit him with the shovel when he was down? If you're right, Al, and using the shovel was done in rage, she would've done it before she left."

He stopped writing halfway through what she said and shook his head. "I think we have to assume Mr. Cheever was too drunk to notice whether or not Warner was bleeding."

"Did the alcohol keep the blood from getting on his clothes and hands? You know yourself there was no blood on him. But he had to handle Mark to get his watch and wallet. There was no way for him to do it without picking up a few bloodstains."

"I don't know how it happened," he admitted. "What I need you to tell me is what we're looking for as far as creating the poison. Could she pop this stuff into the microwave? How complicated would it be?"

Peggy took his notebook and scribbled down a few ideas. "No, she couldn't just pop it in the microwave. The temperature would have to be exact. She'd have to know what to do with it to obtain the pure anemonin from the protoanemonin. Anything less would've created drastic, immediate results. Not the kind found in Mark or Molly."

"Does Ms. Prinz have that kind of knowledge, Peggy?" He fixed her with an intent stare like he was looking for anything that would give away her feelings.

"In my opinion, no. Not only that, she doesn't have the right temperament. Look at all the famous poisonings. All of the perpetrators had something in common. They were sneaky, devious people. They wouldn't have asked Mark to come to the Potting Shed for a showdown. But as you said, I'm not a shrink. That's only my opinion."

Al lumbered slowly to his feet. "Thanks, Peggy. I'll let you know what we find out."

"Was Mark's body released to his wife again?"

"Yeah. He was cremated this morning. I read somewhere his memorial service is later today. Why?"

"I thought I might pay my respects." She smiled at him. "There may be a few more of his conquests there. I'll let you know if I see anyone suspicious."

MARK WARNER'S MEMORIAL SERVICE was held in Myers Park Presbyterian Church. The crowd was so large, police officers had to direct traffic to allow visitors to park on the street. Van loads of flowers were deposited in the chapel until it was overflowing. The remainder were left in the adjacent cemetery and on the church steps.

Peggy was glad she rode her bike. It was easy to leave it at the bike rack near the entrance to the church. Her black suit was no less formal for wearing slacks that allowed her the freedom to pedal.

She pushed her black hat firmly down on her head and stuck a large pearl-headed hatpin in as she walked into the church. It was the same hat she wore to John's funeral. She'd wanted to throw it away after it was over, but her mother's thrifty upbringing wouldn't let her.

The service began, and the talking ceased. At the front of the church was a large portrait of the dead man. His teak coffin was resplendent with large brass handles and covered with a maze of flowers. Friends whispered that Julie put Mark's ashes in the more traditional coffin. She couldn't stand the idea of an urn.

The Warner children and the grieving widow walked to the coffin to lay a final white rose on it. Peggy couldn't believe how small and pale Julie looked in her elegant black suit. She had a firm grip on both children's hands. It was impossible to decipher the expression on her face. The tiny pillbox hat she wore was very chic. Even in mourning, she set the example for the other widows in Charlotte who would follow.

The service was brief. The crowd followed the pallbearers into the cemetery to bury their friend. Peggy looked at the faces of the women around her, especially the tall ones with long, dark hair. It was hard to believe how partial Mark was to that type with his own wife so tiny and blond.

She saw Ronda and Bob McGee talking to Julie. It would've been interesting to hear what was said between the two women. If Ronda was right and Julie knew she was seeing Mark, the looks alone would be more virulent than the poison that killed him. Peggy wondered if Ronda was back with Bob for the funeral or if they'd managed to reconcile. There was a lot to lose for both of them. A divorce would hurt Ronda as much as it would Bob.

Peggy remembered what Ronda told her about being certain Julie was the one who threatened her on the phone. Adding poison to the equation of Mark's death made it possible that Julie could have killed her husband. Anyone could hit a man who was already unconscious on the floor. Of course, she had the perfect alibi. The entire household knew she was home that night with a sick child.

She watched Julie give the two children to Emma. From the look on the housekeeper's face, she could tell how devoted she was to the mother and children. She studied the group from the Warner household with new eyes. Was it possible they weren't as innocent of the situation as they seemed? The police checked out Molly Stone's husband. But what about Mark Warner's wife?

Peggy saw Julie break down into sobs at the graveside. A dozen hands reached out to take her arm, give her a handkerchief, ease her grief. If she didn't love her husband and was capable of killing him, she was a good actress. Remembering how she'd been at the shop, wanting to see the place he was killed, Peggy considered she was probably reaching. Keeley was so close to being arrested for the murder. Her mind was grasping at straws.

She turned away from the rest of the service, commending the body to the earth. It was still painful for her to hear those words. She didn't think any amount of time could make it less. Instead, she studied the flowers and arrangements sent to the memorial. Most were from well-known florists in the city. A few were actually flown in from out of state.

The flowers chosen were always more for color, consistency, and longevity than for meaning. There were daisies and forget-me-nots together in an arrangement. With Mark's reputation, that was a joke. Faithful and loyal love wasn't a priority in his life.

There were plenty of gladioli. Again, sincerity wasn't a virtue either. Someone sent a huge spray of white carnations and red chrysanthemums. *Pure love. Admiration.* Yellow mums and striped carnations would have been more appropriate. *Slighted love. Disdain and rejection. I can't be with you.*

A nice big pot of pansies was appropriate. *Thoughtful recollection.* Their card said they were from a group of people at Bank of America.

She looked up and noticed the service was over. People were paying their respects to the widow and wandering back to their cars. Her quest for yet another Warner woman seemed over, too. If another woman existed, she didn't notice her being there.

She wondered if Keeley or Molly would've come if the circumstances were different. Even being sure the wife didn't know what was going on, a mistress would have to be fairly brazen to come to her lover's funeral. In Ronda's case, she had no choice if she wanted to keep up appearances.

An odd wreath caught Peggy's eye as she turned to go. She wasn't able to see it with the crowd around the grave. In all the funerals she'd attended, she'd never seen another one like it.

The majority of it consisted of withered flowers. None of the other arrangements were in this state. It wasn't caused by the weather. She looked at the tag. The flowers came from a reputable local florist, an acquaintance of hers. She couldn't believe he'd been that careless.

The wreath was dotted with anemones, yellow carnations, and columbines. In the language of flowers, the wreath was a large proclamation of rejected love and pain. She couldn't believe anyone would send such a thing to a funeral. But whoever was responsible knew the truth and might have been the one who put the columbine in Mark's pocket. She looked for a card, but there was only the florist's tag.

"It's an interesting arrangement, don't you think?"

Peggy looked up quickly and smiled at the widow. "Yes. It's surprising."

Julie touched the wreath with her gloved fingers. "I wonder what someone was trying to say. Or maybe the florist just had a bad day."

"That's probably it." Peggy took Julie's hand in hers. "I'm sorry for your loss. Losing a husband is a terrible thing. I'm so glad my son was grown when I lost mine. He was a great source of comfort for me. If I can help in any way, please let me know."

"Thank you." Julie watched as the cemetery workers began to cover the coffin. "There are times when I can't believe he's gone. I guess I'm still in shock."

"I'm sure. Especially with all the difficulty trying to find out what happened to him."

"Yes. That's been hard. It was bad enough thinking some homeless man killed him for his shoes. But now to find out one of his girlfriends did it." A delicate shudder ran through her diminutive frame.

"One of them?" Peggy seized on her words. "Was there more than one?"

Julie smiled. "My husband led a full and active life, Mrs. Lee. He was a very vigorous man. I couldn't keep up with his needs. We had an understanding. He was a good husband and a good father."

"You're a better woman than me. If I'd found out my husband was sleeping around, I'm not sure what I would've done. I guess it's my Irish temper. John would've had a bad headache from the frying pan I hit him with, if nothing else. Men can be such a burden."

"That's true. But it's the way God intended it. Women

are supposed to be chaste, except when they're bearing children. Men don't have those restrictions. I suppose it's all part of the infinite plan."

Peggy agreed in principle. "I wish you well, Julie." She looked down at the green grass still untouched by frost beneath the two-hundred-year-old oak tree. "Oh look, a clover. I'll pick it for you for luck."

Julie stayed her hand. "That's a five-leaf clover, Mrs. Lee. Those are unlucky. Only the four-leaf kind brings good fortune."

"Well, you don't need that then, do you?" Peggy smiled at her. "Take care, Julie."

Making her way back to the bike rack, Peggy dialed the number for the Potting Shed on her cell phone. "I have something I have to check into, Selena. Can you watch the shop for a little while longer?"

"HEY PEGGY! I HAVEN'T SEEN you in ages! What have you been doing with yourself?"

"Hi, Mort." Peggy closed the door to the tiny florist shop in the East End. The scent of carnations, roses, and mums was overpowering. "I've been busy as always. How about you?"

"Me, too." The man continued working on a large floral wedding arrangement. "What can I get for you?"

"I saw some of your work today." She wandered through the shop, looking at the huge striped tiger lilies and masses of baby's breath. "It was a little strange."

He laughed. "But it made you look at the tag, right? *That's* what's important. Are you talking about the Simpsons' baby shower? That cradle made out of bachelor's buttons was an inspiration. The problem was getting so many pale pink flowers. I had to order on-line from a dozen hothouses."

"I wish I'd seen that, Mort. But I was talking about the wreath at the Warner funeral."

"Oh. That." He sighed and lost his smile. "You know

I didn't come up with the idea for that monstrosity. But you do what the customer wants, right?"

"Right." She touched the velvet petals on a rose. "There wasn't a sympathy card on it. Who was the customer?"

"Now, Peggy. You know I can't tell you. Some of my customers rely on my discretion. If people thought I'd take their orders and tell everyone who had them made up, I'd lose a lot of cheating husbands and unfaithful wives."

She laughed as she neared the counter where he was working. "Like a lawyer or a doctor, right?"

"Exactly. I have a reputation to protect."

"Did you ever do business with Mark Warner?"

"I guess it won't hurt to admit it since he's not gonna be much of a customer anymore. But, yeah, he was a big spender. Liked to send the ladies plenty of flowers."

Peggy snapped the end off a red carnation and handed it to him. "What about Mrs. Warner?"

Mort put the flower in place on the arrangement. "If you tell anyone else, I'll deny it."

"So she's bought flowers here before?" She held her breath waiting for his answer.

"Only this one time." He snapped the end off another carnation. "The woman knew what she wanted. I think she *knew* what those flowers meant."

"I owe you a cup of coffee, Mort. Good luck with the wedding."

"Just remember," he said as she was leaving, "you didn't hear it from me."

PEGGY MET WITH AL for a few minutes while he ate a late lunch. She told him everything she suspected about Julie Warner, including what Ronda told her about the threatening phone call.

Al ate his Reuben sandwich and listened politely. Then he pointed his pickle at her and blasted her theory. "I can't believe you were married to a detective for twenty years and don't have any faith in us getting the job done."

"I have faith in you, Al, but—"

"But you're still sneaking around pretending to be a private detective or something!" He took a bite of his pickle. "We know about the threatening phone call to Ronda McGee. We checked it out, but we couldn't trace it. As for all this flower business, I know you don't think the lieutenant is going to listen to a bunch of stuff about funeral wreaths having meaning."

"It's no more ridiculous than making poison from anemones," she argued. "You may not understand it, but it makes sense to people who do. It would be like saying a threat in French was less dangerous than a threat in English!"

"Don't you think we considered Julie Warner as a suspect? We checked her out. She was home with a sick child. A housekeeper saw her there all night, and she talked to her child's doctor at about the same time as the murder. We're not incompetent."

Peggy tapped her fingers on the desk. "The housekeeper would do anything for her. She hated Mark and felt like he took advantage of Julie. Lying to police isn't that big a deal. As far as talking to her doctor, she could've called him while she was standing over her husband's dead body."

Al stared at her. "You really hate this woman, don't you?"

"I don't hate her at all," she defended. "I'm looking for the truth."

"The truth that doesn't involve your friend."

"I know Keeley is innocent. Can you say the same about Julie?"

He wiped his hands on a napkin. "You see, that's what separates a detective from everybody else. I'm surprised you didn't realize it sooner. A detective is objective. I don't have a friend involved in this. If I did, I'd exclude myself from the case. You're too emotional, Peggy. You can't see the facts clearly."

She got to her feet. "Thanks for listening anyway. I have to go to the shop."

Al didn't try to keep her, shaking his head as she walked to the door. "No hard feelings?"

She smiled at him. "No. I know you mean well. You've got a blob of mustard on your chin. You might want to wipe it off before you see Jonas again. Next time, get an extra napkin."

SAM WAS AT THE Potting Shed with Hunter, Selena, and Keeley. They were sitting behind the counter while a few customers walked through the store. Peggy wasn't sure if she should tell them her theory about Julie. It was likely they'd be *too* receptive. After all, as Al pointed out, they were emotionally involved.

As she walked toward them, Steve came in through the front door. The lights in the courtyard were flickering on in the gloomy twilight. Another storm front was getting ready to pounce on the city. The weather warmed in anticipation, but the depressing atmosphere weighed heavily on them all.

"I think we need to have a party," Sam said, giving Peggy his chair. "Hey, Steve. How's it going?"

"Fine." Steve went to stand beside Peggy, squeezing her shoulder. "What's with all the gloom and doom?"

Peggy smiled at him, a little zing zooming through her at his touch. Still, she wondered why he hadn't called.

"The police are about to arrest Keeley," Hunter told him. "My car had a flat, and I chipped my nail trying to change it."

"That's nothing," Selena told them. "I had a man try to return two hundred pounds of fertilizer today. He insisted it smelled bad and wanted some that smelled good."

Peggy laughed. "What did you do?"

"I sent Keeley to the drugstore for some baby powder, then I sprinkled it into the fertilizer. He was happy. I couldn't tell any difference, but whatever works, right?"

"I hate to top everybody's bad day," Keeley added. "But my lawyer thinks the police are about to arrest me, and they probably have an airtight case so they don't look stupid again. I think I get the prize for the worst day. We won't go into the fact that they ripped my apartment into shreds looking for evidence. Then they descended on my car. They're like locusts."

Everyone sympathized with her. Peggy offered to take them all out for pizza if they'd help close up the shop. "Maybe we can sit down and come up with something brilliant to turn all of this around."

Hunter shook her head. "It's too late for my nail, Peggy. And I'll still have to get a new tire. Have you seen those potholes on Trade Street? I was lucky they didn't swallow my car."

It only took five minutes to close the shop after the last customer left. Hunter offered to drive them to a pizza place on Park Road. They all piled into her SUV, ignoring the undersized spare tire in the front.

Steve sat beside Peggy with his arm around her. "Are you okay?"

"I'm fine, thanks." She smiled at him. "Just hungry." *And wondering where you've been.*

The restaurant was deserted since it was Monday night and they didn't have a large-screen TV for football. The group from the Potting Shed didn't mind. They took up two big tables and had plenty to discuss.

"What's next?" Sam asked after they ordered their pizzas and beer.

Hunter shrugged. "Janice gives Keeley the best defense she can in the circumstances. We can't manufacture an alibi. Keeley's already confessed to being there with Warner that night."

"What about his other women?" Selena poured a glass of beer. "Sorry, Keeley, but we know he was a three- or four-timing son of a bitch. And that's not counting his wife."

"Peggy's been looking into that," Hunter answered. "So far nothing's turned up. As far as the police are concerned, Keeley is the number one suspect for the poisoning."

"I was out of town for a few days. I can't believe things progressed so quickly," Steve reflected. "It's odd that the Warners' cat was poisoned, too."

Peggy took a sip of her water. Steve had been out of

town. That's why he didn't call. Of course, he could've *told* her he was going out of town. *Hush! You don't know him that well!* Then it hit her. "What did you say?"

"The cat was poisoned," he repeated, glancing at the group as they stared back at him. "What?"

"What kind of poison?" Sam asked. "Why didn't you tell us?"

"I didn't think about it," Steve answered. "And I don't know what kind of poison. I didn't send a sample away. The housekeeper wasn't interested beyond the fact that he was dead."

"What happened to the cat?" Peggy wanted to know.

"I gave him to the housekeeper. She said she was going to bury him in the backyard."

Peggy nodded. "Then I guess we'll have to dig him up."

15

Chrysanthemum

Botanical: *Chrysanthemum morifolium*
Family: Asteraceae
Common Name: Mum

The Chrysanthemum *genus is made up of 150 species, including the common daisy. Named by Carl Linnaeus, it means golden yellow flower. The name is derived from the Greek words* chrysos *meaning* gold, *and* anthos, *meaning* flower. *Confucius wrote about chrysanthemums in 500 B.C. According to Chinese feng shui, chrysanthemums bring happiness to your home. Chrysanthemum petals are eaten in salads to increase longevity.*

"WHEN YOU SAID dig him up," Steve whispered, "I didn't think you meant *dig him up*."

"Do you know any other way to test what kind of poison is in the body?" Peggy asked as she led the way across the fence that separated the Warners' property from their neighbors. She handed him the shovel and the plastic garbage bag.

"Peggy, this is trespassing and probably other legal terms I don't know." As he finished speaking, the rain that threatened all day began to fall. It didn't bother with a few drops here and there. Instead, it crushed them in heavy sheets.

She pulled her dark hood up over the brown wool cap she'd used to hide her hair. It didn't matter. After only a few seconds, she was soaked to the skin. "We won't get caught. This rain actually works to our benefit. No one's going to be out on a night like this."

He jumped over the fence and offered his hand to help her across. "No one except us."

They crept through the back edges of the estate. Peggy could only hope the housekeeper buried the cat close to the house. There was too much property to search everywhere looking for a small grave. Fortunately, it would be fresh, the ground only recently disturbed. Even in the rain they should be able to find the spot.

"Where do you suggest we start looking?" Steve wondered as they approached the guesthouse and garage behind the main house. There were lights on in the windows of the big house, but the two smaller buildings were dark.

"I'm hoping she buried him in the garden. It makes sense. The ground is soft, and she wouldn't be disturbing the sod. I know the Warners' pay a fortune to have their lawn taken care of."

He shrugged, rain dripping down his face. "That makes as much sense as anything."

"The only thing is we'll have to get up close to the house. They probably have the drapes drawn, so we should be safe. We'll have to be careful how we use the flashlight."

"Okay. You use the flashlight, and I'll dig where you tell me to dig."

Peggy smiled at him. "Thanks for coming with me, Steve. After stealing Mark's body, I wasn't sure if you'd be up for this. Not many people would be willing to go and dig up a dead cat."

"That's not how it sounded to me. I thought Sam was going to hit me when I offered to come with you. All of them wanted to dig up the dead cat."

"They're college students, except for Hunter."

"You must be right," he said. "She was the only one who didn't want to be here."

They walked around the garage and found themselves in the beginning of the formal garden area. It was nicely manicured with carefully laid out paths. Statues and topiaries were illuminated, helping to show the edges of the winding trails.

"There must be an acre of garden." Steve stood still in the rain and looked at the yard. "How are we going to find it?"

"There won't be a lot of digging going on in the garden this time of year. I'm sure they have it cleaned up. Julie's very particular. We should be able to see any place the soil's been disturbed. It'll be easy."

An hour later, they were still looking. The lights went off in the house, but the rain was still falling. A cold wind began to blow in from the north, creating tiny icicles in the trees. The decorative lights picked them out, making prisms in the ice.

Peggy was on her hands and knees, shining the flashlight between rosebushes and birdbaths. A few spots looked promising but ended up being new plantings. Apparently there was more fall work than she'd anticipated.

"I don't know if we can find it like this," Steve said. "Maybe I could ask Emma where she buried the cat. I could tell her I need it for research or something."

"You'd say anything to go home right now, wouldn't you?"

"Yes, ma'am. Even my goose bumps are frozen and wet. And I don't see how we'll find it in all of this. It's like a maze."

Peggy laughed. "Don't worry. We'll find it. And for the record, I don't think anyone would respond well to you asking to do research on their dead cat."

"It was just a thought. My brain is mostly frozen, so it might not have been the *best* thought but—"

"I think I found it!" She interrupted his misery to point the flashlight at a small mound of red clay beside the statue of an angel reading a book. A purple mum was in full flower beside it. "There's even a little cross. This has to be it."

Steve hoped so and applied the shovel carefully. The ground was soft and wet as Peggy predicted. It only took a moment to dig up a small wood box. "Either they bury their wine or this could be the cat."

"Let's open it." Peggy dropped down beside it, already too wet and muddy to care. "It's the right size. How does it open?"

"It slides." He demonstrated, pushing the flat panel open. "And voilà! A dead cat."

She looked at the partially decomposed animal. It was wrapped in a yellow scarf. "Is it the right cat?"

"Looks like it to me."

"Are you only saying that so we can leave?" She glanced up at him.

"No, of course not. It's the same cat. Can we leave now?"

"Steve!"

"Peggy, I'm in a stranger's backyard digging up their dead cat. Why would I bother lying to you now? If it isn't the *right* cat, you'll make me come back again. Trust me. It's the same cat."

She closed the wood panel and struggled out of the mud to get to her feet. "Okay. Let's cover it up and get out of here."

Before they could move, the back door to the house opened. The bright yellow light from inside alerted them. Steve dropped down to the ground beside Peggy, putting his arm around her. Peggy snapped off the flashlight. They crouched down close to the bushes, hoping they wouldn't be noticed.

A tiny figure in a dark poncho walked down the path from the house. The fairy lights in the garden illuminated her footsteps. She walked by close enough to touch Steve and Peggy, but the darkness protected them. Not wasting any time in the terrible weather, she opened the guesthouse and went inside.

"Let's get out of here," Steve whispered. He made sure Peggy was out of the way and closed the hole in a few seconds. "Thank God. Next time you ask me to do something with dead bodies, remind me to say no."

She kissed his cold, wet cheek. "I will."

They ran quietly out of the yard the same way they went in, careful to stay clear of the guesthouse, where one light burned in the window. Peggy felt safe once they put the garage between them and the house. They climbed the fence, sliding on the icy mud as they reached the neighbor's yard. Steve took her arm, and they ran the rest of the way back to the Saturn.

Once they got there, Peggy felt guilty about the mess she was about to make in his car. She hesitated after the door was open. Maybe she should walk home. It wasn't that far. He'd never get all the mud out if she sat down.

"Don't worry about it." Steve pushed himself behind the wheel. The muddy shovel was already in the backseat. "Autobell does a fine job of cleaning the car."

She laughed as she got in. "Am I that transparent?"

He leaned close and kissed her. "Maybe. Or maybe it's that I feel I've known you my whole life."

"It's possible, you know. I'm older than you."

"Good thing." He started the car. "If you were younger, I couldn't keep up with you."

It took two days to get the results back from the independent lab. The cat was poisoned with anemonin.

"But to really compare the poison in Mark Warner, Molly Stone, and the cat, we'll need the source where the poison was created." Peggy put the test results down on her kitchen table.

"I'm not breaking into the Warners' house," Steve said. "I draw the limit at moving dead bodies around the city."

"I could probably get some buddies, and we could break in," Sam suggested.

"Thanks for the offer." Peggy smiled at him. "But it wouldn't do us any good. Even this lab test doesn't prove enough for Al to get a search warrant. Without one, the evidence is useless. Julie would go free."

"What do we need?" Sam grabbed a donut from the cabinet. "What does it take to get a search warrant?"

Peggy refilled Steve's cup of coffee. "It takes hard evidence to make a judge decide they have a reason to search a place."

Shakespeare started barking. When Paul walked in through the kitchen door, all discussion of the murder ceased. His blue police uniform was enough to remind them of the obstacles they faced trying to prove that Julie killed her husband.

"Ever have the feeling people are talking about you?" Paul wondered as he walked into the silent room. "What's up?"

Sam looked at Peggy and shrugged. "Nothing. We were just talking."

"About what?" Paul poured himself a cup of coffee. "If I didn't know better, I'd think you were planning to buy drugs and guns and transport them across the state line."

"That's ridiculous." Sam stuffed another donut in his mouth.

"Good morning, Paul. Are you using your police radar on us?" Peggy took over the conversation before Sam said anything else.

"It wouldn't take much." Paul looked at the three of them. "You all look guilty as hell. I don't know what you've done . . . and I don't want to know. I came by to see how you were doing, Mom."

"I'm fine, sweetie. Would you like a donut?" Peggy kissed his cheek. "How are you and Mai doing?"

He was obviously irritated by the question. "How did you know? Never mind. You seem to have your own little spy network."

"I wasn't spying," she defended. "If you don't want people to know about the two of you, maybe you shouldn't kiss her right outside my door."

"Oh that." Red stained his cheeks as he took a donut.

"We'd be doing a lot better if she didn't feel like she had to hide everything you say and do from me."

"I have to go." Steve kissed Peggy lightly and shook Sam's hand. "Let me know if you need anything. Nice seeing you again, Paul."

"You, too, Steve," Paul said around a mouthful of donut.

Shakespeare started barking again, and the kitchen door burst open. "Don't worry," Hunter told them. "I can get you out of this. Don't say anything. Even if they caught you in the act, they'll have to prove what you were doing."

Paul swallowed the rest of his donut and glanced at his mother. "Is there something you'd like to tell me?"

"Hunter always comes into a room like that." Sam got up and put his hand over his sister's mouth. "We're going, too, Peggy. See you at the shop."

Shakespeare whined and turned around several times before he got comfortable again on the rug in front of the door. The kitchen was silent except for the ticking of the clock near the pantry and the hissing of the coffeepot.

"I need to get to the shop." Peggy got slowly to her feet. The adventure in the Warners' backyard made her knee sore again. It was going to take her a few extra minutes to ride uptown this morning.

"Mom, you act like this uniform makes me some kind of monster. I know you're trying to help Keeley. I could help, if you let me."

She thought about the dead cat in the box that was now buried in her backyard. "I know the uniform puts restrictions on what you can do, Paul. If I do something that's legal, I'll let you know."

"Mom! You're going to end up in jail *with* Keeley if you're not careful."

"I've been careful." She kissed his cheek. "Thanks for worrying about me."

"I don't want to see your name on the arrest sheet."

"You won't. Or if you do, you'll know it was done in good faith."

Paul wrestled with his conscience and his duty. He sat

down at the kitchen table and asked her to join him. "Tell me what you've got."

"Are you sure?" Peggy pulled out a chair.

"I'm sure. Maybe I can help."

She told him everything she knew about the murder, including her new information about the cat. She didn't go into detail about moving Warner's body from the crematorium or digging up the cat. She explained that Steve worked on the cat and left it at that.

Unfortunately, Paul jumped on the legitimate claim of how Steve came across the information about the cat. "We could use that to get a search warrant. If nothing else, it could be for the good of the family. Someone could be trying to poison the rest of them."

Peggy sighed. She'd tried to keep the rest away from him. "It's not quite that simple. Steve didn't send the sample away the *first* time he looked at the cat. He knew it was poison, but he didn't know what kind of poison."

"What do you mean? He went back and got the cat from the housekeeper?"

"In a manner of speaking. You don't want to know the details. But they wouldn't impress a judge, and they might get Steve in trouble."

Paul shook his head. "Then they'd probably get Steve's *partner* in trouble, too, right?"

"Yes." She pushed past that discussion. "The question now is, what we can do with the information we have? I'm sure Julie Warner killed her husband. She probably killed Molly as well. The cat was probably an accident. But the ME will need a base comparison of the poison to know for sure. If I'm right, that's in her house. We can't get into her house without a search warrant."

"And you can't get a search warrant on illegally obtained information." Paul understood her dilemma. "You'll need some other evidence that corroborates what you've already got. But it has to be obtained *legally*."

"I don't know what that could be at this point." Peggy folded a kitchen towel that was left on the table. "Any ideas?"

"Not really. And my advice would be to leave it to Al and Lieutenant Rimer." He got up and hugged her. "But since I know that's not going to happen, I'll think about it today and ask around. Okay?"

"Thanks, honey. I appreciate your help."

Paul left for work. Peggy locked the kitchen door and went upstairs to get dressed. She didn't have classes that day. The university was closed for the Thanksgiving holidays. She was grateful for the extra time to consider the problem and get the Potting Shed set up for Christmas.

She was amazed the police were moving so slowly against Keeley. But every day they had a chance to continue looking for answers was a day in her favor. Peggy wasn't going to let Keeley go to jail when she knew in her heart Julie was guilty of the crime.

She dressed in jeans for the dirty cleanup work at the shop. She tied her Reeboks and slipped the leash on Shakespeare's collar. She wanted him with her, since she might be working late.

There was half a pot of coffee left from breakfast, despite her guests. "Might as well take this with me," she told the dog. "It'll look good in a few hours."

She took out a small green thermos and started pouring the coffee into it. The action made her remember something else important. Ronda told her Julie was at Mark's office the night he was killed. What if she'd delivered the poison to him? The bank videotaped everything for security reasons. If Julie was on one of those tapes, she might be able to place her at the bank at the right time to administer the lethal dose.

"I think I'm going to drop you off at the shop, then take a quick trip over to the bank." She patted Shakespeare on the head. "Let's see if we can't find the legal evidence Paul was talking about."

A FEW HOURS LATER, Peggy was sitting in a small room directly across from the security manager's office at Bank of America's corporate headquarters. She told the security chief someone was stealing her plants. He was glad to play back a few tapes that could help her find the person.

It was a small, white lie. Even her daddy couldn't raise fire and brimstone from it. And it was done with the best of intentions.

The security manager located the tapes from the night Mark was killed. He told Peggy he was glad Mark didn't die there. "Bad feeling when someone dies on your watch, you know?"

"I can imagine." She was better able to empathize than he'd ever know.

The security manager left her alone with instructions on how to stop and rewind the tape. Peggy watched the footage carefully, glancing at the bank's sign-in sheet for the time Julie arrived.

When she got to seven P.M. on the tape, she slowed it down. There was Julie in a fabulous, calf-length black wool coat. She had a colorful scarf tied around her neck and a white pharmacy bag in her hand.

"What's this?" Peggy asked as the tape moved forward.

There was another shot of Julie in the elevator. Then she appeared again, passing Ronda as she went toward Mark's office. Ten minutes later, she got back on the elevator, without the white bag, and left the building. The sign-out sheet showed her leaving at seven-twenty.

"That's it!" Peggy pushed the button to make a copy of that part of the tape. "That's how long it takes to murder your husband. What did you do then, Julie? Wait somewhere until you saw him leave? You thought he was meeting Ronda at the hotel that night. But instead, he went to meet Keeley at my shop. You knew he was still alive when Keeley ran out crying. You had to curb your impatience to see what happened until Mr. Cheever went in and took Mark's things. Finally, you went in and found him, not quite dead. But you didn't want to wait for the poison to finish the job. You picked up a shovel and hit him with it."

Shaking her head over her flight of fancy and the terrible things people did to each other, Peggy took the tape, signed out of the building, and went to see Al.

"You did *what*?" Al demanded when she explained everything to him.

She left out the body moving of cat and man. She couldn't understand why he was so upset.

The door to his office opened, and Jonas poked his head around the corner. "Is it okay to come in? It sounds like the Gulf War out here in the hall. Afternoon, Peggy. Are you causing Al to have a heart attack?"

Al got up from his chair. "As a matter of fact, maybe this is exactly what we need." He glared at Peggy. "My friend has some ideas about the Warner murder."

"And the Stone murder," Peggy added without remorse.

Jonas closed the office door and took a chair close to hers. "I thought I asked you not to interfere in this investigation."

"I haven't interfered," she replied. "I've exercised my right as a citizen to help solve a murder and put the killer behind bars."

"I think you watch too much Court TV." He looked at Al, and they both laughed.

"If you'd be willing to hear me out and take a look at this video, it might make more sense to you."

"Listen, I know your friend is in trouble." Jonas attempted to sound sympathetic. "But trying to blame this on someone else won't help. We've worked up a good case against her. I'm expecting the arrest warrant any time."

Peggy got to her feet and smiled at both men. "That's fine. I'm going to take this over to the DA's office. He and I go way back. He went to school with John, you know."

Jonas shuffled uncomfortably in his chair. He obviously didn't want to hear what she had to say, but he didn't want the DA to hear it either. Finally, he made up his mind.

"Okay. Let's take a look at the tape, and you tell me what you know."

"Lieutenant!" Al was hoping for a good setdown that would make Peggy leave it alone.

"We'll listen to what she has to say and view the tape, Detective," Jonas said again, sotto voce. "Then we'll talk about it. What can it hurt?"

Half an hour later, Jonas and Al sat back in their chairs. Neither man spoke for several minutes.

Peggy collected the tape and put it in her backpack. "Well?"

"It's enough to question Mrs. Warner, Lieutenant." The words sounded painful coming from Al's throat.

"And you're sure about the rest of this, Peggy?" Jonas asked as he reached for the phone.

"As sure as I'm standing here."

He shrugged and called his assistant. "Call Mrs. Warner's lawyer and set up a meeting. I think we have a few questions we need to ask the widow."

THE REST OF IT HAPPENED quickly. Julie didn't resist the summons. She met Park Lamont at the precinct, and the two of them were locked in the conference room with Al and Jonas. During that time, the press waited outside, and the police commissioner paced the uneven floors.

Peggy didn't try to hide. She was convinced Julie killed her husband. She didn't care if she knew who accused her. Julie stared at her a moment when she first arrived but turned away as her lawyer took her elbow to guide her into the conference room.

But when Julie and Park walked out about an hour later, the look on Al's face told her it was all for nothing.

"Well, she's smarter than us." Al leaned against the door-frame. "Her alibi is airtight. She was delivering his prescription for asthma. That's why she went in with the bag but didn't come out with it. We already checked out that prescription bottle. It was clean. We talked to the pharmacist who filled it. She picked it up and dropped it off. That's all. Rimer is gonna blame me for this. Especially now, when we were set to arrest Ms. Prinz."

"He was the one who decided it sounded worthwhile," she reminded him. "What do we do now?"

"*We* don't do anything. For God's sake, Peggy, lay off! We're having enough trouble with this case. Mrs. Warner probably knows the mayor and the DA personally. The police look stupid and incompetent. Doesn't that make you feel bad? Your son is still on the job. John must be rolling over in his grave about now. Doesn't any of that matter to you?"

"I'm sorry," Peggy said when Jonas joined them.

"It was my fault for listening to you. I made the call. The DA already left me three voice mails on my cell phone. Mrs. Warner didn't waste any time complaining."

"I still think there's something wrong about it," Peggy replied, not feeling bad about her part in the fiasco.

Jonas frowned at her. "Go home, Peggy, please. Let us get some real work done."

Al drove Peggy to the Potting Shed. "Looks like everybody is getting ready for Christmas," he observed, stopping the car outside Brevard Court.

"That's what I'm going to do," she told him. "But I have some time. I could buy you lunch."

"Sorry. Can I take a rain check?" He smiled at her. "I kind of feel responsible for getting Rimer into this. I didn't think he'd take you seriously. Hell, I didn't think *I'd* take you seriously. You had some good ideas, Peggy. And you might be right about Mrs. Warner. But without proof, you might as well forget it."

"Does this mean you'll still be serving the arrest warrant on Keeley?"

"Probably. We don't have anything else that makes sense. We can't afford to screw up, but we can't let it hang there either."

"I understand." She opened the door and got out of the car.

Al popped the trunk. "Need any help with that bike?"

"No, I'm fine. I tote it all over Charlotte. I'll talk to you later."

Keeley, Hunter, Sam, and Selena were waiting impatiently to hear what happened. They pounced on her when she walked in the shop.

"Nothing happened." She pushed her bike against the wall and braced herself for Shakespeare's happy lunge when he saw her. "They did the best they could."

Keeley dropped silently into a chair. Hunter stormed up and down an aisle.

"There has to be something else." Sam glanced at his sister. "No one is *that* smart. She made a mistake somewhere."

"If she did, she's covering it up right now." Selena leaned against the counter and sighed.

"I don't know what to say." Peggy went to stand beside Keeley. "They told me the DA is ready to issue a warrant for you."

"Great!" Hunter stopped pacing. "We should get you out of town. If they have to look for you, it will give us more time to trap Mrs. Warner."

"Is that legal?" Selena asked.

"Keeley hasn't been arrested yet," Hunter answered. "Rich people do it all the time."

"But where would I go?" Keeley wondered. "I'm not rich. My mom lives here in Charlotte. It's not like I can take off and go to Paris for a few weeks."

"What about your aunt?" Peggy suggested. "Doesn't she live out in Montgomery County? It'd be hard to find you out there."

"That's true!" Keeley jumped up. "And it's better than going to jail."

"Let's go." Hunter grabbed her pocketbook and keys. "We didn't have this conversation. Keeley needs some time away after losing the baby. You'll each have to decide what to answer if the police ask you if you know where she is.

Technically, she's not a fugitive yet. That could all change very quickly."

"I was working when this happened, and I have no idea where she is." Sam folded his arms across his broad chest. His blue eyes were defiant.

"Besides," Selena said, "I don't know where her aunt lives. Even if I *knew* she was going there."

"Thanks, guys." Keeley hugged them all. "I guess I should go."

"Right now," Hunter agreed.

When the two of them were gone, Peggy looked at Selena and Sam. "I guess it's just us getting the store set up for the Christmas rush."

"I hope this is over before the holidays." Selena tied her hair back with a white scarf. "I hate bad stuff happening over Christmas."

Sam went out to get the blue spruce he bought for the shop. The roots were bundled in burlap so the tree could be planted after they were done with it. They decorated it with seed packages, bulbs, and miniature garden tools. Peggy put a row of red poinsettias around the base.

They stowed all the autumn decorations in the back and took out the giant snowflakes and bells from last year. Peggy had been forcing paper-white narcissus to bloom in the cooler storage area. Several of the purple Christmas cactus that grew in the front window near the counter were flowering.

They swept and mopped. Sam stocked the usual Christmas fare that traditionally sold. This year they added gift certificates as well. Peggy was working on the idea of a club that would send one potted plant a month to the recipient.

It was late when the store was finished. It smelled of lemon oil and spruce. The aisles were tidy for once and stocked almost to the ceiling. There was a little over a week until Thanksgiving and the start of the Christmas marathon.

"That's it for me." Selena sat down on the floor and refused to move.

"I think we're done." Peggy looked around the store with a smile. "Thanks, you two. I couldn't have done it without you. How about some dinner? My treat."

But Selena had to study for a makeup exam she was taking the next day. And Sam had a date.

"Don't make a big deal out of it or anything." He grinned. "But this guy is *really* hot."

"Then what's he see in *you*?" Selena laughed as she put on her coat.

"Some people think I'm hot." Sam glanced at himself in the dark shop window.

"People on the Internet who've never seen you." Selena slapped her hand on the counter. "I'm *good* tonight!"

"At least *I* have a date," Sam scoffed. "At least I'm not a pathetic loser who has to go home and study for a makeup test."

Selena opened the door to leave. "Snappy comeback. Good night, Peggy. You, too, Shakespeare."

Sam looked at himself again in the window. He flicked his fingers through his golden hair. "You think I'm hot, don't you, Peggy?"

"I'm sure I would if I didn't think of you like Paul." She laughed. "Don't pay her any attention, Sam. She's mad that you're not interested in her."

He made a face at himself. "Don't say *that*! How can I work with her, knowing she's longing for me?"

"Go home. I'll see you tomorrow."

He started to leave, then realized she'd be there alone. "I can wait. I don't want to leave you here like this."

"I'll be fine. Someone would have to be pretty daring to take on Shakespeare. Don't worry about it. I'll be leaving in a few minutes anyway."

He left, after calling a taxi to come and get her, insisting she shouldn't ride home late at night, even with the dog. Peggy absently said good-bye as she put together a small train set. It was John's. Each of the cars carried a package of seeds. She watched it race around on the track before she roused herself to go.

She looked up when the front door opened. She meant to lock it behind Sam. Now she might have to deal with a customer. "We're closed."

"I didn't come to buy anything."

Peggy got to her feet and faced Julie Warner.

16

Rose

Botanical: *Rosa hybrida*
Family: Rosaceae

The rose symbolizes completion, achievement, perfection, which is how it came to be so popular for anniversaries, after plays, and at other times of celebration. Meanings of the rose depend on the color, shape, and number of petals. For instance, the red rose means love, desire, respect, job well done. The white rose; innocence, silence, secrecy. The yellow rose; joy, gladness, friendship.

"I THOUGHT WE WERE FRIENDS, Peggy." Julie methodically took off her gloves. They were black leather like the long skirt and short jacket she wore.

Peggy felt threatened. She couldn't help it. She was still holding a garden trowel. Her hand tightened on it. The menace was there in Julie's stance and the dangerous look in her eyes. "Acquaintances."

"All right. Acquaintances then. Why would a *friendly* acquaintance accuse me of murdering my husband?"

"I'm sorry, Julie. I believe you had good reason to hate the man. He made a fool of you, your family, and your marriage vows. But there's never a good reason to kill someone."

"What would you know about it?" Julie slapped her gloves against her thigh as she walked through the front of the shop. "When your husband died, did the papers say he was known to step out with other women? Did the police consider one his many mistresses to be his killer? Did he almost die in the arms of his *pregnant* lover?"

Peggy didn't move. She watched the other woman, wondering how fast she could dial 911 on her cell phone. Shakespeare was growling behind the counter, but he didn't move. What would it take for him to attack someone? Not that she wanted him to randomly go around attacking people in her shop. But maybe she could come up with a signal to let him know when she was in trouble.

"Well, Peggy?" Julie stopped walking and ranting. "Did any of those things happen to you? Or did they only say what a hero your husband was and how he was an honorable man?"

"I can't pretend to know what you've been through," Peggy said in a soft voice. "But why didn't you divorce him? No one made you stay with him."

Julie's laughter bordered on hysteria. "Why didn't I leave him? Let me see. I have two children who are in private school and hope to go to Harvard. I have a lifestyle I enjoy and a home I love. I wouldn't have any of those things if I left him."

"We all make choices, I guess."

"Where's the fairness in that, Peggy? We can shoot a mad dog, but a human being who doesn't act civilized ninety percent of the time can ruin anyone's life he wants. Why should I have given up *everything* because Mark was a bastard?"

"I don't have the answer to those questions. I only know killing him wasn't the best way to handle the problem."

"I didn't kill my husband. Or that little tramp from Columbia. God knows I would've liked to. She actually came to the house and threatened me. She just didn't realize that Mark would *never* have left me. It's not that he loved me so much as he loved to show off." Julie seemed to get control of herself. "Stay away from me and my family. You don't understand what we've gone through."

Peggy's fingers clutched at the trowel. Her Irish temper kicked in. It was all she could do not to use her good left hook on the other woman as she put her gloves on and prepared to leave the shop.

The door closed behind her. Peggy didn't move until the taxi driver knocked at the window and pointed to his watch. Her muscles ached from clenching them so long. She looked at Shakespeare. He was asleep on the rug behind the counter. "Fat lot of help you were. Next time someone threatens me, you jump up and bite them."

The dog wagged his tail. She sighed and put on his leash. She slipped on her purple cape and picked up her backpack. It wasn't until she was in the taxi and close to home that she realized she was still holding the trowel.

It wasn't that Julie was big or overpowering. But Peggy could feel the deadly anger and fear emanating from her. Her words were threatening.

"Thanks for waiting," she said to the taxi driver as he helped her take her bike out of the trunk.

"No problem, Peggy. I look forward to seeing you and your dog now. That eucalyptus rub you gave me really did the trick on my arthritis. Thanks."

"You're welcome. Is this your last fare?"

"Yeah, I'm headed home." He glanced at her house silhouetted against the faintly orange sky. "Nothin' as grand as this, I'll tell you. What does one little woman do rattling around alone in a big place like this?"

She gave him what she owed him for the trip plus her usual tip. "It doesn't seem so big to me. Besides, where would I keep Shakespeare if I didn't have a house this size?"

He laughed and got back in the taxi. Peggy put her bike away and shook her head at the Rolls that slept in the garage. Maybe since the shop was set for Christmas and she didn't have any classes, she could get to the project again. She let Shakespeare run in the yard for a few minutes, but she felt very vulnerable being outside. She finally dragged him into the house and locked the door.

She was able to lose herself in her work, as always. The eighth graft from the night-blooming lily seemed to be taking on the rose. It would be a few weeks before she knew if the experiment was successful or if she'd have to start over. Many of her colleagues preferred the newer bio-genetics, changing the plant on a cellular level. But she preferred the old ways. Plants had been propagated and changed for thousands of years. She didn't see any reason to alter her technique. She got good results, and she was happy with her work.

At two-thirty, she climbed wearily up the stairs with Shakespeare. Luckily, she didn't have to get up for an early class that day. She had a tendency to forget the time when she was with her plants. At least ten alarm clocks were in the basement. All she had to do was remember to set them.

The phone was ringing when she got out of the shower. Shakespeare barked and whined, startled by the sound. His floppy ears *almost* managed to stand up. "It's okay." She stroked his head and neck.

But she didn't answer the phone. When the answering machine picked up, there was only silence on the line. Shivering, she turned out the light and climbed into bed. For once, she was glad to have the big dog beside her. He was the only reason she went to sleep that night.

PEGGY WAS MAKING chocolate mint tea when there was a knock at her back door. It was Al and Jonas. "I'm making some tea. Would you like some?"

"This isn't a social call," Jonas explained. "We're looking for Keeley Prinz. Do you know where she is?"

"No." Peggy didn't mind lying to them. Especially after her visit from Julie last night. "Have you checked her apartment?"

"Yes," Al told her. "And her mother's house. We thought maybe she was out on a job for you."

"No, she can't work yet. She had the miscarriage. Her doctor won't release her for six weeks. Her work is pretty strenuous, you know."

Al ran his hand over his face. "Peggy, don't you think it's kind of weird that you knew the DA was going to issue an arrest warrant for your friend, and now she's vanished?"

She managed to look surprised and upset. "I wouldn't tell her to hide from the police. I believe in the system. You know that, Al."

"What about hiding her here?" Jonas glanced into the kitchen. "This is a big house. A girl could feel safe here. Especially since she knows her friend who owns the house is buddies with the police."

"If you're suggesting you'd like to search the house, go right ahead. I wouldn't hide a fugitive here. That's illegal."

"We might take a look around." He strolled into the kitchen and sniffed the air. "What's that smell?"

"Chocolate mint tea. It should be ready by the time you finish. Ignore the mess. I always do massive cleaning over the holidays when I don't have classes."

He took a cookie she offered him and walked into the dining room.

Al shook his head. "That was too easy. I *know* you, Peggy. You wouldn't let us in if she was here. You would've had some contagious fungus or something that would keep us out until you found another place for her."

"I didn't realize I had such a devious reputation." She held up the plate. "Cookie?"

He refused. "Not devious. Just too smart for your own damn good. Someday you might be sorry you played us along this way. Your friend could really be a killer, and she could turn on *you*."

"That's the least of my worries." She took a bite of a cookie and told him about Julie's visit to the Potting Shed. "Unfortunately, I didn't have my digital camcorder set up to catch all of it. But I won't leave home without it again."

"What she said couldn't really be construed as a threat, Peggy."

"You weren't there, Al." The kettle began to whistle, and she turned off the stove.

"Have I mentioned how stubborn you are?" He picked up a cookie and followed Jonas into the house.

Thirty minutes later, they were gone; a cup of tea in their hands and cookies in their pockets. Peggy fed Shakespeare and went upstairs to get dressed.

SAM, SELENA, AND HUNTER were already at the shop when Peggy arrived. Sofia and Emil hurried over with tea and bagels when they saw her. Everyone had visits from the police looking for Keeley.

"We didn't know what to say," Sofia exclaimed. "You should tell us when something like this happens. What's the story?"

Peggy explained a little, leaving out the part about Keeley going to her aunt's house. The Balduccis didn't need to know, and she didn't want to ask them to lie.

"It's only a matter of time," Hunter said when they were gone. "She can only hide for a few days, then Janice will advise her to turn herself in."

"Do we have any other leads proving Mrs. Warner did the deed?" Sam asked as he moved back and forth in the rocking chair.

"Not as far as I know." Peggy turned on the computer. "The videotape was my last idea. We've got everything except the proof. Who'd have thought two people I know would be charged with the same murder."

"It's weird, I suppose." Hunter picked up her jacket. "Except when you consider the DB was found right here."

"DB?" Selena asked.

"Dead body," Hunter explained. "I have to go. I have a drunk driver in court this morning. Whatever you do, don't contact Keeley. The chances are all of our phones are bugged. Hopefully, they didn't get one in here, too."

Selena and Sam glanced around the shop, looking for listening devices.

Peggy laughed. "Like they have the budget for that! I'll talk to you later. Thanks, Hunter."

Sam left right after his sister. The twin of the blue spruce in the shop was scheduled to be planted in Claire Drummond's front yard that morning. "Let me know if you hear anything. Or if you think of anything else we can do."

Peggy promised she would, but she knew she was out of plans. Everything she'd tried worked, but it wasn't enough. Julie stayed one step ahead. And now that she was aware the police could be looking for evidence, she was bound to make sure there was nothing for them to find.

Keeley's mother called and thanked Peggy for her help. From her tone and her carefully stilted words, Peggy knew Hunter already warned her about wiretaps.

"Don't worry, Lenore," Peggy said, mindful of her friend's paranoia about her daughter. "We'll think of something. Take care of yourself."

The shopping crowd was brisk all morning. Peggy didn't know if it was early Christmas shoppers or people happy to see the warm, sunny weather. Whatever, she was glad to take in the extra money. She thought again about another assistant to help at the shop. It would be nice to have someone she could call if there was an emergency.

Al called her after lunch. She'd been dreading the call all day. It meant they'd found Keeley and taken her into custody. "Can you meet me at Carolinas Medical?"

That surprised her. Was Keeley injured? Surely she wouldn't resist arrest. What if she was shot? "Of course. How is she?"

"She? Oh, you mean Ms. Prinz. She's not here. We haven't found her yet. This is something else. Can you come?"

Peggy agreed to be there as soon as she could. She hung up the phone and looked around the crowded shop. What could she do? Sam and Selena were both busy. Dawn was out of town, and Brenda was taking Keeley's place cleaning and watering plants at the Overstreet Mall.

If there wasn't so much traffic, she might be able to get

Sofia or Emil to watch the shop for a while. But she knew they were busy, too. She racked her brain to come up with an alternative. Without letting herself stop to question the wisdom of her actions, she dialed Steve's number.

Twenty minutes later he was there, putting on an apron. "I take the money and give them a receipt, right?"

"Yes. If they have any questions, refer them to the gardening encyclopedia at the end of the counter. If that doesn't work, get their name and number. I'll call them back as soon as I can."

"Okay. Would you like to take my car? I know you're in a hurry."

Peggy wrestled with her conscience. She swore she wouldn't drive another internal combustion engine machine again. But letting people drive her around in them was just as bad. She took his keys and promised herself she was going to work on the Rolls. "Thanks, Steve. You're a lifesaver."

"You owe me dinner." It was all he had a chance to say before a woman in a bright red suit cornered him to ask about growing tulips on her patio.

Peggy left before she got caught in the middle of it. Al wouldn't call her unless he had a good reason. If it wasn't Keeley, she couldn't imagine what it could be. She felt sure he'd tell her up front if it was Paul. She thought about a dozen more reasons he might call her on the way there. Then she parked the Saturn in the visitors' parking lot and hurried into the hospital.

Al was waiting at the side entrance from the parking lot. "I think this may be the break you're looking for. Lieutenant Rimer is on his way over. I wanted you to hear this first, but let's speed it up. He might not understand me calling you."

They went up on the elevator to the third floor. "For goodness sake, Al, tell me what's going on."

"A doctor gave me a call this morning. It seems he got the test results back on one of his emergency room cases. The man was poisoned by anemonin."

Peggy's eyes widened. "Really? How did it happen?"

"His name is Dwayne Johnson. He's got a rap sheet for drugs as long as your arm. Anyway, this time he picked up some capsules he found in a trash can on Queens Road. Free drugs are the best drugs, you know."

"How is he?" she asked, excitement building in her chest.

"Sick as a dog. But the doctor says he'll be fine. I've got two officers picking up the rest of the capsules from his house. If it turns out the way I'm thinking, we may have to change that arrest warrant. Johnson identified a photo of the Warner house. He says that's where he got the drugs."

"I'm sure Jonas will love that." She laughed as the elevator stopped.

"Yeah, he's just peachy about it." Al smiled at her. "I think you did good on this, Peggy. Even if you should've stayed out of the way."

"Thanks, I think. Why did you ask me to come up, besides telling me this?"

"As awkward as it may be, I'd like you to come with us when we search the Warner house again. I don't know what the hell we're looking for over there. What do you make poison out of?"

She nodded. "I'll give Steve a call and go with you. Does the position pay?"

He scratched his chin. "I'm sure we can get you a small stipend. And you'll have the satisfaction of finding out if you were right or wrong."

"That sounds appealing. Where do I sign up?"

THE CRIME LAB FOUND TRACES of anemonin in the rest of the capsules at Dwayne Johnson's home. Most of them were mutilated and only contained traces of the poison. The quest for the perfect capsule to give Mark seemed to be the only reason Dwayne was alive.

Peggy went with Al to search the Warner house. The judge issued the warrant on the strength of Johnson's bedside affidavit that he picked up the capsules from the Warner trash can. Julie's lawyer argued anyone could've put them there. But since the bank video showed Julie bringing in a pharmacy bag and the poisoned capsules matched the medication she brought Mark, the judge allowed the search.

Julie stayed in the house. Her eyes promised retribution when she saw Peggy.

Peggy shivered, but she straightened her spine and went ahead with the officers. The warrant allowed them to look for anything that could have been used in the commission of Mark Warner's murder.

"There's so much in here," Peggy said to Al. "How are we going to go through it all?"

"Just remember, I only want you to look for the kind of paraphernalia that could be used to create the poison. Let us take care of the rest."

With the Warner children crying in the kitchen, Peggy looked everywhere else first. There was no sign of anything she recognized as useful. Al asked Julie to wait upstairs with the children so they could search the kitchen. Peggy was grateful for his intervention but still couldn't find anything.

"I think she had too much of a lead, Al," she told him. "If there was anything here, she got rid of it. Maybe we should search the dump."

"Great." He glanced around the kitchen. "We'll never get another warrant for this. They found a long dark wig upstairs in Mrs. Warner's closet. That could help us make the case for the police in Columbia."

"But not if we can't find a beaker or anything that the poison was in." Peggy thought about the cat being poisoned. If it was an accident, Julie had to be out in the open somewhere in the house. If not in the kitchen . . . "What about the basement? This house must have a basement."

Al looked for a door, enlisting the aid of the officers as they finished searching the rest of the house. "If there's a basement, she must have to climb in through an outside window."

"Some of these older houses had cellars instead of basements." Peggy began stomping her foot on the floor in the kitchen. "If there's a door cut in the floor, it should sound different."

Al and the officers joined her in stamping their feet across the floor. Peggy took a moment to smile at the sight, then she stomped down hard on a spot near the pantry. "I think I found something."

The door cut into the oak tongue-and-groove floor was hard to see. They didn't need a rug to hide it. The carpenter who'd created it did an excellent job. The lines between the different cuts in the wood were so thin as to appear almost invisible. Peggy found a spatula and used it to pry up one end of the door. It opened smoothly and quietly. She pushed back a new steel support brace that held the door open.

Al instructed two of the officers to stay upstairs with the Warner family. "We're so close. I don't want to have to look for Mrs. Warner like I've had to look for Ms. Prinz."

"Have you found Keeley yet?" Peggy asked as she started down the narrow stairs.

"No. But I expect you knew that."

The space under the house was more a cellar than a basement. It was crudely wired. One naked lightbulb hung over a rough workbench. A large Bunsen burner was pushed back from the edge. Various sizes of glass beakers and bottles stood on shelves.

"Holy smoke." Al couldn't believe his eyes. "Richards, get down here with that camera. Nobody touch anything until CSI gets here."

Peggy poked around in the shadowed corners. Close to the workbench was a smaller table. It was covered by yellow scarves. Five jars of honey, five small pumpkins, and five oranges adorned it. On the wall behind it was a small picture of a beautiful black woman dressed in yellow scarves. She appeared to be dancing.

"What is that?" Al asked.

"Oshun," Peggy told him. "That explains the yellow scarf around the cat. She's part of the Santeria religion. And from what I hear, she can get *very* angry."

"The *what*?"

Peggy left the cellar as she heard Emma come in the back door. The housekeeper put her bags of groceries on the table and rushed toward Julie as the officers were putting handcuffs on her. Her children were crying and clinging to her.

"No, no," Emma was muttering. "Oshun wouldn't let this happen."

"It was you," Peggy said in amazement. "It wasn't Julie, was it? *You* killed Mark. You did it out of love for Julie and the children, of course. You killed Molly because she had the nerve to come here, face Julie, and threaten her. You tried to kill me because I was asking too many questions."

Julie stared at Peggy, then swept her tearful gaze toward her housekeeper. "Emma? Is that true? You wouldn't, would you?"

"You're better off without him," Emma told her. "And his disrespectful whore deserved to die, too."

Jonas and Al glanced at each other. Al shrugged his hefty shoulders. "Don't ask me."

"Are you saying Mrs. Warner *didn't* kill her husband?" Jonas asked Peggy.

"*I'm* not." She nodded at the housekeeper. "But I think *she* is. Emma's a believer in Santeria. They have a lot of basic knowledge about plants and poisons. I think when you dust for fingerprints in the cellar, you're going to find Emma's prints, not Julie's."

While Julie cried, a defiant Emma proudly confessed to the murders. Peggy slipped out the door. She'd done her part. She didn't want to hear the rest. Two more squad cars joined the group, and a Channel 3 news van pulled smoothly up. She was glad Steve's car was parked on the street.

Her cell phone rang. "Peggy?" Steve's voice sounded desperate. "There's a man here who wants to order two hundred tulip trees. I don't even know what the hell a tulip tree is. Are you coming back soon?"

She laughed. "I'm on my way. Don't let him leave the shop."

FOR THE FIRST TIME SINCE John Lee died, the blue spruce in Peggy's house was decorated for Christmas. She decided to do it in grand style by inviting half of Charlotte to help her. The drop-in party was so large that the police sent complimentary officers to help with parking and traffic.

"It's the least we can do since you went to so much trouble to make us look like idiots," Jonas told her as he put a star on the tree.

"Don't listen to him." His wife, Georgette, smiled at Peggy. "He got a big commendation for solving the murder here and helping with the Stone case in Columbia."

"I never listened to him anyway," Peggy replied. "He can testify to that. But I'm glad everything turned out okay."

Jonas asked her, "How did you know? The whole Santeria thing. It didn't look like anything to me."

"I was in Cuba last year touring a new botanical garden they're working on," Peggy replied. "One of the gardeners was involved with Santeria. If Emma had chosen any other orisha, I wouldn't have known. Sometimes things just seem to fit together, don't they?"

She left the Rimers by the tree with a cup of eggnog for each of them. The house was so full, she wasn't sure if there were enough food and drinks. She walked toward the kitchen, stopping every few seconds to talk to someone she knew.

Jane Cheever and her father arrived. Joe was in a wheelchair, but his faded eyes twinkled at Peggy. "Greetings, my dear. What a splendid party. Thank you for inviting us."

Peggy hugged him. "You're just like your old self!"

He glanced at his legs. "Not quite, but I'm working on it. My daughter tells me that I owe you a great debt."

"No, she owes *me* a great debt." Hunter came in behind them with Sam at her side. "But I'm sure we can work that out. How pitiful am I that I had to come to a party with my brother?"

"You mean, how pitiful am I that I had to come with *you*!" Sam groaned.

"Never mind." Peggy stepped between them. "Go and get some punch and put an ornament on the tree. Walk around like you don't know each other. No one will notice."

Hunter leaned close to her. "Any eligible men here?"

Sam did the same. "Yeah. Tell me first, Peggy. She can have my leftovers."

"I'm sure there are plenty for both of you. Now, scoot!" Peggy helped Jane take her father into the foyer where everyone was milling around the food and the tree.

Keeley was helping Steve look for the bottom plug behind the tree that would turn on the twinkle lights. Lenore was watching her and smiling. Peggy introduced her friend to the Cheevers.

"It's nice to meet you." Lenore took Joe's hand. "Peggy's told me so much about you."

"And this must be your daughter." Joe looked at Keeley. " 'The brightness of her cheek would shame those stars, as daylight doth a lamp.' "

She stopped searching the bottom branches of the tree and smiled at him. "Uh—thanks. Nice to meet you. I guess we'll always have something in common, huh? We were both accused of the same murder."

Joe agreed but added, "True. And, most importantly, we were both innocent."

"I found it!" Steve yelled, taking pieces of spruce out of his mouth as he climbed through the tree.

"Eureka!" Joe raised his glass and smiled.

"Let's light it up," Peggy suggested. "Would you do the honors?"

"Of course." Steve put the plug in the wall, and the tree came alive with lights. There was a round of applause and a great deal of oohing and aahing. A spontaneous burst of "O Christmas Tree" followed but died quickly when no one knew more than the first two lines.

Paul came up and put his arm around his mother. "Looks good. I didn't know if we'd ever do this again."

She hugged him. "I didn't know either. But it feels good, doesn't it?"

"Yeah. I think Dad would be happy to see it."

Peggy wiped a tear from the corner of her eye but kept her smile. "Where's Mai?"

"Probably trying to get through this crowd. She headed for the eggnog." He looked past the people surrounding them. "There she is. She's really great, Mom."

"I know. And I'm so glad you found each other."

"How's it going with you and Steve?" He glanced at the other man who was accepting congratulations for his part in lighting the tree. "Is it serious between you?"

Peggy laughed. "I'm not sure what that means. But he's very nice, and he makes me feel good. It doesn't hurt that he's willing to dig up dead cats either."

"Don't tell me!" Paul hugged her and smiled. "I never thought my mom would be dating, but it's okay. I wanted you to know. I know you don't need my permission or anything, but—"

"It means a lot to me that you said something." She kissed his cheek. "Thanks."

"I think I see Al and Mary trying to get in the door," he said. "I'll go see if I can help them. I didn't know you knew so many people. Is that the mayor?"

Peggy didn't answer as she turned to speak with someone else. At the height of the party, she retreated to the basement. An alarm clock was ringing, but it wasn't necessary. She'd been waiting for this moment for the past few weeks. A lovely red rose was beginning to open in the darkness beside the pond where its cousin, the water lily, was perfuming the air.

"Hey, you aren't supposed to be down here with your plants when you have a million people at your party." Steve put his arm around her. "Looks like your experiment worked. That's great! This just came for you."

He handed her a small box that was wrapped in gold foil. She looked at the card attached to it. *"You've done it. Congratulations, Nightrose. Merry Christmas! Nightflyer."*

Peggy slipped the box into her pocket and smiled at Steve. Nightflyer didn't show up again at the gaming site. She had Sergeant Jones close the investigation. But Nightflyer wasn't gone from her life.

"Are you okay?" Steve asked.

"I'm fine," she answered, focusing on him. "Let's go back to the party."

Peggy's Garden Journal

Autumn

We all know that autumn is a good time to plant bulbs for the spring. It's also a good time to check your garden for damage from summer storms, heat, and insects. Take the time to go through your garden and notice what's changed. Time to trim back plants that have grown straggly over the summer. Mulch around trees and bushes to protect for the coming winter. Bring in plants that can't withstand the cold.

In the house, it's the same. Plants will grow more slowly once the weather changes, even inside. The sun is less warm even in sunny windows. It's a good time to cut back unruly growth and use cuttings to begin new plants.

Autumn can be a good time for those outdoor projects, too. With the heat of summer gone and the kids involved with other projects and school, maybe you can get that bench built near the oak tree or create the trellis you've wanted for your climbing roses.

Take time to enjoy the cool breezes and warm sunshine

before we're all inside reading our seed catalogs during the winter months. Happy gardening!

Peggy

Care and Feeding Guide

ANEMONE

Anemones have clear, beautiful colors such as red, pink, and purple. One anemone bulb has lots of flowers. If you pick faded flowers right away, they will flower continuously until the end of their cycle.

Anemone bulbs should be dry and without mold when you buy them. The best planting season is autumn. However, some species are not hardy for the cold climate. If you grow such species in an area where the temperature reaches below 0°F(−18°C), plant them in spring.

If you plant hard-dried bulbs in soil and let them absorb water abruptly, they get cracks on the surface, which may cause infection or promote mold. Therefore, pretreatment is required.

Plant them in vermiculite first and let them absorb the moisture in the air for two days without giving them water. Gradually water them with water spray until germination and then plant them in soil.

Anemones like full sun or partial shade. Wait until the surface of the soil gets dry, and water thoroughly. Take care not to let it get too dry. After the flowers have faded and the foliage has turned yellow, stop watering.

Mix fertilizer in the soil before planting, and give liquid fertilizer while the plants are growing. If you want to reuse the bulbs, give another fertilizer when the flowers start to fade.

You can leave the bulbs in a container in dry-summer regions. However, it is recommended to dig the bulbs out after the aerial area dies back if you live in a climate with rainy summers or cold winters (below 0°F or −18°C). Be sure to thoroughly dry bulbs after digging them up.

AFRICAN VIOLET

African violets will bring color to your home with continuous blooming, but they require some general guidelines.

Water carefully. Don't let water get on the leaves! It will cause dead spots. The secret is to water well and allow to dry out afterward. Pour room temperature water into the trays or pan, and after about twenty minutes go back and drain off whatever is left in the tray. They can't sit in water for a long time because the roots will rot. As is true of any plant, they must breathe oxygen from the roots.

Don't leave dead flowers or leaves on your plant, and don't subject them to sudden temperature changes. You can buy good African violet potting soil in small bags at the store. It is made of a mixture of primarily pine bark and sand. This soil will allow for good drainage, unlike the peat mixtures. Peat mixtures, however, are perfect for many other plants.

Suckers are little baby plants that grow on the main stem of the plant. Be sure to pick them off. You can sit your plant in the kitchen window to receive the morning sun. African violets need a certain kind and a certain amount of light, and they will flourish perfectly. Spread the plants out so that the leaves don't touch anything.

PANSY

The plants are on the small side: Most types grow well close together in a mounding habit to just eight or nine inches in height, with a spread of one and a half to three feet across. The foliage is a rich, attractive green, while the flowers are five-petaled beauties that come in a range of vibrant shades.

Because pansies are hardy annuals, they are tougher and more versatile than their somewhat dainty appearance might suggest. They can be grown in either full sun or partial shade. They tolerate heat better than most other violas and are highly resistant to cold. You can establish them outdoors as much as a month prior to the frost-free date in your area, provided the plants have hardened off. Blooms can be expected in spring, summer, and sometimes fall (after a late-summer rest) in cold-winter regions, and in winter and spring in milder climates. Generally speaking, gardeners in cooler northern climates will enjoy flowers longer than their counterparts in the South, where higher soil and air temperatures tend to abbreviate the blossoming season.

Pansies can serve a variety of aesthetic and practical purposes in the landscape. Use them for mass color or as festive trim in borders and edgings, as a flowering ground cover for spring-blooming bulbs, for showy display in pots and window boxes, or to fill in bare spots in the garden at the beginning and end of the growing season.

Because of their incredible tolerance, the pansy is forgiving of too little or too much water. Light fertilizing will keep them strong. They will grow abundantly without much care.

Tips for Choosing Spring Flowering Bulbs

• Select the best you can find. Expect to pay more for them, especially from good sources. Unhealthy bargain bulbs may bloom once, but many won't survive the winter. Those that do may not bloom for years. On-line stores may be more expensive than local nurseries, but many offer top-quality bulbs that you can't find locally.

• Planting time is usually before the first hard frost but can be any time before the ground freezes. The idea is to plant early enough in the season to allow the root system to become well established but late enough so that little or no top growth occurs.

Grafting

Grafting is the process by which a part of one plant (usually a piece of stem) is surgically attached to another plant (usually a root or stem with roots). These parts grow together to form a single grafted plant.

This is usually done to strengthen a plant that is less than hardy in an area or to create a new type of plant. Learning to graft is a difficult and painstaking process but can be rewarding for the patient, dedicated gardener.

What plants are usually grafted? Roses are frequently grafted to create new colors or scents. Fruit trees are grafted to produce more fruit or combinations of fruit. Vegetable plants are grafted to create more and bigger yield.

TIPS FOR SUCCESSFUL GRAFTING

Use a sharp knife to cut the wood. A grafting knife should be razor-sharp. A dull knife can cause failure at grafting. You can buy knives specially created for this purpose. These knives have one side sharp, one side flat. Start at the base of the knife blade and use a single cut. Don't saw at the wood. Splinters, bumps, or unequal cuts will prevent a good match and reduce your success rate.

Collect budsticks from young, firm stems of the plant you want to graft. Wilted budwood won't make a successful graft. Place the sticks in a plastic bag with a damp paper towel or a little moist peat moss, then seal the bag with tape. Store it in a cool spot, out of the sun. It will last several days.

Cut surfaces will dry out quickly and hurt your chances at a good graft. It's important to cut, match, and wrap the graft as quickly as possible. Some gardeners put the cut ends in their mouths to keep moist while they're working. But beware of poisonous plants! Don't let cut ends come in contact with soil.

After joining plant and budstick, wrap grafts with clear poly-ethylene budding tape. Stretch the tape almost to the point of breaking. Then seal with tape. A graft is usually wrapped three to six weeks, depending on the type of plant being grafted. A callus should develop on the cut surfaces. This is the healing tissue of the plant. It's a small drop of white or tan spongy material. When you see this, the graft is ready to be unwrapped. Cold-weather grafts should be left longer. In colder climates, fall grafts are sometimes left wrapped until spring.

Not all of your attempts will work, but this can be an in-teresting way to create your own new plants!

Longwood Gardens: Home of the Antares Night-Blooming Water Lily

"Longwood Gardens was created by industrialist Pierre S. du Pont (and is sometimes referred to as the DuPont Gardens) and offers 1,050 acres (425 hectares) of gardens, woodlands, and meadows; 20 outdoor gardens; 20 indoor gardens within 4 acres (1.6 hectares) of heated greenhouses; 11,000 different types of plants; spectacular fountains; extensive educational programs including horticultural career training and internships; and 800 horticultural and performing arts events each year, from flower shows, gardening demonstrations, courses, and children's programs to concerts, organ and carillon recitals, musical theater, and fireworks displays. Longwood is open every day of the year and attracts more than 900,000 visitors annually." [www.longwoodgardens.org]

Longwood Gardens is located in Kennett Square, Pennsylvania. For more information, visit their Web page, www.longwoodgardens.org, or write: Route 1, PO Box 501, Kennett Square, PA 19348-0501, USA, or call: 610-388-1000.

A Good Place to View Antares and Other Night-Blooming Water Lilies

http://williamtricker.safeshopper.com/23/182.htm?533

To Get Your Seed Catalogs

http://www.burpee.com/
World famous seed catalogs

http://www.seedman.com/
Plants from around the world

http://www.stokeseeds.com/cgi-bin/StokesSeeds.storefront
Good prices on seeds to get your garden started

www.parkseed.com
Giant seed and garden catalog from South Carolina

Happy fall planting!